Bloodswell

Jane Houng

QX PUBLISHING CO.

Bloodswell

Copyright © 2012 QX Publishing Co.
First Edition, November 2012

Author: Jane Houng

Distributed by: The SUP Publishing Logistics (H.K.) Limited 3/F, C & C Building, 36 Ting Lai Road, Tai Po, N.T., Hong Kong

Printed by: Elegance Printing & Book Binding Co., Ltd. Block A, 4/F, Hoi Bun Industrial Building, 6 Wing Yip Street, Kwun Tong, Hong Kong

ISBN 978 962 255 113 8
Printed in Hong Kong.

To Leo, the bear

My love will grow

Vaster than empires, and more slow.

A hundred years will go to praise

Thine eyes, and on thy forehead gaze;

Two hundred to adore each breast,

But thirty thousand to the rest:

An age at least to every part,

And the last age should show your heart.

For, lady, you deserve this state,

Nor would I love at lower rate.

From *To His Coy Mistress by Andrew Marvell*

While parents are alive,

One must not travel afar.

If one must, one's whereabouts

Should always be made known.

From *Analects of Confucius, Book II*

CONTENTS

CHAPTER 1
A blood-red Harley-Davidson

I'm singing *Bloodswell* in a dark smoky scruff of a room at China Chicks Music Centre. The studio is down an alley behind a bustling street market near my home in suburban Hong Kong. A projector beams our life-size images onto a wall screen opposite: I see Wing rocking on bass guitar and Mimi pounding the drums. My coal-black hair shimmers under the spotlights. Motes of dust shiver. *'Silk sheets, You're neat,'* I trill, nose-bump close to the invisible one I'm secretly in love with. And I grip the mike with snaking fingers, throttle it with desire, while Wing's bass notes thrum and Mimi's gleaming cymbal clashes.

Then my mobile vibrates against my leg and starts bleeping.

It's a text from Peggy: **noodles or rice?**

I hit reply, text: **rice,** then give the thumbs up to Wing and Mimi, who haven't stopped playing.

Chi sin. Crazy. I'd so been in the zone, I hadn't noticed the time. Wing will kill me for dumping her in the middle of a Rock Band session, especially as she has paid for two hours. But Peggy is my best friend and in Chinese History class today, she told me that the hungry ghost visited her home last night. 'I felt a cold burst of air on my forehead and the lights flickered,' she said. 'Can you come round tonight? Big brother's on a late shift. I don't want to be alone.'

'It must've been the wind,' I said.

'No way.'

Whether Peg's flat is haunted or not, it's okay with me 'cos I'm not scared of ghosts. Don't believe in them. So I told her I'd come round after Ma left for work. I didn't tell her I'd be jamming with Wing and Mimi around dinner time, 'cos she'd feel hurt. It's not my fault Wing doesn't want her in our band – Peggy is tone deaf.

Wing and Mimi are still rocking so I turn the volume down, give the slice-my-throat 'cut' cue and shout down the mike, 'Hey, gotta go soon. Peggy's in a fix.'

I check out Wing's face. But she seems cool about it. 'What's up? Another bad trip?' she says, her hand glissing up the neck of the guitar and striking a funky chord.

I snigger.

Mimi thwacks the cymbal. I turn the volume back up. We finish the song.

It's as humid as a steam bath outside. I take my hoodie off, tie it round my waist and stride past mounds of fruit and flapping fish towards the high street. Past the jars of deers' dicks in the window of the Chinese medicine shop, and the glittering chandeliers of the lighting shop, and the sweet-smelling bakery where Ma's bread is sold. Then I cross at the zebra, cut through the queue at the bus stop and enter Peg's public housing estate.

The last time I was here there'd been a suicide. Some couple had been arguing about their daughter. The Pa said he'd pay any amount to send her to a direct subsidy school, even if it meant a lifetime of eating vegetables. And the Ma lost it, went for him with a cleaver. And the Pa grabbed their daughter and jumped from the balcony. From the fifteenth floor, I think. When I arrived, POLICE: KEEP OUT tapes cordoned off the area where the two covered bodies were lying. But the flashing blue lights had attracted a crowd. After the ambulance left, uniforms paced around measuring distances and cleaners swept up shards of glass.

Tonight there's just the half-blind guard and his flask of tea. He recognises me; I don't have to sign in at the counter or anything, and I go up to the twenty-third floor in a lift that stinks of scallions.

I walk along the dank corridor towards flat number 2369, past bolted bottle gates, pots of burning incense, dinner hitting sizzling woks.

I ring the bell, press harder, rattle the gate, knock on the door. There's no answer. Press the bell again. Nope.

Now Peg's not perfect. She used to be a ketamine queen. Until she quit. So when she doesn't answer, I'm on edge. She should be back from the takeaway by now.

Don't panic, I tell myself. Just phone her.

I listen to two loops of her ringtone before she picks up. 'Let me in,' I say.

'Come to SG,' she says. Her voice sounds kind of squashed.

Something's up. Peggy's not at the takeaway. She's at Secret Garden, a 24/7 Korean BBQ restaurant where you eat *kimch'i* and cook slivers of raw meat on a gas stove in the middle of your table. It's the place where, after rave parties, we used to chill out before going home. *What's she doing there?*

I make a run for it. *Shit.* Just missed the lift. And it's going down. I push open the fire door to the emergency exit; it'll be quicker to walk.

The rubbish bins and rat bait are familiar. How many times have I sat on a cold concrete stair, Peggy's pale face propped on my shoulder? A scattering of cigarette butts marks the spot where I forced her to make a pact with me to quit drugs a few weeks ago. We sliced our index fingers with a razor, sealed them flesh-to-flesh and licked dribbles of our mingled blood.

I'm on the main street again, weaving my way through the crowds. The pavement is packed with tight-lipped workers, shoppers and jostling bags of shopping. Mums and maids drag kids to tutorial classes. Neon signs glare, taxis and minibuses honk. There's a seventy percent discount at I.J.'s boutique but I'm just set on getting to the Secret Garden a.s.a.p.

I turn into a side street. It leads to a cul-de-sac which borders a park at the bottom end. SG is only a couple more minutes away. My flip-flops strain between my toes as I run down the hill. As I round the corner, I see someone pinned against the park wall by three guys. There's a girl screaming: it's Peg!

Fear churns my stomach, but I race towards her, hurling expletives like I'm crazy. As I get closer, I recognise Brew, a drug pusher, rumoured to be a pimp too. He's the one holding a knife to Peggy's throat.

'She's here,' Peggy shouts, trying to break free.

One of Brew's mates swings round to face me. He has a deep

scar across his forehead, dyed brown hair and a tattooed chest.

Brew's head jerks in my direction. 'Check her out,' he shouts. Scarface and a skinny guy grab my arms and drag me towards the wall.

'Get off, scumbags,' I scream.

There's a shooting pain from my elbow as my arm hits the wall, the burning of flesh as my body hits the pavement. Skinny rolls me on my back and grovels in my bum bag for valuables. '*Wa!* An iPod!' he says, pocketing it. Scarface laughs and lights up a cigarette.

Gaau choa! There's no way I can live without my iPod Touch. But I don't have the strength to wrench myself free. 'Help, help,' I yell, kicking wildly. Until Scarface pulls out a knife and points it at my jugular. Suddenly I'm trying to shout but no sound comes out.

Meanwhile Peggy is wrestling with Brew. Unlike me, she's built like a tank. With a *kung fu* cry, she has got him in a kind of arm lock and he yelps with pain.

At that moment, a motorbike comes screeching around the corner, its HID headlight dazzles. There's the squeal of brakes and the rider leaps off, rips off his helmet.

'What are you doing?' a gravelly voice shouts. I peep over Scarface's shoulder and nearly faint with surprise: it's him! The guy I've got a thing about. The guy who picks Tiffany up from school. He's riding a Harley-Davidson. A blood-red Harley-Davidson.

'I'm Steel,' he says. 'What are you doing with my friends?'

He looks fit. Drop-dead fit.

The three druggies are stunned. So stunned, they freeze.

Next moment, Steel has pounced like a tiger, jerked Brew's arm from Peggy's neck and thrown him to the pavement. There's a sickening crunch.

Skinny tries to make an escape through the bushes but Steel leaps on top of him, shoves his chin skyward and pins him down.

Scarface releases his grip on me, whimpers, and tries to make a getaway.

'Not so lucky, bro,' Steel says, grabbing him by the neck and dragging him back through the bushes.

'Okay, okay,' Brew says, sitting on the pavement nursing a bloody nose. 'We did them no harm.'

'Oh yeah?' Steel says. His backbone is arched and his bright eyes are smouldering with rage.

Steel. MY friend. My heart pounds.

Peg and I stand side-by-side. Her toilet-brush haircut glistens with beads of sweat. 'It's an old debt,' she tells me breathlessly.

'Let's talk later,' I say, grovelling in my bum bag.

Steel watches. Skinny and Scarface squirm under his paws.

Brew moans.

I slap two red hundred-dollar bills into his hand.

Peggy's brows are furrowed.

I suddenly remember my iPod. Then, it's almost like Steel has read my mind 'cos he's throttling Skinny and shouting, 'Have you got anything to give back?'

Hurriedly, Skinny pulls my iPod and Peggy's purse out of his pocket. Sweat drips down his face. That's when I notice that Steel's skin is bone dry. It has the smooth sheen of lacquered door guards in temples. That's when I realise he speaks weird. In a kind of posh has-been way.

'Leave them alone, will you? Or I'll be back,' Steel says, releasing his prey and flicking back a loose strand of his sleek black hair.

The druggies slink off into the park.

Peg and I brush ourselves off.

'Hey, Steel, thanks a lot,' Peggy says.

'Thank you,' I say. Parrot-like.

Steel's eyes level with mine. Soften. He swings a long leg over the Harley and slips the motorbike helmet back on his head. 'Those guys are dangerous,' he says. 'You should keep away.'

Then he snaps the visor shut and, with a rev of the throttle and a snort of the exhaust pipe, accelerates away.

CHAPTER 2
Lovesick

'Wake up, Anna. Rise and shine.'

I hear Ma's voice a thousand miles away. She tweaks my ears, Buddha ears, which will bring me good luck. She believes.

She opens my curtain, goes back to the kitchen. Did I tell you she's a great cook? Without her I'd probably starve to death.

Dull sunlight and the comforting smell of *congee* rice porridge permeate the air. Ouch, my elbow hurts. I patched it up at Peg's place. The plaster has some dried blood on it. Better if I hide it from Ma.

I cover my face with my quilt and try to snatch a few more seconds of the amazing dream I was having about a motorbike rider free-falling down a waterfall. It's Steel. He's wearing a pair of tight jeans, black Converse All Stars sneakers and a bright yellow T-shirt. The bike catapults over the crest and Steel somersaults through the sparkling spray.

My friend, he said. But how did he know Peg and I were in trouble? Why did he come to rescue us?

Facts. What are the facts? I think, slurping the shredded pork *congee* with preserved egg that Ma has stayed up to prepare for me. I run through what I know about Steel for the zillionth time:

He picks Tiffany up from school in a brand new black BMW SUV;

He parks under the branches of the banyan tree near the school gates;

His SUV has tinted windows and the number plates LANTAU1;

A friendly black Doberman dithers around on the back seat.

Tiffany only joined my form this term, just after Chinese New Year. Only one more year (and a bit) before school's out. Yeah! Usually Mainlanders keep themselves to themselves, they suss that we Hongkongers kind of look down on them. But Tiffany goes one step further – she doesn't hang out with anyone.

For the first few weeks, I presumed Steel was her boyfriend. But whenever I saw him, I got goosebumps. It was Peggy who noticed he stared at me through the rear-view mirror of the SUV when we walked past. And that's when I started obsessing about him.

Then, last Thursday to be exact, the Phone Catch incident occurred. From the gates, I saw Steel standing on the pavement adjusting a side mirror. He was much taller than I imagined, slim, sharp-nosed. 'Like a movie star,' Wing said. In the excitement, just as we were passing behind him, I accidentally lost the grip of my mobile. But before it crashed to the pavement, Steel had scooped it up.

'Cute,' he said, dangling my Little Kitty phone charm before handing it back to me. I was struck by the lightness of his eyes. They were golden. Liquid gold.

'Thanks,' I murmured. Steel grinned nervously. Then Peggy grabbed my elbow, Wing tutted, and we tripped off.

Since then, my brain has been on Phone Catch action replay. Until last night, that is. Now it's looped to the Harley-Davidson dream. And you know what? I'm in free fall, plunging down that glittering waterfall. Out of control.

Ma has gone back into her room; she's dead tired from being on nights. She works on shifts at a bakery in the light industrial centre just down the road.

Her door is ajar. I pop my head round to say 'bye' but she's already asleep. Her pretty face is resting on her pillow. I get my double eyelids and cherry lips from her, my height from Dad. So Dad used to say. Apparently.

For once, I'm itching to get to school. I'm going to approach Tiffany, befriend her, find out what Steel told her about last night. That's the plan. Anyway.

When I walk into the classroom, it's buzzing with chit-chat and air-cons. There's a gaggle of girls peering over Wing's laptop. But Tiffany's desk is empty.

'Have you seen Tiffany?' I ask.

Peggy shrugs. 'Nope.' She looks tired, her eyes have bags, her skin is sallow.

'Were you spooked overnight?'

She shakes her head unhappily.

A minute before registration, Tiffany stalks in the classroom and sweeps past my desk like an icy blast from Beijing. What's new?

I hunker down in my seat and wait for first break, when we go to the snack shop.

We're four tables away from where Tiffany is sitting. Alone. Peggy is telling Wing and Mimi about last night.

I casually glance over while piercing a carton of lemon tea with a straw. Tiffany is engrossed in her iPad. As usual, she's immaculately turned out. Not a spot of grime on her white uniform. All tight tits and bum. Her face is as fine-featured as a Barbie doll. She has phoenix eyes that sweep upwards, whitish skin, rouged lips. I feel a stab of jealousy: of course she's Steel's girl. She's so beautiful, so lithe. Like him.

The sun pierces through a cloud and she puts on a pair of sunglasses.

Wing starts gossiping about her to Peggy and Mimi. 'Have you noticed how she glares if you go anywhere near her desk?' she says.

'Yeah, weird,' Mimi says. With the humidity, her glasses have slipped halfway down her nose.

'*Ting bu dong ta shuo shenme,* can't understand a word she says,' Peg says with a Canto accent.

They all nod.

I smirk.

Wing is fingering a spot on her chin. 'Remember the trip to Mai Po Marsh when she hid herself under an umbrella the whole time?'

'When I asked her if she felt sick, she gave me this really creepy look,' Mimi says, gnashing the metal braces in her teeth.

'Vain,' Peggy says, narrowing her eyes into slits.

Wing and Mimi seem to agree. Then we stand up 'cos the bell

is ringing.

For the rest of the day, Tiffany and I aren't in the same classes. And at home time, Mimi asks us to wait while she reports a lost phone at the office. So, by the time the four of us leave school, the SUV isn't on the street.

I go to Peg's place, as promised. After a drink, she switches her computer on for me. She tells me she's tired, she needs to take a nap. 'Maybe the hungry ghost is feeding on your *qi* energy,' I joke.

She lies on her bed and closes her eyes while I surf the Web. *Should I send a friend request to Tiffany?* I ask myself.

My Facebook homepage is up. I type her name: Tiffany Tang. Then change my mind. (*Wa!* She only has five friends. Sad!)

On impulse, I type in 'Steel', then 'Steal', and in desperation, 'Stele' but nothing comes up for him.

I flop beside Peggy, fantasize about his smooth muscular stomach and snapshot his nervous smile. His eyes become gold nuggets glinting in the sun.

I zoom in on Peggy's face. *Was it really an old debt I paid for last night?*

She's asleep. Her lips twitch and her cute childish dimples remind me of the day we first walked back unaccompanied from primary school together.

We marched down the busy street in step, interlocking fingers sticky with sugary egg waffles bought from a street hawker, the starched collar of my blouse rubbing my neck. The toothless medicine man waved, the shirtless newspaper man hawked, the bad-tempered guard in the lobby of Peggy's block snoozed. Her block was back-to-back with block C, 'C for "crap",' Peg and I joked, covering our mouths after saying the naughty English word.

We made up a story about the blocks being giants' legs cut off at the crotch, standing around wishing they could walk someplace else.

Then her Ma's blob of a face appeared from an iron-grilled window high above. Time for Peggy to go up to her rabbit-hutch flat with its damp walls, chipped floor tiles and sluggish toilets. Time for me to take the shortcut to the adjacent private estate.

Tsuen Wan was an okay place to live until the manufacturing business went over the border to China. Now it's a higgledy-piggledy jumble of high rise and warehouses, temples and flyovers, Mom-Pop shops and shopping malls.

These days Peggy is often home alone 'cos her parents only come back from Guangzhou once a month to pick up their old age allowance. Her big brother is supposed to keep an eye on her, but he works late and chases skirts.

Peggy's phone rings, she wakes; it's someone called Jane. I feel a tinge of jealousy. *Who's she?*

After demolishing some instant noodles, we play computer games, have a smoke, text Wing and Mimi. Around eleven we go out for a late-night snack at a local *dai pai dong*.

'How about we go to China Chicks?' I say. Shrimp carcasses are scattered around our makeshift table.

Peggy narrows her reptilian eyes. 'I'd rather play a game of snooker.'

'What's it like in there anyway?' I say. I've never been to the parlour she likes to hang out in. Not interested. In ball games, that is.

'Cool.'

'Just for one song?'

'And I wonder which one would that be,' she says.

I start singing and she kind of croaks along:

> *'Feel the power,*
> *Taste my glory,*
> *Crossed swords,*
> *Blood love,*
> *What's your story?*
> *Drip drop,*
> *Stitch clot,*
> *Silk sheets,*
> *You're neat,*
> *Bloodswell.*
> *All's well.*
> *Ding dong*
> *Bell.'*

CHAPTER 3
Black rainstorm

The weather has turned bad, there's a rainstorm alert. It's really blustery outside and on the way to school I'm drenched by passing storm clouds.

Tiffany is at her desk (dry as a bone). She sits three rows behind me. Her head is down and she's plugged into an iPod. She's studying a Geography textbook while twirling a gold-capped pen between her thumb and first finger.

She looks up and we exchange glances. Hers is as cold as the Tibetan plateau, her lips a crack in the permafrost. By the time I have twitched my face into a fake smile, her nose is back in her book.

I prod my umbrella into an overflowing stand, dry my shoes with a cloth, and silently curse.

Maybe it's my imagination, but throughout double Maths there's like two lumps of coal searing my back. At break, the Ice Queen is nowhere to be seen. Next class, Teacher Pang plonks a pile of exercise books on the front desk of my column. Tran takes his, and passes the rest to me. I swing the books to the desk behind me and meet Tiffany's eyes. They're unblinking, aggressive, as if we're in a battle and she's defending her territory. *Why's she so angry with me?* I fear the worst.

First class after lunch is Chemistry and in the lab we work in twos. I rack my brains for a scheme to be Tiffany's partner. Maybe Peggy could pretend to be sick and skip the class for me. Annoyingly, she refuses. 'I'm already in enough trouble,' she says.

The afternoon stretches in front of me and I'm sweating with the high humidity, and sinking fast. When the sky becomes a mass of black clouds and raindrops splatter at the windows, Teacher Pang has to switch on the lights 'cos it's so dark.

Then the sky is torn by jagged streaks of lightning. Blasts of thunder split our ears. The school intercom system crackles into action and the principal's voice bleats from above: 'I have been informed that the Observatory will issue the Black Rainstorm signal at 2 pm. All students are required to return home immediately. Those of you who take school buses should listen for further instructions.'

Everyone cheers and starts to pack their bags. Except me, that is. For the first time in my life, I don't want to leave school! I loiter around my desk, peeved that I still haven't connected with Tiffany, and trying to muster enough courage to turn back and speak to her. Peggy is leaning on the wall near the classroom door, wondering what's taking me so long. Teacher Pang is waiting by the air-con to switch it off. I reluctantly walk towards the exit.

'Let's go to my place,' Peggy says. The floor of the corridor is a patchwork of puddles.

'I think I'd better get home,' I say, dragging my feet. Ma will probably be off work until the rainstorm alert is lifted and she'll go ballistic if I'm not there.

'What's up?' Peggy asks. We're out of the school gates,

hunched under our umbrellas. The rain is falling in sheets and my feet are already soaked from rivulets seeking drains.

The SUV is on the street, windscreen wipers swishing at full pelt.

'I wanted to talk to Tiffany,' I say, more shrilly than expected.

Peggy is battling with her umbrella; a gust of wind has blown it inside out. 'Why didn't you then?'

When I don't answer, she stops on the pavement, faces me, and laughs. 'You fancy Steel, right?'

I grab her arm and forge ahead, using my umbrella like a shield against the driving rain. From the corner of my eye, I see a fogged-up window of the SUV opening and my heart leaps.

Steel leans over the passenger seat towards us. 'Can I drive you home?' he calls, looking straight at me.

At that moment, my attention is diverted by Tiffany. She barges in front of me and, with a snort of contempt, flings the passenger door open and jumps in. The door slams shut. The window closes. 'You're forgetting about Janet,' I hear her shout.

There's a heated exchange of words.

'*Chi sin*,' Peggy says.

We're just about to move on when the window opens again. Steel's left arm is warding off Tiffany and he's beckoning us inside. Peg and I clamber into the back seat.

'Thanks a lot,' I say, leaning my sodden umbrella against my leg.

There's a stony silence as the SUV cruises down the road. A *yin yang* medallion dangling from the rear-view mirror swings like a pendulum when we turn corners.

'I'm Steel,' he says.

Tiffany tuts.

'Yeah, we know,' Peg says.

'And thanks again for the other night,' I say.

'Don't mention it,' Steel says. The mirror reflects his eyes. They're bright. Alert.

'So you like motorbikes?' I say.

He nods. His shoulders seem stiff. 'You were in danger. Peggy too.'

'Just passing by, were you?' Peggy says airily.

Steel nods slowly.

'Your car has unusual number plates,' I say, desperately trying to keep the conversation flowing.

Tiffany rolls her eyes.

'Yes,' Steel says. 'Have you been to Lantau?'

'Yeah, Disneyland. Shopping in Tung Chung.'

'What about the south side?'

'Yeah … ' I say, and a childhood terror flashes before me.

'Like it?'

'I was just a kid.'

'So?' Steel says, grinning.

'Ma rented a holiday flat for a weekend. I turned on the shower and a gigantic spider popped out of the spout.'

'Ugh,' Peg says, and cringes.

'I've had this huge phobia about bugs ever since,' I say.

Tiffany titters, and turns on the radio. There's a weather

warning. Blah blah about staying inside and avoiding areas where there may be landslides.

The traffic lights change to green and Steel presses on the accelerator. We've almost reached the front gates of my housing block.

Ma is home. The TV is on and there's the familiar smell of garlic, ginger and sesame oil. 'I'm making your favourite *tofu* dish,' she says, throwing shreds of ginger into a sizzling wok. On the table, there are the end cuts of loaves that the conveyer belt in her bakery has rejected. I'll eat the fresh food. She'll eat up the old, and the crumbs. Frugal. Thrifty. That's my Ma.

After eating, I wash my small porcelain bowl and matching soup spoon. I tell her I've got loads of homework, and escape to my bedroom.

I Google 'Lantau' but soon get bored, so chat on Facebook instead. Wing wants another session at the Rock Band studio next week. Mimi says it's my turn to book.

I re-stick one of my pop star posters that is peeling off the wall. I select from My Favourites list in iTunes, plug in my earphones and turn the volume up full blast.

Half way through *I Want to Get Laid,* a thought pops up in my mind: *How did Steel know where I live?*

CHAPTER 4

Pet therapy

A long-haired grey and white cat with a flat face is purring on my lap. I stroke her fur and she curls herself up into a ball, two front paws covering her face. I check her name-tag: 'Fluffy'. How original is that?

Peg and I are chilling out on orange floor cushions. Her cat isn't so friendly. Whenever she puts him on her lap, he jumps off. I suggest she befriends another – there must be around thirty of them in the play corner, chasing balls of wool, scratching sisal posts, sleeping, cleaning. The lights are dim and the music is low 'cos apparently cats don't like bright light and noise.

Pet therapy, that's what I've come for – some love and affection. Wing told us about the place. It's on the eighth floor of Causeway Bay Plaza. Sounded so cool Peg and I caught the MTR here straight after school.

It's been two long weeks. Two eternal weeks of sleeping through class, tossing and turning at nights. Steel. Where are you? In my dreams, I eat and drink his smooth skin, his cat-like sleekness, his glinting golden eyes.

Aloof. Snobby. That's what Peggy says he is. But I'm not so sure. He seems the lonely type to me.

Since the Secret Garden incident, Steel hasn't picked Tiffany up from school. The white-turbaned Indian who chauffeurs her in the morning does. So now I'm convinced he's *not* interested in me.

Why should he be? He's so cool. So handsome. So grown-up. I'm still wearing white ankle socks and school uniform.

I haven't managed to befriend Tiffany either. When I approach her she tenses up and turns away. Once, she actually scowled at me. I've found out some interesting stuff about her family though. She lives in Kowloon Tong, an up-market residential area, where Bruce Lee had a house. Her Dad writes letters to newspapers about preserving Hong Kong's wildlife. And Taoism. Can't say I know much about either. Taoism is an ancient Chinese religion. Followers love trees and rocks and living in harmony with nature.

'You're thinking of Steel again,' Peggy says. We've left Cat Corner and are eating smelly bean curd on the street. She's right. She sounds kind of jealous though. Maybe it's 'cos she has never had a guy interested in her.

'What's wrong with fancying a guy anyway?' I ask her later, sitting on my bed, Japanese patches stuck on the soles of my feet. They're supposed to draw out the toxins in your body.

We're back at my place, a stone's throw from the government housing estate where Peggy lives. She likes coming here 'cos it's all of nine hundred square foot and right above the 24-hour 7-Eleven shop and the MTR station. My room stinks of nail varnish 'cos we've just painted our toenails black.

Peggy flares her nostrils. She sniffs roughly and says, 'Let's have a ciggy.'

We light up. I light three incense sticks on my bedside table to mask the smell. A few puffs later, the key of the front door is turning. *Gaau choa!* Ma has come back from the wet market. We hastily stub our cigarettes out and I check my bedroom door is locked.

When there's the sound of cooking, I go to the bathroom to clean my teeth and go into the kitchen to say hi. Chunks of pork and white radish are neatly prepared on the chopping board. Spinach is sizzling in the wok and the aroma of fried scallion and garlic make my stomach juices churn. 'Dinner will be ready at seven,' Ma says, 'then I must be out of the door.'

Peggy takes the cue and leaves. I give her our 'I'll call you later' sign.

The TV is on. Ma and I have our bowls to our mouths cleaning out the last few grains of rice. We're watching two policemen carrying a stretcher out of an old building in Mongkok. The narrow steps are slippery and the body of the victim is covered. It's the third murder in a spate of similar killings.

The victims – to date – are women who operate out of one-room flats. Prostitutes. They avoid using pimps by renting their own place and advertising their services directly.

Ma's eyes are suddenly fixed intently on mine. She reminds me not to let strangers in, she wishes I'd stay at home more.

'Don't worry, Ma. I'm a big girl. No way I'd open the door. Stop bothering me. I've got tons of homework,' I lie.

When she smiles I feel a twinge of guilt. She's worried for my safety, I know. But she's even more concerned that I'll fail my exams, not get into uni and start selling my body instead. And her future depends on me 'cos she barely earns enough to keep us, and our relatives in Hunan. She's forty-two, a single Mum and not very skilled at anything. When she was my age she moved down from the countryside to work at a massage joint in Shenzhen. My Dad – thirty years older than her and with a family in Hong Kong – took her as his 'second wife'. When she got pregnant, Dad bribed the immigration guys on the China side. Ma crossed the border and two months later gave birth to me. In this flat. Dad's wife was mad to death when she discovered why her husband spent his weekends in Tsuen Wan. So Dad stopped visiting.

A few months later, Ma was so desperate for money she phoned Dad to ask for help. But the wife picked up and told her to go to hell. Then Ma found a job in the bakery, and, on the advice of a workmate, applied for the right of abode.

My first memory is of her smacking me across the face, really hard. 'That's to remember to keep your family background a secret,' she said. And the day before I started kindergarten, she whipped me ten times with a bamboo cane. 'That's to remind you to speak Cantonese,' she said.

I was thirteen when Dad died, but he left some money in a secret bank account for my education. There's enough money for uni in there. Unless someone's nicked it.

I've never forgotten those beatings. Maybe Ma's way of teaching stuff is good 'cos although I'm kind of shy, I've got some good friends and nobody knows my history. Except Peg.

CHAPTER 5
Visitations

When the bottle gate clunks closed and Ma's footsteps fade down the corridor, I text Peggy: **your place?**

yeah, she replies, **bring gaga.**

The Lady Gaga DVD is a rip-off copy from Shenzhen. On the cover Gaga is nude. But her three naughty bits are hidden by white stickers. She's a *gweipo* – a Western woman – and I don't really know what she's singing about. But she's cool. Cool and smart. Peg and I love her curvy body, pouty lips and white skin. We adore her sexy dancers too. We're watching them now, jumping and jiving with them, in our bras and panties.

The door-bell rings.

'Turn the volume down,' Peggy shouts, rushing to put a T-shirt on.

'Expecting someone?' I ask, an image of the dead prostitute flashing through my mind.

Peg purses her lips. Says no, frowns, then says maybe yes. Her mother has arranged for a priest to come and appease the hungry ghost.

She peers through the eye-level spy-hole of the front door, confirms it's a Taoist out there, 'with another guy. With ... Steel.'

'Steel?' I cry, my heart jumping into my throat. I push Peggy aside to take a look. She's right. It is him. He's dressed in a grey gown, white leggings and a stiff black hat.

I snatch my clothes and bolt into the bathroom, dress frantically, straighten my hair, rub off the bright red lipstick that Peggy painted on me and silently scream at my face in the mirror.

Steel seems totally unfazed when I emerge. It's as if he knew I was inside all along. The priest and Peggy are standing in the centre of the room with their backs to me. Steel, who's facing me, gives me a shy smile. To my horror the TV hasn't been switched off: Gaga is still gyrating on the screen. I reach for the remote and fumble for the red dot, feeling my cheeks burning with embarrassment. Steel smiles knowingly.

When I'm done, he tweaks the priest's elbow. The priest turns towards me. He's as tall as Steel, as slender, and has the same varnished sheen to his skin. He has a wispy beard and light eyes. His hair must be really long 'cos there's a lumpy bun under his headdress. The blue silk gown he's wearing is hand-embroidered with suns and moons and *yin yang* symbols. 'This is Master Tang,' Steel says, addressing me.

Master Tang acknowledges my presence with a grave nod. 'I'm here to perform a ceremony that will pacify the hungry ghost who's haunting this flat,' he says, glancing around the room.

'Master Tang is from the Luen Institute,' Peggy whispers to me.

'Where's that?'

'Ten minutes' walk from here, up by the Western Monastery.'

'How long has there been a presence?' the priest asks.

'Since the last Hungry Ghost festival,' Peggy replies.

Master Tang sniffs the air, looks at the ceiling and studies where the windows are. 'The *feng shui* is good here. There's a through wind and nothing is obstructing the exits and entrances. But THIS could do with more tender loving care,' he says, pointing to the family shrine hung on the wall above the dining table. The curled mug shots of Peggy's grandparents gaze through a thicket of charred incense sticks. Only one of the red lights bordering the joss house is working and three mouldy oranges are the only offering on its ledge.

Peggy laughs nervously.

'The souls of the dead need the prayers of the living,' Master Tang says, digging into his shoulder bag. He arranges pyramids of apples, fresh oranges and pomelos on the ledge, lights three new incense sticks and bows three times.

'Is the hungry ghost one of my relatives?' Peggy asks.

Master Tang and Steel swivel their heads as if searching for something. They stare at each other as if comparing mental notes, then simultaneously answer: no.

Behind their backs, Peg and I exchange glances, raise eyebrows.

There's a sudden creak – like a spurt of bamboo growth, a contraction of wood on a dry day – and Master Tang crouches down, as if ready to pounce. For a minute or so, it's so quiet you could hear a toothpick drop. I gawp at Steel. Gobsmacked.

'Nothing to worry about,' Master Tang says, straightening up.

Peggy snorts.

'This hungry ghost doesn't have enough food and water to

survive in the afterlife. We need to conduct a ceremony,' Master Tang says, straightening his headdress.

He starts shuffling round the room. Steel follows directly behind, chiming a metal gong and intoning incomprehensible chants and prayers. Before they reach Peg's bedroom, we hastily tidy up the clothes and make-up that's strewn all over the floor.

After an age of circling round the flat, Steel bangs the gong loudly and Master Tang announces that the ritual is completed.

Steel is fishing around in the capacious sleeves of his gown. He retrieves a selection of trinkets. They're tiny jade animals strung on red strings. 'Which Chinese animal were you born under?' he asks me shyly.

'A sheep.'

Peggy is a monkey. Steel sifts through the bracelets to choose an appropriate talisman for us both. Mine is a dog: dogs protect sheep.

When I put out my palm to receive it, my hand shakes involuntarily. Peggy helps me with the clasp. Then I do the same for her, silently vowing never to take mine off.

'Wear them at all times,' Master Tang says. 'They will keep you safe.'

There's an awkward silence until Peggy asks Master Tang if he would like some tea. He declines, says they should leave.

'My Ma says don't mess around with ghosts,' my voice blurts. Little Miss Tactless, or what?

Steel swings round, eyes flashing. 'That's good advice,' he says, dead serious.

'Not that I've seen one,' I say, flummoxed by his reaction. 'Anyway, Ma says if you're a good person, you can't see them.' My voice trails away with embarrassment.

Master Tang nods sagely. His mouth opens and shuts, as if he isn't sure how to respond. Steel is also searching for what to say. But then his iPhone rings and he's talking to someone about their next appointment. 'We've really got to be going now,' he says.

Master Tang offers Peggy a handful of yellow and red posters decorated with strange calligraphy. 'They're lucky charms to paste around your home,' he explains. Then they bid good-bye.

Steel gives me one last curious smile.

As soon as they are out of the door, Peggy throws herself down on the sofa and lights a cigarette. 'Ghostbusters or what? Wait until we tell Mimi and Wing.' She rubs the tail of a dragon tattoo that's peeping out from underneath her shorts.

We smoke in silence for a while. I'm still not sure what to think. 'It was as if they could really see the hungry ghost,' I say.

Peggy takes a long drag from her cigarette. 'I'm not so sure.'

'I just don't believe in ghosts. Do you?' I say, suddenly questioning why I bother lighting incense for Dad at the family shrine when Ma asks me to.

'Nope.' Peggy stubs out her cigarette and reaches for the Gaga DVD sleeve.

I tell Peggy I have to get home early tonight, which is true. I haven't started packing yet.

It's already dark outside. Rainwater is rushing along the roadside drains and a dirty splash from a passing taxi soils my socks. But I don't care. I'm on a high. Steel has come back into my life. He's some kind of Taoist. Weird, but true. And he can see ghosts.

Does that make him a bad person?

Ma's not home yet. The family shrine is glowing red; I prop a couple of apples on the ledge, just in case. Then I boil up some frozen dumplings, go into my bedroom, check my emails, surf the Web.

At first I don't think there's anything unusual about the wind gusting around the block. I absent-mindedly raise a hand to stop the curtain from billowing onto my computer screen. Then the lights suddenly flick off and it's pitch black.

I search for my desk light switch. A click of the switch and I'm screaming and my chair has crashed onto the tiles. 'Cos there's a spider hanging from the ceiling. A hairy spider, the size of my fist, dangling on a thread and making a mechanical clicking sound.

The desk light switches itself off again and the spider's eyes glint a luminous green. In my haste to escape, my legs smack into the fallen chair and I stumble to the floor. That's when spindly legs grip my arm and I feel a sharp sting. I imagine the spider squeezing itself into the deep hole it's dug in my flesh, but I'm too terrified to pull it out.

'Ma,' I shout, in vain. 'Cos Ma isn't there, of course. I remember my mobile is on the dining table and cry out with relief. Miraculously, the spider releases its grip. But then I feel its shaggy body brush against my cheek, imagine it bouncing back to launch another attack.

I pull myself to my feet, pound towards the front room, screaming as something flaps around my face. My whole being is focused on finding the doorknob, on escaping, on seeking light. I fling the door open, race around flicking on the lights, shrieking.

The key turns in the front door, I'm rigid with fear. But it's only Ma, armed with presents for our Chinese relatives. I rush to her, wrap my arms around her, sweating and sobbing.

'Little Anna, what's wrong?' she says, blinking under the ceiling spotlights.

A little voice warns me not to tell her; I bite my lip to restrain myself. 'Bad dream,' I mutter, brushing down my arms and legs.

Ma sighs, lowers her heavy bags on the table and clicks the TV remote. 'We have to be up at five-thirty tomorrow morning. So how about you just go back to sleep?'

I sit on the sofa for a while, numb with shock. There's a Korean serial showing – the Korean fiancée is suicidal 'cos her boyfriend has left her for another girl. Ma tootles around, packing, wrapping, eating up old food. Gradually, I summon up enough courage to go back into my room.

'Night, Ma,' I say as casually as I can, turning the doorknob, switching the light on, leaving the door ajar.

The curtain is hanging meek and quiet; there's no sign of the spider. For a few seconds, I think it must have been a dream.

Until I spot it, lying shrivelled on its back, motionless, on top of my computer keyboard.

I phone Peg. She doesn't believe me.

CHAPTER 6
A walking corpse

I'm surgically attached to my iPod, listening to some grunge. I'm cold and hungry and feeling as rotten as a bad egg.

A low mist is moving across the paddy fields, blending them into a single grey smudge of land and sky. How I hate the Chinese countryside.

On the train, there aren't even enough hard seats for all the passengers. Noisy peasants are sitting in the corridor outside the compartment, seemingly oblivious to the stench of toilets. Piles of seed husks, tea leaves and fruit peel litter the floor. At Shaoguan station an old lady with two live chickens parks herself on a vacated seat opposite me. The chickens are hanging upside down, legs trussed with rope, wings flapping. If they don't stop squawking soon I might completely lose it.

I'm not speaking to Ma. She looks hurt. Which reminds me, annoyingly, that I did agree, finally, to visit my grandparents in Hunan over the Easter break. Her relatives are the only ones we have.

'Next time I'll take you to the mountains where *Avatar* was filmed, I promise,' she says.

Big deal. Everything is always next time.

I press fast forward to skip a track. *And what about the spider last night?* An itchy red welt on my forearm proves the attack really happened. *Is it pure coincidence that I told Steel that spiders were my pet hate?*

Fragments of the conversation I had with him in the SUV, Tiffany's scowling and tittering, and the *yin yang* medallion swing through my mind. 'Yeah, weird,' I hear Mimi saying.

Then I remember Tiffany rolling her eyes. Can she tell I've fallen in love with Steel? Is she his girlfriend after all?

It seems like the spider bit me deliberately.

I'm desperate to find out more.

Instead, I've been banished to China for a week.

Usually, the only time Ma and I go to Hunan is to celebrate Chinese New Year. It's the Chinese province where Ma comes from. We consider the little village in the middle of nowhere where she grew up to be our ancestral home. That's 'cos, despite my surname, we're not recognised as members of my father's clan. Last February we didn't come 'cos Ma was sick. So she wants to make up for it this month. She says Grandma is feeling her age and Grandpa's legs are gammy. She says they could do with some help with the spring planting.

I remenber that their peasant house is stuck in the middle of a field the size of a football pitch. You have to walk along dirt paths alongside knee-high furrows to reach it. The last time I was there, it was so fricking freezing I had to wear all my clothes in bed, and cuddle up to Ma. Our toilet was a chamber pot in the corner of the room. Every morning, Ma sloshed the contents into a cesspit at the back of the house. The sewage was later used to fertilise the fields. I was infested by worms which poked in and out of my arsehole all night. Never again would I visit, I vowed!

The train has stopped at a station again. Unshaven grey men push steaming trolleys shouting, 'Beef jerky, fried duck's tongues, pig's intestines,' and passengers stick their heads out of the windows, bartering, spitting and emptying their flasks of tea. Ma pours some boiled water in a carton of pot noodles and passes it to me. 'Next stop, Changsha,' she says in her please-don't-answer-me-back-in-public voice. I slurp the noodles loudly and burp. No one bats an eyelid. This is China, after all.

At Changsha we transfer to a local train and it's so crowded I'm forced to stand in the aisle and hang on to a grubby rail. The compartment is even dirtier and smellier than the last one. When a cleaning lady mops between my legs and carelessly smears accumulated spit and debris over my new trainers, the worst swear word I know buzzes around my head.

Then there's a two-hour taxi ride up into terraced hills, through a labyrinth of tunnels and along bumpy muddy roads. All the peasant houses have black brick roofs. It's been unseasonably wet and there's a rumour that our fields are flooded.

Young guys around here drive motorcycles. Girlfriends ride as pillions, their legs folded together and swung awkwardly to one side of the chassis. To prove they are virgins, or what? *Oh yeah.* Ride on!

In the taxi, I ponder about Steel coming to Peg's place to exorcise the hungry ghost. *Did he know I was there too?* The more I ponder, the worse I feel.

But when I see my grandparents, I can't help perking up a little. They're so pleased to see Ma and me; tears drip down their faces. We don't hug or anything (Chinese don't do hugging) but Ma is laughing and crying and blowing her nose on soggy tissues. The house has radiators now, and windowpanes. And one flushing toilet! Still no curtains.

Grandma bustles around the kitchen stuffing rice stalks under the iron stove and lighting them. She skins a scrawny chicken, guts a freshwater fish. Ma and her sister exchange recipes for spicy pork while they chop the vegetables. Grandpa sits on a straight-backed chair smoking cigarettes with Uncle Bai, whose wife, Aunty Gu, is talking to me in a rough local dialect which I barely understand.

Just before dinner, I try to send a text and, amazingly, there's a network. **wotcha peggy**, I write, **there's human shit on the fields here.**

hold your nose, she writes.

back on sunday, I reply. (Amazingly, before leaving the railway station Ma managed to buy return tickets at a not too rip-off price from a scalper.)

cool.

But that's as cool as it gets. Every meal my tongue is scalded by chillies. Every night I have to sleep with Ma in a rickety bed on a rock mattress. During the long days, I have to listen to my relatives' sing-song dialect, unless they remember to switch to Mandarin for my benefit. Swatting the clouds of flies buzzing around the rooms fails to dispel the horror of the Spider Attack.

Then my logical mind develops a reason for it, and I hate myself even more.

Tiffany. It was Tiffany. 'Cos she's Steel's girlfriend.

It's the last night and we're sitting around the table in a large draughty space on the ground floor. It's freezing cold and the radiators aren't working. Everyone is wearing baggy coats and pompom hats. Grandpa is stomping around in muddy boots.

On the wall opposite there's a large portrait of Chairman Mao, and a Chinese almanac. Chicken and pork bones are scattered on the plastic tablecloth, a murky soup is congealing in a wok and there's the *crack-crack* of melon seeds being prised open and spat out. Uncle Bai takes a long drag of his cigarette and stubs out the butt on the tiled floor. I think they're talking about the price of pork. As long as I nod demurely from time to time, no one bothers to translate.

The wind picks up and rattles the windowpanes. It seeps through the gaps in the window frames. Outside is as black as sesame paste – the nearest house is a five-minute hike across the field. I'm nodding and idly wondering what Steel is doing, when in the distance there's the steady clang of a gong coming towards us. Ding-DING, it goes. Insistent. Growing louder.

Aunty Gu pauses mid-sentence into her recipe for lotus root and pork bone soup. Everyone is alert and listening. Then Grandma hobbles towards the door and switches off the only light: a bare bulb hanging from a wire above our heads.

'Ah! It's Saturday,' Uncle To whispers.

'They haven't come by for a while,' Grandma says, tip-toeing back to her chair. Uncle Bai's cigarette glows in the darkness.

'Ma?'

She squeezes my hand, puts a finger to her lips.

The gong dings float on the wind towards us, interspersed with two men chanting 'Yo ho, yo ho' in unison.

The chant gradually dies away and Aunty Lan motions towards the window.

'Keep away,' Uncle To hisses.

'They're taking the path past Old Zheng's tonight,' she says.

'Keep away woman,' Uncle To barks. 'You know what bad luck it is if they see you.'

'They're nearly out of sight,' Aunty Lan says, undeterred by her brother's rudeness.

My heart is thumping as I follow Ma to the window. I can just about make out a procession of two, or three, men in bulky black robes. The one at the back is unusually tall. Is that a big hat he's wearing? The one in front is carrying a lantern and banging the gong.

Uncle Bai takes a noisy slurp from his flask of tea and laughs nervously. The eerie spectre has now disappeared beyond the horizon. Nothing moves except wispy clouds fleeting across a full moon.

'Mrs Lim says that since her son has been back, her rice yield has doubled. And last week her daughter-in-law delivered a son,' Grandma says.

'It always brings good fortune to the family,' Grandpa says.

'What does?' I ask Ma, in Cantonese.

Grandma has switched the light back on. Ma gives me a tell-you-later smile and says it's time for bed.

'Do you think the tradition is still going on in Hong Kong?' Aunty Lan asks.

'Probably,' Ma replies. 'It's so expensive to ship bodies by plane. And smuggling is rife, especially in the New Territories.'

Uncle Bai and Aunty Gu nod.

'What tradition?' I say. Impatient now.

All eyes are on me. Grandpa speaks first. 'Of walking corpses,' he says, slapping his thigh. A piece of mud from under his boot comes loose.

'Walking corpses?' I remember that's what they call those stiff Chinese vampires with pale green furry skin, long tongues and razor-sharp fingernails. They hop around killing humans to absorb their life essence in old horror movies.

'I don't get it,' I say.

Ma explains the origin of corpse-walking. When Chinese people die away from home, their relatives often arrange for their bodies to be carried back to the Taoist temple nearest their ancestral village for funerary rites. This tradition has been going on for thousands of years. Corpse-walkers in Hunan are famous for having the power to walk corpses for days on end, up and over mountains, through villages. Apparently, the corpses march in step with the living.

'That is so, completely, weird,' I say.

'It's magic,' says Grandpa quietly.

Chinese superstition, I think.

Grandpa grunts.

'Surely the bodies are just piggy-backed,' I say.

Aunty Gu titters.

But I'm insistent. 'Anyway, why bother carrying them back?'

'Because they died away from home, their souls haven't left their bodies,' Ma says. 'They're not peaceful. So their descendants aren't either.'

'They are the undead,' whispers Aunty Gu.

'Like hungry ghosts?'

'No,' Uncle To rejoins. 'Hungry ghosts died close to home, so their souls have left their bodies. But their family members didn't prepare a proper funeral so they are fated to wander around the earth feeding on the living.'

'What do you mean, a *proper* funeral?'

'You know – blessings, spirit money, paper gifts, food,' Ma says. There's a touch of irritation in her voice.

'So I've just seen a corpse being transported back home?' I ask, shuddering.

Ma nods.

'Why did you switch the light off, Grandma?'

'Corpses sometimes get away and kill strangers,' she replies.

Uncle To is shaking his head. 'We shouldn't have looked. One of them may come back to attack us.'

Uncle Bai cracks another melon seed between his teeth. 'That's why I always ask my wife to keep a good supply of chicken's eggs and sticky rice in the house.'

Aunty Lan smiles. 'And a big black guard dog.'

Ma is looking at her watch: it's already past midnight and we have to be up at five to catch the train back to Hong Kong. For once, I look forward to sharing a bed with her.

Upstairs, I text Peg immediately: **just seen something gross.**

what? she replies.

tell you tomorrow.

'Have you seen a walking corpse before?' I ask Ma later, snuggled by her side.

Ma sighs. 'Only on TV.'

I toss and turn for a while. 'Ma, I really don't get it. I mean, let's say you ... pass away in Hong Kong, will I have to arrange for your body to be transported here? How can I organise that?'

'Go to a Taoist temple. Ask a priest,' she murmurs, already half asleep.

CHAPTER 7
Yuanfen

No matter how much I blow my nose, it leaks like a water pipe. It's red and sore: the consequence of a shitty week in Hunan. Now it's the first day after half-term and I'm going to walk straight up to Tiffany, grab her arm and ask for an explanation.

But I'm in for a mega-disappointment. The Ice Queen turns up the millisecond before registration, grabs her school exam timetable, and disappears.

It's the first break. Peggy, Wing, Mimi and I are sitting at our table in the snack shop drinking Taiwanese bubble teas. Peggy is in such a strop I decide to call it quits and go home. I'm dying to check out the movies about walking corpses that Ma has told me about anyway. I want to swing by the video shop on the way back, and do a search on YouTube.

So when the bell rings for the next class, I say I'm feeling too sick to stay, and make a quick exit.

There's a bench under the banyan tree outside the school gates. I sit down to suck up the glutinous pearls of the Taiwanese tea, feeling frustrated and flu-ey. It's an overcast day, dull as my thoughts. I'm just about to phone Ma when a yellow sports car catches my attention. The driver is … Steel; he's driving a Mercedes Sports Coupe! He slows the car down, everything slows down, my stomach flutters. He waves from the driving seat and gives me a bashful smile. He parks on the other side of the road between two cars and cuts the engine. Then he's crossing the road, walking towards me, standing above me.

I suck up a glutinous pearl too fast, it hits the back of my throat and I explode into a coughing fit. I shake my fringe over my eyes to hide my embarrassment.

'Fisherman's Friends are good for coughs,' he says, close now, reaching into his jacket pocket. The butterflies in my stomach are flapping their wings. His thick black eyelashes quiver. The cough sweets click as he shakes the crinkly packet. His fingers are long and elegant; his fingernails have half-moons.

'Thanks,' I say, as coolly as I can manage. My chapped lower lip cracks when I smile.

Steel tears off the right-hand corner of the packet. I cover my face to suppress a cough and crank my other hand forward. Steel shakes the packet (*please, one, just one, and not on the ground, I pray*). A lozenge plops onto my open palm. Restraining an instinct to store it as precious treasure, I pop it into my mouth.

Steel's head is cocked to one side. Awkward. Stiff. This isn't easy for him either. 'Have you got time to talk?'

All the butterflies in my stomach flip over, cataleptic. I suck the sweet furiously, feel my cheeks colouring and repress the urge to chop my ugly nose off. 'I have to go home. I'm sick,' I say, sniffing to prove it.

But my butt stays glued to the bench.

'Yeah, you don't look so well.' Steel locks the Mercedes with a zap of his remote. 'But how about the two of us have a bite to eat first?'

'I'm not very hungry.'

He looks across the street, eyes up a noodle shop.

'But I s'pose I could eat some *congee*,' I say, before I can stop myself.

The noodle shop is empty, apart from a cleaning lady who is mopping the floor. *Mahjong* tiles clatter from a loft above our heads.

Steel sits opposite me. I sneak a look at him as he studies the menu. He reminds me of a racehorse at Happy Valley: smooth, sleek, and leggy. I love his mop-top coiffed hair. He's the prince of my dreams, despite the spider.

He orders two bowls of *congee* – one plain, the other with pig's blood – then unwraps my chopsticks and dunks them in a bowl of boiled water. He takes off his jacket and loosens the collar of his shirt. (It's hot, hot.)

I sip some bubble tea trying to drum up the courage to say something. Like kamikaze pilots, the millions of questions I've wanted to ask him for weeks are bombarding my mind.

But Steel speaks first. He leans towards me, elbows on the table, head in his hands. 'Anna, I'm sorry, I mean, really sorry. About the spider. You must have been scared to death.'

'How … how do you …?' A knot of sadness wraps itself around my throat and I can't finish what I want to say.

Steel's tone softens. 'Look, Anna. That's why I'm here. To explain.'

I still can't speak. But I can feel his golden eyes on me, pleading for my forgiveness. It takes a long moment for me to realise that I'm really upset.

'It wasn't me,' he says.

'What do you mean?' I ask miserably.

'Tiffany. It was Tiffany. She doesn't like you.'

'Oh.'

He frowns.

I still need time for the truth to sink in.

'She doesn't want us to see each other.'

'But why?' I say, prepared for the worst.

Then I can't bear to hear what the answer may be. I mean, how could she, like, magic a spider in my room?

Steel smiles guiltily. 'You'll understand fully one day.'

'How about now? I don't intend to sound so tetchy.

Steel slowly meets my eyes, and says, 'She's telekinetic.'

'What?'

Enunciating each syllable slowly, he says, 'Te-le-ki-ne-tic.'

A no-answer buzzer buzzes in my brain. 'Pass.'

'She has the ability to manipulate matter. It's a psychic skill.'

I'm coughing again, foraging for a tissue.

'She's promised me she won't do it again.' Steel says, offering me another Fisherman's Friend. I can't stop spluttering.

The food arrives. The *congee* is piping hot.

'You caught your cold in China, I suppose,' he says, stirring the cubes of pig's blood in an effort to cool them down.

My head jerks back in surprise. How does he know I went? I haven't told anyone, except Peg.

Steel stares at me, a touch of mischief tweaking at his

cheekbones.

I blow my nose to give myself more time, decide to conduct an experiment. 'Yeah, I went to Shenzhen with Peggy.'

His eyes narrow, his lips flatten. 'Yeah?' he says. As if he knows I'm lying.

I jiggle the straw of my bubble tea and take another swig.

He slides his elbows forward again. Entreating. Concerned. 'Can I trust you?'

My conscience kicks in and I feel a tinge of guilt, and regret. Regret for telling a lie. *How I long to share all my secrets with someone. With him.*

So I turn his question round. 'Can I trust you?'

'Do you want the honest answer?' he asks, suddenly playful.

'What do you mean?'

'What I say, as usual.'

I feel a tinge of frustration. This conversation isn't going anywhere.

But he's smiling again, looking at me as if to say, 'Come on, ask again.'

My heart quickens. 'Can I really trust you?'

'Yes. You can.' He emphasises each word.

I suddenly feel angry. I want to scream: *But you've got a girlfriend. And she's horrible to me.*

'Let's say she finds it hard to control her emotions,' he says, as if reading my mind. 'Come on, you know I like you.'

I feel myself blushing.

'You do know, don't you?'

Then why did you disappear out of my life for so long? I think.

'I've been busy, really busy. Some family problem but … but … '

He grips my arm. Ardent. Beseeching. 'You're beautiful,' he says.

I feel my face turning red hot.

He laughs. 'Your cheeks match your nose now.'

And then I'm laughing too, with relief and confusion.

The cleaning lady drags her mop into a back room. There's only an old hag at the counter totting up the previous day's takings on an abacus. The *congee* is cool enough to eat.

'I know you like me too,' he says, 'After all, we are old souls.'

'Old souls?' I say, shriller than expected.

His face suddenly clouds over. 'It's not easy for us,' he says, looking down, blinking furiously.

'What do you mean?'

'It's just … '

'Please tell me.'

But he has clammed up. 'This isn't the right time,' he says apologetically. 'Come on, you should eat.'

He offers me a spoonful of his *congee*. It smells good.

'I'm infectious,' I say.

'Doesn't bother me,' he replies, balancing a cube of pig's blood between his chopsticks.

I pull my head up to meet his molten eyes. 'Is it something to do with your religion?'

Steel rocks his chin from side to side. 'Yes. No. Partly,' he says.

'You're a Taoist, right?'

'A novice.'

'Did you honestly see a hungry ghost at Peggy's?' My voice is firm.

He flinches. He folds his legs under the table. I noticed when we crossed the road that he's wearing shiny patent leather shoes. 'Yes,' I did,' he says.

'How come?'

'I just can. Others can too, see the fifth dimension, I mean. Ghosts live in the fifth dimension.'

My questioning eyebrows elicit further explanation.

'Mathematicians have proved it exists,' he says, shrugging his shoulders.

'I never was good at Maths,' I say. 'But does that mean you're, you're … ?' My tongue has tied itself into a knot.

Steel leans back on the bench, sighs, glances at me, then glances away. 'Anna, please believe me when I tell you that I am not evil.'

There's such sadness in his voice, I refrain from continuing the conversation. Instead, my fingers reach for the trinket on my wrist. The jade dog feels smooth and comforting to my touch. 'So, I'm safe, with you?'

He grimaces. 'Yeah, you could say so.'

I eat up the rest of my *congee,* willing myself to have the courage to ask the question that's burning on my lips. It bursts out: 'Tiffany is your girlfriend, right?'

'You really think she's my girlfriend?' he says, as if waking from a trance.

I feel embarrassed to acknowledge it.

He sighs. Sighs again. 'A girlfriend is someone you love, someone you want to share your deepest intimacies with, your most secret self. Tiffany is NOT my girlfriend.'

I blow my nose to stop it dripping. The tissue smothers a splurge of emotions.

Steel gives me a look of deep sympathy. He reaches out for my wrists. His fingers are cold. 'And that someone is you. You and I have *'yuanfen'*: a binding force that draws us together. You and I are soulmates.'

A shot of adrenaline streaks up my spine. I don't say anything 'cos I don't have any breath to say it with.

Steel laces his fingers tightly round mine. 'There you are. I've said it. But it's not the best time to tell you. I've got a lot going on at the moment.'

Gaau choa! My phone is ringing: it's Ma. She's at home, wondering if she should take a couple of hours off work to take me to the doctor's.

A billion thoughts are competing for space in my head.

'You really should go home and rest,' Steel says, his eyes kind and affectionate. 'Can I drive you?'

I shake my head, although inside I'm screaming, *Yes. Yes.* 'How do you know where I live, anyway?' I ask.

But he's already standing. He puts on his jacket and picks up the bill. 'Let's talk more tomorrow,' he says, retrieving the Mercedes remote from his pocket.

CHAPTER 8

A confession

My bleeping phone wakes me from a deep coma. It's a text from Peggy: **i am coming round to hear more about the walking corpse.**

Eiya! It's already dark outside. I've slept the afternoon away.

My head is woozy but my heart is rejoicing. *Steel said I was beautiful. He said he liked me. He said I was his soulmate, that we have yuanfen. (Weird!)*

This obsession, this fascination, is a first for me. A few guys have kissed me at rave parties but that's as far as it's ever got.

I sit up, switch on my bedside light and text back: **ok.** But then I'm coughing and Ma is knocking at my door, asking how I'm feeling. She forces a cup of smelly Chinese medicine down me.

'You've still got a temperature,' she says, after zapping my forehead with a thermometer. 'No school tomorrow. Doctor's orders.'

I nod. That's fine with me!

Ma is dressed up for work, ready to leave. 'There's some fried rice in the wok. Heat it up in the microwave when you're hungry,' she says, pulling my Buddha ears and closing my door to keep the air-conned air inside.

My phone rings; I s'pose it's Peggy. But it's not her number – I don't recognise it. *Could it be ... ?* I sit up, flick back my fringe and take a deep breath. 'Hi,' I say, as coolly as circumstances will permit.

'Hi,' Steel says. 'Just wanted to check that this is your number.'

'How did you get it?' my voice croaks.

'Tiffany gave it to me.'

Tiffany? My heart thumps in my chest. A few seconds pass as I try to gain control.

'Don't worry, Anna. She's got this thing about numbers,' he says, chuckling. 'I'll call tomorrow morning to see how you are.'

'Thanks,' I say. Stunned.

'Take it easy.'

'I will.'

Neither of us hang up.

'Tomorrow then,' he says.

'Yeah. I should be fine by then.'

I call Peggy immediately. She says she's on her way to my place. 'Did you give Tiffany my number?' I ask.

'Why the hell should I do that?' she snaps.

I'm not sure if I can cope with her if she's in one of her moods. 'Peggy, how about you don't come round,' I say. 'I need to rest more.'

'You don't want to see me?'

'Of course I do. It's just that … I'm infectious.'

She's breathing heavily. I can hear buses, cars, a motorbike grinding down the street. 'We can chat on the phone,' I say.

'So Steel called you?' she says. Aggressive-like.

'I bumped into him on the street after I left school.'

'And?'

A voice inside warns me not to say anything more. 'Nothing special.'

'Did you tell him about the corpse?'

I don't answer.

'I bet he's carried one himself. I mean, it's the kind of stuff Taoist priests do, isn't it?'

'Peg, please.'

'You know what? I think your in-laws are half-wits.'

'I told you, I saw it with my own eyes. I heard the carriers' voices. Ma saw it too.'

'And you say you're not superstitious?'

'I'm not, but ... corpse walking has been going on for centuries in China.'

I hear the click of her lighter and a sharp intake of breath.

'Anyway, what about your hungry ghost? Is it still around?' I say.

'No,' she says flatly.

I give her time to drag on her cigarette.

'Listen, Anna. I tell you, there's something really strange about what's been happening to you recently.'

'Yeah, you're right.'

'I'd keep well away from that creep Steel if I were you,' she says.

'Why?'

'He ... he doesn't seem normal.'

Peg's just pissed. We rarely bicker and it doesn't feel good. I decide to terminate the conversation. 'I'm going to get a bite to eat then try and snatch some more Zs,' I say.

Peggy takes another drag and exhales slowly. 'You're weird,' she says. And hangs up her phone.

Mad dog!

There was a bleep while we were talking. I check it. It's a text from Steel: **don't forget to take your medicine.**

I start punching in a reply: **thanks.** No, delete. **thanks a lot.** Nah. **thanks for your care.** No way.

Is Peggy right? Is there something about him that's kind of abnormal?

I concentrate on my phone. Enter then delete, enter then amend (not cool to be too forward), enter then hover over the send button. In the end, I decide a simple **thanks** will do. I hit the send button and collapse on my bed.

The traffic seems especially loud tonight, the honking irritates me. Aggravates. I eat. I leave the dirty dishes in the sink then decide to wash them after all. I put some soothing eye pads on my eyes so they won't be too puffy tomorrow. Threads of my conversation with Steel weave round my head incessantly. Peggy's words too. Eventually, to stop the babble, I pull my quilt to the sofa and watch some cartoons.

When I wake again, it's already 3 am. But I'm feeling better. Sweaty, but more clear-headed. Excited about tomorrow.

Tomorrow then. That's what he said.

While stripping in the bathroom for a shower, I catch a glimpse of my body in the mirror. It's neat, slim, hairless except for the usual places. I cup my hands under my breasts and push them up. My nipples harden. I smell strong, stronger than I can remember. But that doesn't embarrass me. I sit on the toilet and after peeing, slide a finger up my vagina and press against thin layers of muscle, to enjoy a pleasurable itch. I explore the sensation more with the spray of water from the shower head.

I have a confession: I'm not sure if I've ever experienced an orgasm. I don't think I'm quite right down there. Here's another: I'd give my virginity to Steel. I think. If he wants, that is.

It's another grey rainy day. Low hanging clouds slither ghost-like down the mountain behind the housing estate. The top of the high-rises are shrouded in mist. I trip along the wet paving stones and my heart is singing:

> *'Feel the power,*
> *Taste my glory,*
> *Crossed swords,*
> *Blood love,*
> *What's your story?'*

Steel and I have arranged to meet in Starbucks. He called again, shortly after I woke up this morning. Ma was already fast asleep.

Half an hour later, my daily special coffee stands half-drunk in front of me. Next table, a group of noisy students are working on a group project. Within earshot, there are two men in suits, and a *tai-tai* wife feeding cheesecake to her fat toddler. Steel is sitting upright, opposite me, on a red velvet sofa. He has ordered a tomato juice but hasn't touched it. He's fingering his phone – the latest iPhone model – tapping the fingers of his other hand on the table top. On his wrist, he's wearing a designer-label watch. He seems distracted and I'm wondering why.

'I probably can't stay much longer,' he says.

'Are you hungry?'

'I don't eat sandwiches.'

'How about some pig's blood *congee*? You liked that.'

Steel gives me a sickly grin. 'Please be nice. Today is not going well for me.'

His eyes are dark and brooding. Actually, I feel a bit insulted. I'm even beginning to wonder why he suggested we meet. But I sense his bad mood is nothing to do with me.

Suddenly he lightens up. His eyes are focused on mine and he looks apologetic. 'Sorry about my mood, Anna. I'm so glad you're feeling better today. Let's talk some more.'

'What about?' I say, postponing my inquisition, not wanting him to swing back into being a Grouch.

Steel leans forward, cups his chin with his elegant hands. 'There's something I want to tell you. But you must promise not to tell anyone else.'

I'm with him immediately, excited by the sudden intimacy.

'I love your dress. The pattern is called polka dot, isn't it?' he says, snatching a quick look at my cleavage.

I can't help laughing. 'That's not what you wanted to tell me,'

I say.

He looks serious again. 'I'm worried about my big brother,' he says, then looks at me with startled eyes, as if he regrets confiding in me.

'You have a brother?'

'Yes. Two actually. And a sister.'

I take a sip of coffee. 'What's the problem?' I ask, a tiff miffed that the conversation is not about us any more, that it seems to be going off at a tangent.

'He's disappeared. Left home. And Dad has ordered me to find him.'

'*Wa!* Have you reported it to the police?'

Steel sucks air between his teeth. 'Not appropriate,' he says, drumming his fingers on the table.

I add another sugar to my coffee. Stir. The students pack up and leave.

'And Tiffany is giving me a hard time,' he blurts.

'Is that why you haven't been picking her up from school?' I ask, a bit confused-like. Yesterday he said she wasn't his girlfriend, but now I'm not so sure. I'm suddenly on tenterhooks waiting for his answer.

'Yes,' he says simply.

'She hasn't been spooking you with spiders, has she?' I say jokingly.

Steel laughs miserably and shakes his head. 'She's afraid of what I could do back to her.'

Something clicks inside. 'So you have a psychic skill too?'

Steel squirms uncomfortably on the sofa. His eyes are searching mine again. 'To be honest, yes, I do. I have a few. Can you guess one?'

'I have a suspicion.'

'Try me.'

I close my eyes. The first thing that comes into my mind is a spurting shower head.

'Shower head,' he says.

'You can read my mind,' I squeal, and my heart skips a beat. I bang my mug on the table – louder than intended – and feel a rush of blood to my cheeks.

His eyes are pleading now, his dark eyelashes fluttering. He takes my hands in his. 'Anna, you're right.'

My hands instinctively recoil but he grips them strongly. I'm blushing with embarrassment and indignation.

'Don't freak out. It's alright. There's nothing to be afraid of. I don't usually bother reading people's minds, but I like to read yours. And the closer I am to you, the more I can pick up.' He leans back on the sofa and sighs, as if an enormous burden has been lifted.

I stare down at the paper tissues on the table and just see fuzz.

Steel chortles to himself, then bursts into a peal of laughter. 'I love it when you blush,' he says.

Which makes me blush even more.

He looks dead serious again. 'I KNOW you are a good person. I KNOW you are my soulmate.'

I shake my head forcefully. This conversation is going way

over the top.

'You're going to quit smoking. I hate the smell. And smoking is hazardous to your health.'

'Really?' I'd never considered it, until now.

'And you took drugs only once. That takes a lot of willpower.'

I blink with surprise at his logic. But decide to engage. 'It was such a revolting experience. I should never have tried.'

'Now you're worried about Peggy relapsing. That's really nice of you.'

'I blame myself, a little bit. 'Cos Peggy became addicted. I even stole some money out of Ma's purse to pay for one of her debts.'

Steel relaxes his shoulders. He pushes my mug away and, on the table top, traces a large circle with his index finger. He draws a backward 'S' shape inside the circle, and pretends to colour in one half. 'Everyone has a touch of evil in them,' he says, drawing a mini circle in both halves and shading the second. *Yin* and *yang*. Male and female. The symbols of life and death. 'There's a circle of evil in every pure spirit. All Taoists know that,' he says, using his finger to alternate between the two small circles.

I'm speechless. One minute I'm stressing out about Peg. The next minute he's teaching me Taoist philosophy.

Steel smiles sadly. 'So we are both neither perfectly pure nor perfectly evil,' he says.

I flick my fringe over my eyes. It's a delay-response tactic. 'Ye—es,' I say.

CHAPTER 9
What's up with Peg?

Steel teases a lemon slice out of his glass and downs the tomato juice in one. His phone vibrates and he picks up immediately. 'You're breaking up. Wait a second,' he says, grim-faced. 'Sorry' he mouths to me, and moves towards the entrance of the coffee shop for better reception.

He comes back looking pained and concerned. 'Has Peggy called you today?' he asks.

'She texted me this morning to say she was going to cut class.'

'And since then?'

I shake my head. I know 'cos I've just been checking my phone for messages.

'Try to phone her,' Steel says.

I try. No answer. That's not like Peg, at all. She always picks up, 24/7.

'Peggy is in danger,' Steel says. Dead serious now. 'We must leave at once.'

I sit bolt upright, shocked. 'What's up?'

'Let's just get there a.s.a.p,' he says. Anxious. Agitated.

'Where?'

'Bamboo Grove Housing Estate. You know, near the Panda Hotel.'

'What's Peggy doing there?'

Steel doesn't answer. Next minute, we're on the street flagging a taxi. An ambulance siren wails past us, blue and red lights flashing. 'We need to hurry,' he says, phone in hand. He has covered his head with a hoodie and is wearing sunglasses.

As usual, the roads are chock-a-block. We're nose to tail most of the way to the housing estate. A delivery van honks and cuts in; our taxi driver swears and shakes his fist.

We arrive in a sweat at the main gates and scoot across the main quadrangle. Steel's long legs stride across the puddles. Bedraggled flowers droop in the rain.

While I'm panting like a dog, Steel's mouth is shut, his hair unruffled.

No sign of Peg.

'Call her again,' Steel says. Block K is towering up above us. Poles of washing stick out at right angles from cluttered balconies, like Tibetan prayer flags. Steel darts his head from side to side as if his ears are radar antennae locating a low-flying aeroplane.

'Are you ghost busting?' I say, beginning to feel irritated, wanting to know what's happening.

'I wish,' he says. That's when I see the worry lines in the corner of his mouth. 'No, there's a murderer on the loose.'

'Another murder? Here?' I say, incredulous.

Steel is distracted by his ringing phone. He fumbles to answer it and I can hear a loud voice at the other end. When he hangs up, I can tell that he's really mad. 'Anna, we're too late,' he shouts.

Eiya! In my mind, a policeman is covering Peggy's bloody corpse with tarpaulin. 'PEGGY,' I wail.

'No, she's not the victim,' Steel says, then hesitates. 'I don't think so anyway.'

'Where is she?' I yell.

'Calm down,' Steel says, gripping my arm, softening his tone. 'Master Tang should know soon.'

His phone rings again. He picks up right away, listens intently, sighs with relief and gives me the thumbs-up. 'Peggy is safe,' he says to me. 'Try calling her now.'

Peggy answers. Her words are slurred and I suspect what she's been doing immediately. At Steel's request, I put her on speaker phone.

'I've just seen a guy flying,' she says. 'He was jumping from block to block, like Superman.'

Steel yelps, as if in pain. I've no idea why.

'Peggy, where are you?' I say. Still completely freaked out.

'I was on the back stairs with Jane,' she says, slurring her esses. 'There was a crash of doors and a pounding of feet and someone was legging it up towards us. Two strides one flight, speed-rail fast.'

Another voice, an unfamiliar one, joins in the conversation. 'I dragged Peggy up to the roof and we hid behind the stairwell.'

'Who's that?' I say.

'Jane,' Peggy says. 'My friend.'

The way she emphasises the word 'friend' hurts. A lot. I can't speak for a moment.

'We met when you were in Hunan,' she says. Even in her fug, she realises I deserve an explanation.

'Peggy, why didn't you pick up?'

I hear Peggy asking Jane. 'In the rush,' Jane says, 'we left our phones on the stairs.'

'Where are you now, exactly?' I shout.

'Cool it,' Peggy says.

'See if I care.'

'I'm in Jane's flat. On the thirty-eighth floor. We were on the roof, hiding, I don't know how long for. It was sweltering up there. When suddenly the fire door burst open. It almost flew off its hinges. And this guy, I'm telling you, this guy, he was smeared in blood, and he kind of, shot out. He jumped up to the ledge, roared, like a lion, and leapt into the air.'

'He was smeared in blood?' I say.

Peggy is laughing insanely. Steel kneads my arm and gives me a cut-the-call sign.

'Peg, I have to go now,' I say.

'What's new?'

'I'll call you later. Okay?'

She's still laughing when I disconnect.

Steel looks at me, his eyes implore me to calm down. 'She'll come round,' he says.

My pulse begins to return to normal. But my stomach feels heavy, full of bricks. Police sirens are wailing in the distance, growing louder, and there's the flashing of ambulance lights outside the main entrance of the block. People are milling around, shouting and phoning their friends.

'We should get out of here, quickly,' Steel says. He grips my arm, pulls me towards a back exit.

I'm in a daze. It's like everything is running on fast forward.

We're back on the street. 'You're not going to like this,' Steel says, 'but I have to leave you now. Go home.'

'Wait,' I cry. It's all too confusing. I feel lost.

'You'll be okay. Just go home.'

'What about Peggy?'

'She'll be fine,' he says, with a touch of impatience.

'I'm feeling faint,' I say, my head truly spinning.

'I'd take you back with me, but ... '

'But?'

'No. Wait,' he says, suddenly excited. 'Yes, do come. Please come.' Insistent now. 'You'd be doing me a great favour. Dad is really mad with me. He'll have to be polite if you're around.'

I'm in a quandary. It's not often that we Chinese invite each other home when parents are there.

'He knows all about you anyway,' Steel says.

'WHAT?'

But Steel has already entwined my arm in his. We take a taxi back to the car park where his car is.

'And if you're coming back with me, there's something we have to do. Now,' Steel says, in the lift going up to the sixth floor.

We are alone. Out of the public eye. For the first time.

Instinctively, we know it's a special moment. A moment for us. I want him to touch me. He seems to want to touch me too. He takes his sunglasses off, wraps both arms around me, nestles his mouth in my hair and breathes deeply. 'You smell wonderful,' he says.

My eyes are closed, but there's a constellation of twinkling stars in the blackness. I'm flying through a moonlit sky, yearning for his kiss. I feel his hand on the back of my bare thigh. My body hair bristles, goose bump by goose bump, as he slides his hand upwards and plants it firmly just below my panty line.

He says he's sorry, it won't hurt, it'll fade. Then he twirls me round so I'm facing away from him, lifts the skirt of my dress and sighs with pleasure.

The lift lurches to a stop and I stumble out, as if falling out of a dream.

CHAPTER 10
Family secrets

Wa! Steel has a Porsche. A bright red Porsche. The car freshener smells of Christmas trees. Cool!

I sink into a white leather seat. The car feels brand new.

Next minute we're speeding down the highway between buses, lorries and cars. Drivers give us approving looks. 'How many cars do you actually own?' I ask.

Steel jangles a bunch of keys on a key ring that hangs from his belt. 'I haven't counted. My family share a fleet.' He presses down the accelerator to overtake a Lexus.

'Ever thought of competing in the Macau Grand Prix?'

He smiles happily, for a moment. I love his smile.

It's raining; the nine hills of Kowloon are lost in a blanket of cloud. Steel flicks on the radio to show off the sound system and we catch the tail end of a news bulletin:

Reports are coming in of a murder in Tsuen Wan. Stay tuned for further updates on the events as they unfold.

Steel flips over to a music station.

'Hey, I want to listen to that,' I say.

Steel frowns. 'Anna, before we arrive at my place I should explain a little bit more about what's going on, with my family, I mean.'

'First things first,' I say. 'Tell me how you knew that Peggy was in trouble.'

'You want to know how Master Tang knew she was at Bamboo Grove. Am I right?' Steel says.

Inside my head, or what?

'Yes. And who was the blood-splattered guy who jumped off the roof?'

Steel shrugs uncomfortably and switches the windscreen wipers up a notch. 'I'm not a hundred per cent sure. But Peggy was definitely in danger for a while.'

I suddenly feel miserable: Peggy was so far gone she was hallucinating.

'Look, there's something you should know about Master Tang,' says Steel. 'You've met him, right? I introduced him to you.'

'You're his apprentice.'

'Yes. He's teaching me all he knows.'

'Oh my God!' I cover my mouth with my hand. 'Yes, of course, Master Tang. He's your Dad. There's a family resemblance.'

Steel grimaces. 'Actually, he's not my biological father. I'm adopted.'

'And your brothers, and sister?'

Steel nods. 'We all are.' He leans forward and reaches for my hand. His is ice cold. 'My parents adopted us, the four of us. Three of us in China, one in Hong Kong. We're not siblings but we all live together as a family.'

'Wow,' I say, totally amazed. Westerners adopt babies all the time. But when Chinese do, they usually only take in children born of a blood relative. That's 'cos we think our family blood is special and unique. You can't expect loyalty from strangers, can you?

'Actually, it was my Mum who sensed that Peggy was in danger,' Steel continues. 'And she told Dad. She's a visionary clairvoyant. Pieces of future events come to her in dreams.'

'That's incredible,' I say, flashing back to the toothless soothsayer at Wong Tai Sin temple whom Ma took me to after Dad died. To reveal my destiny. And hers.

'So, you can read my mind, and your mother is clairvoyant. Talented family,' I say.

Steel looks at me long and hard before speaking. 'Yes, we all have psychic skills,' he says. 'Dad is the most powerful, by far. He's a high priest. He's an expert in *feng shui,* geomancy, and faith healing too. That's because he has studied *I Ching* for cent— decades. He understands the power of prophecies and the secrets of immortality.'

I'm suddenly not sure if I dare face Master Tang again. 'What did you say you want me to do when we get to your place?' I say.

We're stuck in a traffic jam on Waterloo Road. Residential blocks loom on either side. The car windows are fogged up but the rainstorm has blown away.

'We'll have to play it by ear, I'm afraid,' Steel says.

'Anyway, I'm clearer now,' I say. 'I understand a lot more. Like why you told your Dad about me, and … '

'There's something more. A lot more. You're going to be surprised, really surprised,' Steel says, his voice quavering.

I take a sharp intake of breath. 'Try me.'

'Okay,' he says, decelerating as we approach a zebra crossing. We're in a built-up shopping area teeming with pedestrians. 'My elder brother, Max, had a huge row with Dad about his girlfriend. Two weeks ago he stormed out of the house and we haven't seen him since.'

It seems both brothers are into telling their Dad about their love lives.

'In our family we have to. It's important, especially for Max and me,' Steel says, reading my mind.

Strange.

'Max had a girlfriend for years. Everything was going fine, but then he met this other … girl at a nightclub. When Dad found out, he forbade Max from seeing her again. But Max did, secretly, a few times, and she led him on and … '

'Don't tell me. She's pregnant.'

Steel's lips are turned down. His face seems drained of blood. The Porsche lurches forward as we zoom back into the fast lane of a highway.

'Slow down,' I wail, clutching the seat.

'Okay, okay,' he says grumpily.

'Was I right?'

'I wish … oh, what am I saying?'

'What's the big deal?'

The speedometer dial hovers over the hundred miles an hour mark. *Calm him down,* I think, scared of losing my life.

Steel turns to me. He seems anxious. 'The big deal is … oh

dear, there's not enough time to tell you everything. It'll have to wait. It's so complicated.'

It's my turn to shrug my shoulders.

'But wait, you've got to know this.'

'What?'

'I have another brother, a little brother called Freddy. He's a nuisance.'

'I've always wanted a little brother,' I say wistfully, sensing that this is not what Steel wants to tell me.

'And … '

We've arrived in Kowloon Tong. Steel turns at a set of traffic lights and we're driving along a tree-lined street. Houses with gardens are tucked behind walls.

'And my sister … ' He stops at another set of traffic lights.

'Yes.'

Steel narrows his eyes and turns in my direction. 'My sister, you know her too. In fact you know her pretty well: she's Tiffany.'

So she's not his girlfriend! … Or is she? My mind is reeling. I run my hands through my hair. 'Your adopted sister, right?' I say, stressing the word, 'adopted'.

'Yes. Not related by blood.' Steel says, not giving anything away.

I take a deep breath.

'Phew! What a lot of family secrets!' I say.

Instinct tells me they're not a couple. Instinct tells me they're not a couple. I repeat this like a mantra in my head.

Until Steel turns to give me a disparaging look. 'Anna,' he says. 'Stop it.'

I want to shrivel up and die on the spot.

The traffic lights change, and we turn off the road on to a gravel driveway. A pair of wrought-iron gates starts opening automatically. We drive through a garden, with lawns, palm trees and clusters of blossoming bushes. A uniformed servant is using a net to sieve leaves from a swimming pool.

Ahead, there's a humongous house. White and square, it looks as if it has been transplanted from a foreign movie. It has a Beijing-style red front door with brass knockers, and two stone lion statues guard the entrance. The arched windows are draped with heavy curtains.

'*Wa!* This is your home?'

'You like it?'

Steel parks the Porsche in a garage alongside a row of luxury cars and motorbikes. A turbaned Sikh is polishing the SUV. He twitches his waxed moustache to greet us.

I'm cursing that I'm wearing such a revealing dress. 'I really shouldn't have come,' I whine, putting on my denim jacket and buttoning it up.

Steel checks the handbrake. He takes his sunglasses off and puts them into the glove compartment. 'Don't worry. You look great.'

CHAPTER 11
A blood-red handprint

There are so many cats. Cats and cute kittens, rolling, chasing, cleaning, frolicking and stalking butterflies. Tabbies, black, white and mixed. Sleek-haired and long-haired. 'I think we keep the SPCA in business,' Steel jokes as we crunch our way up the driveway.

'How many do you have?'

'Only around twenty here. We've over forty in Lantau.'

'Lantau?'

'Yes, we have a homestead over there.'

In the far corner of the garden with his back to us, a boy with curly dark hair is tapping a long white stick. The black Doberman I last saw slobbering out of the back window of the SUV is padding beside him, sniffing the ground.

'There's Freddy,' Steel says.

'He's blind?'

'No. That's a divining rod.'

'What a big dog.'

'That's Sport. Watch out, he's very friendly.'

At that moment, Freddy starts running towards us, waving the rod above his head. He's wearing sunglasses. He calls the cats by name as they bound away from him. Sport lumbers behind.

'I'm measuring the acidity in the rain,' he shouts.

'Yes, Doctor D. Anna and I are going inside. You should too.

The sun's come out,' Steel says.

Freddy cocks his impish face at me. 'Are you his new girlfriend?'

I feel flustered.

'None of your business,' Steel says, hustling me towards the front door.

But Freddy follows us, tapping his divining rod against my calves.

Steel swings round and snaps, 'Freddy, stop it.'

'Can I show Anna my mineral collection? I've got samples of actinolite, biotite, calcite, diopside, epidote, flourite, garnet … '

Steel interrupts him mid-flow. 'As if she has nothing better to do with her time.'

I turn and flash Freddy a fake smile. His skin has that polished plastic doll look. Like Steel. Like their Dad.

A bald manservant dressed in a white silk *kung fu* jacket opens the front door and a wave of cool air wafts over me. *Eiya!* It's a white marble palace inside. Clusters of chandeliers sparkle from the high ceiling and vases overflow with pale water lilies. A willowy woman with thick long hair, a flowing gown and bare feet floats down from a polished stone staircase, her hands outstretched.

'Anna, how lovely to meet you,' she says. Her voice is gentle and welcoming. Her lips are full.

'Hi Mum,' Steel says, kissing her on the cheek. She hugs him warmly.

Freddy plonks himself on the floor and kicks off his trainers.

I bend down to untie mine.

'Here you are,' Mrs Tang says, lifting out a pair of golden slippers from a shoe rack.

Steel is behind me, ready to help me take off my jacket. 'I'd rather keep it on,' I say.

'How about you wear this instead? Mrs Tang says, unhooking a pashmina shawl from a coat rack. It's so pretty I can't resist the offer.

A uniformed Filipino maid appears from another room. 'Freddy, come and have a drink,' she orders.

'Red meat juice?' Freddy says, shoving his divining rod into a porcelain umbrella stand.

Steel glances nervously at me as an unwilling Freddy is escorted away.

Mrs Tang smiles dreamily. 'Your father is waiting in the library,' she says to Steel, who frowns. 'I'll have a little chat with Anna before I go to meet Tiffany.'

Steel opens and shuts his mouth.

'From school. I promised to take her shopping.' Mrs Tang turns to me. 'What would you like to drink, Anna?'

'Nothing thanks, I'm fine.'

Steel goes his separate way as I follow his mother into a spacious sitting room. Silk cushions adorn plump sofas and chairs. Many are occupied by sleeping cats. Plush carpets form a colourful patchwork over a matt parquet floor. The heavy damask curtains are closed.

Mrs Tang turns up the lighting a little and sinks into an

L-shaped sofa bordering a long antique coffee table. The table is painted with merchants, trotting horses, swirling willow trees, arched bridges and market stalls: it's a lively village scene in ancient China.

'Please call me Peach,' Mrs Tang says, neatly crossing her legs.

'Peach.'

She leans forward to open a drawer of the coffee table and presses a button. Gentle *pipa* string music strums through overhead speakers.

'Beautiful. It's beautiful here,' I say, caressing the graceful varnished arms of my chair.

Peach smiles happily. 'Thank you,' she says. 'I designed this room myself. Do you like the lamp stands? I'm worried they're a bit too *Art Deco*.'

What's she on about? I glance around the room for a clue. The lamp stands are silver and shaped like animals: tigers, cows, deer, snakes. Rosewood cabinets display statues of Tang dynasty horses. There's enough blue-and-white porcelain and cloisonné bowls to open an antique shop.

'All the animals you see are indigenous to Hong Kong,' Peach says, stroking a purring cat.

I take a sip of water from a glass that a maid has given me.

'Have you fully recovered from your cold? Steel told me you caught it on a ghastly train journey from Changsha.'

I'm gulping like a goldfish.

Peach laughs merrily. Her face is as soft and round as her name. Her flushed cheeks are glowing with good health.

'Sorry if I'm being a little indiscreet.'

I feel myself blushing.

'He's told me how sweet you look when you blush,' she says, and laughs again.

I'm sure I'm now a shade of puce.

Suddenly, Peach turns serious. Her eyes – light, like Steel's – are searching for mine. 'I know he'll be mad at me for telling you this, but later you may thank me for getting to the point.'

I'm all ears.

'Steel has found you early. It's a challenge for him. But he's such a dear, loving … creature, and you are very good for him … '

'Very good for him … ?'

Even Peach is floundering a bit. 'You are good for his soul. And you ARE soulmates. I'm sure of it,' she says.

I'm stunned. Whacked on the head like a fish at the market.

'You do believe in reincarnation, don't you?' Peach asks softly.

'I'm not sure. I mean …'

'I'm sure Steel will explain everything when he's ready. Give him time. There's no hurry. It doesn't bode well for either of you if he's too impulsive.'

'I see,' I say. Not seeing at all.

'Just remember, he's a romantic. Romantic with a capital R.'

There's the buzzing of a machine; it's some kind of intercom system. A black cat blinks, stirs and stretches. 'Oh, that'll be Rajaram telling me that the car is ready,' Peach says, looking at her watch. She switches off the music.

Tiffany and school seem a gazillion miles away.

Peach stands, smile and points to a remote. 'I don't think Steel will be long with his father. How about you relax here for a while? Watch some TV?'

'That would be lovely,' I say.

Peach comes closer. I catch a whiff of her flowery perfume. 'Anna, I like you very much,' she says, taking my hands in hers and smiling. 'You are most welcome to come and stay whenever you want.'

What, with Steel? A voice inside asks.

'Yes, with Steel. After all, you are both over the age of consent now.'

My heart races.

Peach comes forward, wraps me in her arms and laughs. 'So stiff, Anna. Stiff as a wooden soldier,' she says. 'Relax.'

I'm alone, with a glass of water. I gulp some down, and adjust the shawl to cover my chest. For a second, I can't think where I am. Everything has changed so fast. A kitten meows, looks at me questioningly, then jumps on my lap. It purrs when I stroke it, and falls back to sleep.

The house is so quiet, it bothers me. I replay Peach's words in my mind and feel hot. I look around the room. A tapestry covers one of the walls. It's thick and lush: a 'Three Kingdoms' hunting scene. In a leafy forest, brave warriors battle on rearing horses with swords and bugles. A startled deer with beady eyes flees towards a mountain. It's a timeless scene fixed by bobbin and yarn. Frozen motion. There's something about it that makes me shudder.

A giant plasma screen is hanging from another wall. I depress the 'on' button and the TV springs to life.

No implement was found at the murder scene but there are signs of foul play. It's reported that the victim was a single woman who lived alone in the flat. The emergency services were alerted by a neighbour around 10 am. The police have reason to suspect that the killer is the same person as the one who killed a prostitute in Mongkok last week. Tune into the main news bulletin at seven for a full report.

In the excitement, Peggy has slipped from my mind. Her insane laughter suddenly haunts me. I want to phone her but my mobile is in my jacket pocket in the hall. I'll call her later.

I flick through the channels, and find one where the picture is a grid of images of rooms. There are twelve of them; it seems to be some kind of internal security system. I move the highlight frame from one to the other, notice that one image is moving, like a video. I click on it and zoom in. There's someone kneeling in front of an imperious-looking man with long flowing hair and a richly-patterned embroidered gown. *Eiya!* It's Steel, with Master Tang, his father. I look behind my shoulder, half-expecting someone to be hiding behind my chair. But there's no one. I stand up. Sit down again. Hesitate. Guilty as a peeping Tom, I press the audio button.

'But Dad ... ' Steel pleads.

'No excuses,' Master Tang shouts, spittle spurting from his mouth. 'You should have been tracking him. You know how lusty he is.'

'But ... '

'No buts.'

Steel is *kow-towing,* banging his head on the floor. 'Sorry, I'm so sorry.'

Master Tang lowers a clenched fist; the armrest of his giant wooden chair is shaped like a lion's head. 'I understand why you'd far rather be spending time with Anna. I respect why she means a lot to you. But YOU are the one I have chosen to find Max. You must find him and convey my message.'

'Yes, yes.'

'Can I trust you to make it your top priority?' Master Tang bends forward and glowers.

'Yes, yes.'

'Repeat what you are going to tell him.'

'That you have spells to help him. That you will give him one last chance.'

Master Tang is nodding. 'But if it happens one more time, I have no option but to track him personally, and revert him immediately.'

'Understood.' says Steel, banging his head on the floor.

Master Tang stands up and sighs deeply. Above him, a halberd hangs from the wall, and a sword with a jewel-encrusted hilt. 'Now tell me more about Anna. Is she definitely your soulmate?' His voice is calmer now.

I cover my face with my hands and scrunch up my eyes.

'I'm sure of it.'

Master Tang pauses for a moment and strokes his beard. 'Proof. I need physical proof.'

I look between my fingers and see that Steel is standing.

'I have it.'

'Which method?'

'The handprint.'

Master Tang strokes his beard some more. 'In that case, we should commence your training in the art of love.'

I fumble for the remote and with shaky fingers press the off key. *What did Master Tang just say?* I suddenly feel short of air.

Silence. A clock ticks. I have the creepy feeling I'm being watched. I look around for somewhere to hide.

Then I hear footsteps coming down the staircase. The doorknob turns and the door creaks open. It's Steel, looking like his world has come to an end.

'Hi,' I say, smiling weakly, standing up.

He paces towards me with a grim expression.

'Steel?'

He slumps in an upholstered chair. 'Anna, I don't know if I can see you for a while,' he says.

The door creaks again and Master Tang enters. I recognise his gown from Peg's place. He motions towards me. He's wearing black cotton slippers. He extends an arm towards me and shakes my hand. 'Anna,' he says. 'I believe we have met before. Please call me Kung. It's appropriate that you call me Kung from now on.'

His hand is cold but his voice is warm. Beads of sweat are dripping down my brow.

Steel rattles some car keys. 'Dad, I'd better be getting Anna home.'

Kung frowns.

'Okay, I'll ask a driver,' Steel says resignedly, looking at me with pleading eyes.

'Good,' Kung says, and presses a servant's bell.

'Sorry Anna, I can't drive you back today,' Steel says.

I shake my head and shrug my shoulders. Speechless.

A tall yellow-turbaned Sikh is standing at the door. He's the one I saw in the garage. Kung turns to me. 'This is Ishvar,' he says.

'Good to meet you,' I say. My voice sounds faint and thin. Greeting chauffeurs is a first for me.

'Do you need to go to the bathroom before you leave?' Steel asks.

It's only then that I realise I'm bursting.

The bathroom is something else. Someone has painted tropical fish, swirling seaweed and frothy waves all over the tiled walls. There are mirrors everywhere. The sink is a Chinese goldfish bowl. Dried pink corals and pointy starfish adorn the shelves.

A splash of red on my thigh reflected in the mirror behind me catches my attention. I screw my head round to examine it, but it's right at the back of my leg. Resting my foot on the toilet seat, I pick up a shell-encrusted hand mirror from the top of the cistern and angle its reflection to where I want to see.

The top of my thigh is red. It's an imprint of Steel's hand! Raw, blood-red raw, but not at all sore.

I take another look. Then remember our car-park kiss.

It takes me a while to compose myself.

Steel is waiting outside the bathroom. 'Sorry,' he mouths, with a bashful expression on his face.

Kung and Ishvar are waiting in the hall. Kung obviously wants me to leave a.s.a.p.

'Goodbye, Anna. I'll call you tomorrow,' Steel whispers.

Kung has to remind me to change my shoes and pick up my jacket.

CHAPTER 12
Grounded

'Where have you been?' Ma shouts. She's dressed in her work clothes.

'I'm tired,' I say, dropping the house keys on the table next to a bowl of congealed vegetables covered with plastic wrap.

'Of course you are. You're sick. You should be at home. Resting. Studying.'

'I'll start studying right now,' I say. Anything to placate her.

But she's insistent. 'WHERE have you been?'

I sit down, twiddling my thumbs under the table.

Ma stands opposite, hands on hips, and glares. Wayward strands of over-permed hair blow in the electric fan. 'I know. It's a boyfriend, isn't it? How many times have I told you? NO BOYS!'

'Ma, I'm nearly nineteen,' I shout.

'Nineteen, twenty, twenty-one. I don't care. I forbid you to have a boyfriend until you graduate from uni.'

'Ma, I might not even get into uni.'

That's a red rag to a bull. 'WHAT?' she screeches. 'You just don't work hard enough. You're lazy. A lazy good-for-nothing. What would your father have said? He was an educated man.'

I unwrap the cellophane from the *pak choi* and dip my finger in the soya sauce.

'Go to your room,' Ma shouts. 'No dinner until you apologise.'

'For what?'

'For … for being a horrible daughter,' she shrieks, stamping into her room and slamming her door.

There's only five minutes before she has to go to work. The fan whirrs. I can hear her sobbing. Sighing, I delete her missed calls. While I'm at it, I check for Steel's number. I still don't know it. *Chi sin!* He's registered as a 'private caller'.

I pad over to Ma's bedroom and knock on her door. 'Ma, I'm sorry. Okay?'

A couple of minutes later, she emerges. Her face is tight and drawn. 'I do worry about you,' she says.

'Ma, there's no need to. I'm fine.'

'I want you to promise me one thing,' she says, reaching for her shoulder bag.

'I will work, even harder, I promise,' I say.

'No, it's not that. Have you heard that there's been another murder? Just ten minutes away from here. There's a madman around, a killer. I want you to promise me to stay in at nights. You're certainly not allowed to go to Peggy's.'

'Maaaaaaa!' I wail.

'Yes. I mean it. You should be studying anyway. How many weeks to your exams?'

'Please Ma.'

'No,' she says firmly. 'Do you promise me?'

'Oh, Ma. Please?'

'Promise me?'

Why does she fuss so much? 'Promise,' I say. Fingers behind

my back. Crossed.

The following evening I'm at Peg's place, lying on my back on her bed. She's retouching my toenails. Cartoon Network is blabbing in the background. The red glow of her well-stocked family shrine beams from the living room. Of course I had to come and see her. I need to check she's okay. I forwarded my home line to my mobile, which Ma didn't confiscate (ha ha), so she'll never find out.

Peggy's brother hasn't been back for a couple of nights. Peggy looks pale. She says she's depressed. She's convinced the man who leapt off the building was the murderer. She's asked me to forgive her for taking K.

'A pact is a pact,' I say resolutely. 'Drugs ruin your life. You know that.'

'I feel kind of jealous that you are seeing Steel,' she confesses, placing the nail brush back in the bottle.

'But you're still my best friend.'

She nods sadly. 'I don't think you're telling me everything about him.'

'Can I trust you?' I ask. 'Will you promise not to tell anyone else?'

Peggy props half of a toothpick between two of my toes so the varnish doesn't smudge.

'Promise,' she says, narrowing her eyes.

I tell her about Steel telling me I am his soulmate. About Tiffany being his sister. Their amazing house. I don't tell her about the red handprint branding my leg. *Too weird.*

Peggy lights a cigarette, offers me one. I tell her I've quit. She hunts under her bed for an ashtray. The acrid smell turns my stomach.

I bend forward to check that the varnish on my little toe isn't smudged. *What's Peg looking at?*

'How come they're so loaded?' she asks.

I shrug my shoulders. 'Can I do yours?' I say, pointing to her feet.

'Never mind,' she says, digging her toes into her plastic slippers.

The interrogation isn't over. 'How did you know I was at Bamboo Grove anyway?'

'I didn't,' I lie.

I put my trainers back on. I want to get home. I feel a tad guilty about deceiving Ma. I should also catch up on some beauty sleep.

But there's something bothering me. 'Peg,' I say, 'do you believe in reincarnation?'

Peggy snorts. 'What *is* going on?'

'Just asking.'

She stubs out her cigarette. 'My Mum does.'

When I get home, I grab a Sarsae drink, switch on my computer and Google around about reincarnation. According to one website, if you want to catch a fragment of a past life, this is what you do:

Find a quiet place where you won't be disturbed;

Lie on your back, arms gently by your side;

Bend your legs at the knee;

Concentrate on circular breathing (practice makes perfect);

Clear your mind.

Sounds easy, right? I shower quickly (*Wa! The handprint is still there!*), swill down my last set of antibiotics and dim my bedroom light.

I lie on my bed, bring my heels to my bum and focus on the motion of my stomach as it rises and falls.

In the distance, I hear two people shouting at each other. Then it's quiet.

Nothing. No past lives. No fragments. Just a rumbling stomach. And my mind wandering back to Steel *kow-towing* to his father. And what Peach said.

Crazy.

I practise some more circular breathing.

Then I must have fallen asleep.

CHAPTER 13
Broken promises

It's raining. Again! The sun peeps through fast-moving clouds. School looks especially drab. The stairs leading up to S6 are wet and the walls drip gunk. In the corridor just before class, Wing and Mimi collar me.

'We heard about you going to Steel's house.'

'That Tiffany is his sister.'

'That she's telekinetic.'

I boil with rage. Peggy has split on me! I thought Wing and Mimi were intercepting me to fix a date for another Rock Band session. Instead I've got them on my back, nagging me to keep away from Steel.

I glance into the classroom. Peggy's not yet at her desk. 'I wouldn't believe everything people tell you,' I say.

'It all sounds so strange,' Wing says.

Mimi's glasses are steamed up. You know what?' she says breathlessly. 'They sound paranormal, to me.'

Paranormal? Steel? Tiffany? I twitch.

But before I can log into my brain, Tiffany swings by like a blast of chilled air. She has bobbed her hair; it frames her sharp oval face. 'I want to talk to you at break,' she says, her eyes boring into me.

Mimi cringes. Wing steps forward, her body stiffening in defence. Tiffany snarls. Classmates gather round. It's getting really tense, until Teacher Pang turns up.

I march into the classroom. As soon as registration is over, I drop my head on my arms and pretend I'm still not feeling well. I don't budge when first break comes. When someone taps me on the shoulder, I ignore it.

'Sorry,' I hear Peggy say.

'School is for sleeping,' I say. 'I'm tired.'

She leaves the classroom, followed by Wing and Mimi.

Of course I check that there's not just Tiffany and me left in the classroom.

Double Maths. Double sleep.

When I eventually raise my head, my nose is blocked. I blow it. *Gaau choa!* My nose is bleeding. Spots of blood dot the tissue. I raise my hand and make a quick exit to the toilet.

I'm bending over a sink, pinching my nose to stop the flow, when Tiffany comes in.

'Tiffany the Telekinetic,' I say.

'Listen here,' she hisses. 'Keep away from my home, or else.'

'Or else?' I say, rising to meet her fiery eyes.

'Or else … I'll do some serious damage.'

'How about a rattlesnake next time?'

'Ha! You've seen nothing yet,' she says, seizing my bloody tissue and throwing it into the bin. 'If I were you, I'd take heed of my warning.'

'Why shouldn't I see Steel? What business is it of yours?'

Tiffany guffaws. 'He's not available.'

'What do you mean?' I say, flustered.

'What I mean is, he has a girlfriend already.'

He told me he really liked me, I think, pathetically. *We're soul-mates.*

Tiffany's eyes level with mine. Spots of rage dimple her cheeks. 'And she's far more suitable for him than you.'

'I don't understand.'

'There's a lot you don't understand. The less you understand the better. Steel is dangerous. You really should keep away.'

'That's not what your mother told me.'

I seem to have struck a nerve. 'Just go back to the hovel you came from,' Tiffany yells. Her body is arched and tense. For a moment I imagine her pinning me against the wall and shredding me with her fingernails.

But she has struck something deep inside me too. 'He has a girlfriend already?' I blurt.

'Yes, her name is Janet, and she's ... she's my best friend. They've been lovers for years. She's very angry, and very powerful. So I'm warning you now, if you contact Steel again, you're both in deep trouble.'

I feel a strong urge to cry. 'I don't believe you,' I shout, pinching my nose extra hard 'cos it's still bleeding.

The bell rings. Tiffany raises a fist.

Two classmates waltz in the toilet.

I step sideways, and bang my funny bone on the wall. 'Ow!'

Tiffany stalks out. 'You just wait,' she growls.

At least I know now that, for sure, she's not Steel's girl. But the rest of the day is a right-off. I'm home now. The moment I shut the front door, I'm fighting back tears. Bowls of half-eaten food are scattered around the table. Ma must have left for work in a rush 'cos the balcony doors are ajar and there's a pile of crumpled clothes on the ironing board. Snivelling, I stomp into my room, search in my desk drawer for a letter pad and tear off a piece of paper. *Shit.* It's pink.

So that's it. My relationship with Steel is over. Finished. He has a girlfriend, a lover. *They've been lovers for years.* They must have met at primary school. How can I compete? Me, a virgin with zero experience.

My life is completely out of the range. I'm abnormal. Gross. I want to stay at home forever. Stay single. Become a nun.

I draw my bedroom curtain, switch my table light on, and my mobile off. I pick up a pen and start writing. I'll send Steel an old-fashioned love letter, that's appropriate for such a Goth. I'll address it to his home in Kowloon Tong.

Darling Steel … no, too romantic. *Dear Steel* … drop a line, chew my pen. I bombard my brain with commands: keep it short, unburden your heart, leave things open, be honest, don't give everything away …

My heart is sinking fast.

I like you. Nope, too pedestrian. *I love you.* Aargh! Way too forward, cross it out. *I hear you already have a girlfriend. I can't believe you two-time.* Scratch scratch.

I screw up the letter, hurl it into the bin, clutch my face and start crying. Before Steel, no boys have shown much interest in me. The real me. Their minds were just on one thing. Steel is so sweet, such a gentleman. I feel he cares for me, a lot. He might be really upset if I finish with him.

What did he say about our being soulmates?

Whatever he said, I feel he's the first guy that I can really talk to. He's soooo understanding. So grown-up. (Yuk!) And I adore him. He's so handsome.

Tears slop down my face.

How I wish I had a Dad to talk to. I mean, of course you can't talk to your Dad about … about relationships. But as a member of the opposite sex, he could … he would … Then I'm crying even more 'cos I don't really know what Daddies do for their daughters. And memories of my own Dad are just a blur.

The wind has picked up. It's whistling around the high-rise. My table light flashes on and off, like a strobe. I leap to my feet, heart pounding. *OH NO. Not again!*

I rush out of the room, slamming the door behind me. *Gau ming!* Save me! A spider could easily crawl under the door. Panicking, I run to the bathroom to fetch a towel, roll it into a sausage and stuff the gap.

I'm still kneeling on the floor when I hear strange noises – the swish of the shower curtain, a thump as something heavy hits the bathroom floor. In the dark, I sense a presence, a weighty squelchy mass. There's a foul smell. Bile clogs my throat. I swivel round as an amorphous shadow looms in front of me.

There's another thump. It's even louder. Then the door swings open and a ghastly figure wearing a Qing dynasty gown jumps in my direction. Its arms are outstretched and covered in sores.

It's blind, with a greenish face and straggling white hair.

It jumps again, bangs its leg on the dining table, roars in pain, and flips the table up. A glass water jug smashes on the floor and dark sauce splatters across the tiles, like old blood. Bowls roll; I scream. The corpse stops, sniffs and jerks its mouth open. Whooping with joy, it bounds towards me.

I'm going to die, I remember thinking. Then: *it doesn't matter anyway. Steel doesn't love me.*

But I'm running for the balcony. I wrench open the glass doors, cymbal crash them shut and stumble for the lock. But the doors don't lock from outside, *duh!*

I'm a deer, a terrified deer with beady eyes. Cornered. Trapped. About to be slaughtered.

No, I'm not. I'm Anna Wang. And I'm ripping off my T-shirt, tying it around the door handles, knotting and knotting until there's no more material to knot.

The corpse jumps towards the balcony, splats into the door and collapses on the floor. It jerks back on its feet, pounds the glass with its fists; its lips are contorted with rage. Then it turns, hops around the room – as if bouncing on a trampoline – and hurls itself at the glass. This time, a pane shatters, a jagged hole yawns open. The corpse punches at the splintered shards, then howls in pain, cradling a bloody hand.

With another whoop, it seizes the door handles and tries to pull them apart. My T-shirt stretches, stretches, and stretches, but the knots hold.

I gasp for breath. A cool wind blows on my face as I clutch

the balcony railings. They're low enough to climb over if I stand on the stool.

I stand on the stool, see matchbox cars and the distant flicker of street lights below. The dots beckon me. *Jump,* says an inner voice. *Better than being eaten alive.*

The corpse is howling with anger, like a wolf. It shakes the door handles violently. With a roar, it makes one final effort to pull the doors apart. I hear the sound of my T-shirt ripping. One inch. Two inches. The balcony doors fling open.

Gripping the railing, I swing a leg over the top. Wind laps at my face. I swing the other but the corpse is upon me. It snatches my leg mid-air, lunges for the rest of my body, the stool falls away and I'm gripping the railing with all my might.

The corpse is pulling me apart; I'm losing my grip. I grit with iron teeth, grind metal in my throat.

There's a wail of dismay. The corpse releases my foot and I'm catapulted dangerously into the blackness, but rebound, crumpled, against the railing.

I hear a familiar voice; it shouts, 'Be Gone!'

And I turn and see the corpse pinioned against the balcony wall. By Steel.

CHAPTER 14
Revelations

Steel's eyes sear like golden lasers from his swirling black gown. 'Hold on,' he cries. The wind is blowing my hair awry. Ninety feet below me, certain death.

Steel slaps a piece of yellow rice paper on the corpse's forehead and it slumps in a heap, inert.

He rushes towards me and I swoon, engulfed in his arms. And he's swaddling me in his cloak, carrying me like a baby, to bed. 'Tiffany, I'll kill you,' he says, through clenched teeth.

He lays me on a cool white sheet. He kisses my raw fingers. Blood oozes from my fingernails but I'm so shocked I don't feel any pain.

My body seizes up – *where's the spider?* – but there isn't one. Steel pastes back my sodden hair, strokes me, implores me to calm down.

'What have I done?' I wail. I'm shivering now, shaking uncontrollably. And then I remember that I was writing a letter, a letter to Steel. And Tiffany threatened me in the school toilet. *But I made up my mind to finish with him,* I plead. Tears are splashing down my face.

'Please don't leave me,' Steel moans. His eyes are moist and he gives them a brusque wipe. 'I can explain everything, tonight, I promise,' he says.

I close my eyes. My heart is thumping. My head is throbbing.

'Relax. Breathe normally. Everything will be okay,' Steel says, unfastening his cloak and gown. He's wearing a T-shirt and shorts underneath. He lies by my side and enfolds me in his arms.

My toe hurts. A lot. I touch it; it's bleeding. It has dripped all over the bed sheet. Steel suddenly stiffens, growls, grinds his teeth.

'What's happening?'

But his muscles are supple again. 'You trod on a piece of glass, my darling,' he says, slipping the toe in his mouth and slithering his tongue around it.

My darling, he said.

He gently lowers my foot, and, after a moment's hesitation, puts my fingers in his mouth.

Then he lies by my side again. I close my eyes, rest my face on his chest and listen to his beating heart. He caresses my hair with long tapering fingers. The pincers that claw my chest gradually loosen their grip. Steel and I become soft-shelled, fluid.

But another surge of fear seizes me and I sit bolt upright. 'What about the corpse?' I cry, my voice shrill and tight.

'It's in a coma.'

'I don't understand.'

Steel unbends my waist, eases my back to the bed. 'I used a Taoist spell. To make it comatose. It won't bother you anymore.'

I close my eyes again, sinking into the warmth of his arms. I concentrate on breathing normally.

'I'm so very sorry,' Steel says. 'You have my word it'll never happen again.'

I nod. I so want to believe him.

'Tiffany must have the key to the morgue,' Steel says, as if to himself.

'Morgue?'

'Yes. That's where the corpse came from.'

'What?'

'Tiffany must have woken it up, offered it the opportunity for a good feed and carried it here.'

'A morgue?'

'Near here. Beneath a Taoist institute.'

I groan; it's painful to move my foot. Steel nurses it in his hands.

'And how did you get here?' I ask.

Steel strokes my legs. 'I read your thoughts.'

'Reading thoughts is one thing. Suddenly appearing is another.'

'Mmm. Good point.'

'Looking for Max?' I say.

Steel shakes his head, frowns. 'Don't be mad at me.'

I start crying again.

'I must explain more about Tiffany,' he says. Then doesn't.

'Go on then.'

'She's furious because I'm seeing you. That you and I are a couple. But I've told her I'm going to finish with my girlfriend.'

My stomach turns to granite. 'She's called Janet, right?' I say.

'Yes. I mean, no.' Steel sighs. 'She's not my soulmate, like you.'

He sighs again, wrings his hands. 'Oh, it's so embarrassing to talk about it.'

I feel tears splashing down my cheeks.

Steel blinks, his long black eyelashes flutter. 'Janet is my girlfriend,' he says defiantly. 'But it's an arrangement that all us v—, we all have, in order to control our lust.'

I recoil from him but he grips my arm, draws my body closer to his.

'You're shocked, really shocked, I know,' he says, 'but if you trust me, everything will be okay.'

I breathe deeply, trying to quell my pounding heart.

'Shocked about what?'

'That I'm a vampire.'

A ten thousand volt electric shock surges through my body. 'WHAT?!'

'A vampire.'

'But … but, you don't look … '

'Yes, I've been converted.'

I'm gulping for air. 'Converted. From what?'

'Converted from a corpse.'

I'm going to vomit. I'm sure of it. Steel's eyes are imploring me, begging me not to.

I clutch my face, and silently scream at my wall.

'Go on, scream,' Steel says.

I scream. Scream again, less piercing now. Then I'm trembling uncontrollably.

He's lying on his back. His glossy hair is splayed on my pillow.

'Touch me,' he says quietly.

With a shaking hand, I reach for his dark hair. It's as thick and dry as doll's hair. His skin is as fine as eggshell porcelain. My fingertips trace the ridge of his cheekbones. His eyelashes bat like butterfly's wings.

'I can't believe it,' I gasp. 'And you're so beautiful.'

He takes my hand in his and places it on his heart. 'I'm yours. I'm truly yours, I promise.'

Together, gradually, we breathe more easily.

Once my heart is beating steadily, I'm ready to listen to his amazing story.

'So, Tiffany is too. A vampire, I mean,' I start.

'Yes, all my family are.'

I laugh, incredulous. *Of course, Janet is a vampire too.*

'There are hundreds of us in Hong Kong. But we haven't come out. Yet. We want to. But we fear humans. What you may do to us.'

'Really?'

'Of course. Vampires are the undead. Like corpses, hungry ghosts, and fox spirits. Fortunately, Taoists are willing to keep their knowledge about us secret.'

I wrap my arms around my knees. My toe has completely mended. There's not a trace of blood.

'I don't get it,' I say. 'Taoists help the undead?'

'Indirectly, yes. They help people to pacify ghosts. They help people, usually poor people, to arrange corpse-carrying of relatives back to ancestral villages. That's how it's been for thousands of years,' Steel says. 'Then, around three hundred and fifty years ago, Kung discovered how to convert corpses into vampires.'

'Your father?'

Steel nods. 'Kung's last human life was in the Ming dynasty. In his later years, he was banished by the emperor to a remote corner of China, far away from his native home in Jiangsu, and became a Taoist priest. When undead corpses arrived at his temple, he prepared them for burial. The ceremony involved placing a powerful Taoist spell on their foreheads to put them in a coma.

'But he began to pity the corpses that hadn't deserved to die – young soldiers, construction workers, tributary brides. Their souls were still intact because they had died far away from their ancestral villages. Some of them pleaded with him not to be made comatose. After some experimentation, Kung devised a method to convert the good souls into vampires, so that they could live again.

'In 1620, at an annual Taoist gathering, Kung proposed that all corpses, upon arrival at the temples of their ancestral homes, should be screened. The honourable ones should be given the option of being converted into vampires. Their souls could be extracted from their bodies before they were passed to their relatives for burial. Kung's conversion method was approved, on one condition: that vampires had to be reverted back to corpses if they murdered humans. His method is now used at Taoist temples all over China.

'Kung died a year later, hunted down and killed by the eunuchs who had ousted him from his position of Chief Advisor to the Emperor. In his will, he stated that his body wasn't to be sent back to Jiangsu. Instead, he was screened and converted into a vampire. During the ceremony, a priest discovered something remarkable: that Kung had been the renowned Taoist celestial master Chang Tao Ling in a previous reincarnation. Out of respect, it was decided that Kung should be made a member of the Taoist Council, even though he was paranormal. The Council still exists today. Kung is also the chairman of the Taoist Vampire Society, which was set up during the Qing dynasty, when the number of vampires grew rapidly.'

'Why?' I'm lost.

'There was a sudden increase in emigration and thousands of Chinese died in accidents overseas – on the American railroads, the Australian gold mines, the high seas. There were also civil wars and terrible famines in China. The Taoist morgues became clogged with corpses, the human world inundated with ghosts. It was chaos.'

'Why ghosts?' I shudder as amorphous shapes cloud my mind. My world will never feel the same again.

Steel laughs. 'You have to understand that ghosts have no souls. That's why they're so envious of us.'

'No soul?'

'No. As a punishment for being evil, usually, it's held in the underworld by Yan Wang.'

'Yan Wang ... ?' I recollect a terrifying flaming effigy which is sometimes paraded down the streets at the end of the Hungry Ghosts festival.

'The god of the underworld. When Chinese people die in their native provinces, their souls are separated from their bodies and judged by him. If the person has been bad, Yan Wang bars their souls from entering the afterlife. Their bodies roam around the fifth dimension of the earth as ghosts.'

'So, are all ghosts bad?'

'Most of them. They're often harmful to humans. Tormented with cravings and unfulfilled needs. One type – hungry ghosts – has been barred from heaven because their descendants have not followed the rituals for the dead in the afterlife. And all types are dangerous to vampires: they gang up and attack us.'

'Why?

'Because they want to enslave us to hunt for them, have sex with them, kill for them.'

Steel pauses for breath. Mine is caught somewhere down my throat. I let my eyes do the talking.

'Do you drink blood?' I ask.

Steel laughs uncomfortably. His teeth are six inches away from mine. He could lunge at my jugular and drink me dry. 'Yes,' he says, his eyes suddenly simmering with desire. 'But if vampires bite and kill a human, the Taoists consider it murder and we are reverted into corpses.'

I'm giddy with disbelief. 'Have you eaten recently?'

Steel pauses, sighs. It seems he has taken my question seriously.

'Yes, last weekend,' he says.

'Where? Who?'

Steel draws me towards his chest. 'Too many questions,' he says hoarsely. 'You need to rest. How about you close your eyes and try and sleep?'

The living room clock chimes. *'Eiya!* What time is it?' I say, remembering the mess outside.

'I'll clear up,' he says. 'Lie down here for a while. How about I cook some instant noodles?'

'Ma will be back soon.'

'Don't worry. Everything will be clean and back to normal, apart from the smashed water jug. I'll even wash the dishes.'

He draws back the bedroom curtain. A full moon glows in the dark sky; the outline of his elegant body is etched in silver.

He's right. I should rest. I've got school tomorrow, I mean today.

But how can I? When so much has happened? When my world has lost its roundness?

I must have dozed off. 'Cos next minute Steel is stirring beside me, there's the clanging of the outside gate, and a key turning in the lock.

'Be quick,' I say.

But there's no need. Steel is in his gown, at the door, through it, on the balcony. He swings the corpse on his back, shrouds it in his black cloak, gives me the victory sign, jumps on top of the railing and leaps off.

I rush outside, peer down, sick to the stomach with what I

may see. But Steel is clutching a drainpipe way below. He springs off it and lands feet first on the ground, the head of the corpse lolling to one side.

With another bound, he's gone.

CHAPTER 15
Money can't buy love

T.G.I.S. Thank God it's Saturday. Ma's at work. I slept until late afternoon and now I'm on the back of Steel's Harley-Davidson on the way to a party at his place in Kowloon Tong.

My arms are clasped around his middle, my hair is streaming in the wind and we're whizzing in and out of traffic. I hook my chin on his shoulder, and shout:

'So you're immortal.'

'Yes.'

'You have supernatural strength.'

'Yes.'

'You have psychic powers.'

'Yes.'

'You can appear and disappear.'

'Yes.'

'You have bloodlust.'

'Yes.'

'You can mend wounds with your saliva.'

'Yes.'

'You vaporise in sunlight.'

'Yes.'

We accelerate up a hill. The high-rises of Mei Foo estate zip past. The wind glues my lips to my teeth so it's hard to speak.

So it's true. Steel is a vampire.

And I'm completely cool about it.

We dismount from the motorbike and take off our helmets. My hair is as flat as an Annan waxed duck. But I don't care. Much.

'How long have you been one?'

'Eighty-eight years,' he says. Bashful-like.

'You don't look that old.'

'Vampires resemble how we looked on our last day as a human.'

'So, you were twenty … '

'Twenty-five.'

My blood approves.

The motorbike key jingles as he attaches it to his chain. 'Do you still want me?' he asks softly.

'Of course I do,' I say.

How I love his eyes!

Night has fallen. Steel's house is lit up like the Star Ferry at Christmas time. Fairy lights dot the blossoming trees and bushes that border the garden. Only one or two guests have arrived.

'Tiffany's not coming too, is she?' I ask.

Steel furrows his brow. 'Yes, I'm afraid she is. But tonight will be a good chance to sort things out once and for all.'

Arched bowers of luscious white roses have been erected for the occasion. Steel and I walk hand-in-hand underneath them. The flames of hundreds of candles throw shadows on his face.

'Some party,' I say.

'More like a wedding, hey?'

I blush. He laughs happily, his eyes glint in the candlelight. He waves at his parents who are looking in our direction. On the terrace behind them, members of a Filipino dance band are tuning up – there's the twanging of guitars, a snatch of harmony on a keyboard, the testing of a mike.

'Can you dance?' Steel asks.

'I prefer to sing.'

'Then you must join our family band. We have a great sound system upstairs. Instruments too. We've converted part of the second floor into a music studio.'

'*Wa!*'

Waiters march out of the house in a line carrying silver salvers of food. They secure them on top of hot plates fired by gas burners. My heart sinks when I see Tiffany mooning in a skimpy bikini. She dives into the swimming pool, all tight butt and wobbly breasts. The splash alerts a Western chef who is stoking a barbecue.

But then the opening bars of the first song hit the balmy summer evening. *Fun-ky.*

Peach catches our attention and beckons us to where she's standing. A weird combination of excitement and anxiety tingles through me. 'Welcome,' she says, and gives me a hug. 'I believe you've met my husband.'

I nod. Kung smiles. 'Thank you for joining our celebration,' he says.

Peach gives me the once over. 'Steel told me he'd be bringing you on his bike, so I've prepared some party dresses for you,' she says.

'Mrs T … Peach, you shouldn't.'

'I'll be changing too,' Steel says. 'And Mum will be upset if you don't accept her offer.'

Steel leads me up the marble staircase and we enter a lavishly furnished room. It's the size of my flat! Taking pride of place, there's a four-poster bed shrouded in chintz. To my right, an ensuite bathroom. To my left, a cluttered dressing-table, with ebony brushes, ivory combs, a cloisonné box of hair accessories, a tray of moisturisers, eye shadow, mascaras, lipsticks, perfumes and a jewellery chest spilling over with gold necklaces and earrings.

'Make yourself at home,' Steel says, with no trace of irony.

Someone knocks at the door and two barefoot Indonesian maids enter, their arms laden with flouncy dresses in various shades of green, my favourite colour.

'I can't,' I say.

'Look at your face in the mirror,' Steel says, and then we are bent up laughing at the reflection of my gaping mouth.

The maids lay out more clothes on the quilted cotton bed cover – pleated silk skirts, stylish gowns, strapless tops, wraps, jackets. They lift the bedspread to reveal a row of matching shoes. One of the maids starts unbuttoning my blouse.

Steel averts his eyes, says he'll meet me outside the room.

Even though I say it myself, I look quite a babe. Even the lipstick tastes good. Steel is waiting at the top of the staircase, an elbow casually propped on the banister, a diamond cufflink glittering under a crystal glass chandelier that hangs above.

Apart from a white bow tie, he's dressed completely in black, and looks as sleek as a panther.

I glide towards him in silk slippers and a figure-hugging *qipao* dress. My hair is swept into a chignon, revealing a white rabbit skin stole and dangly emerald earrings.

'You look great,' Steel says, approaching my neck and inhaling deeply. 'And you smell divine.'

He whips an iPhone out of his pocket and switches it to camera mode. I rest my head on his, feeling a million dollars. *Flash. Click. Click!*

'We look good together,' Steel says, checking the photos.

He's right. Our glowing faces and sparkling eyes shine back at us. We look like a prince and princess.

'Let me accompany you downstairs,' he says. 'Before I eat you up.'

'Are you okay?' I say, backing away. His body is suddenly stiff, angular. *And I thought he was joking.*

'Fine,' he says, smoothing back a strand of coiffed hair.

There's quite a crowd chatting and drinking on the terrace and in the garden – guys and girls, grown-ups too. Everyone is exquisitely dressed, even Freddy is wearing a suit. Cats in colourful collars romp on the grass. I could swear that as I stepped out on the tiles, for a fraction of a second, the music stopped and everyone turned to stare at me.

Steel's hand feels smooth and cool. 'A glass of champagne?' he asks, signalling a barman behind an elegant table laden with bottles.

'What are your parents drinking?' I ask, pointing to their glasses.

'Bloody Marys,' Steel says, with a tricky grin.

Freddy bounds towards me and hugs my legs. 'Malachite, opal, potash feldspar, quartz ... '

'Push off,' Steel says, lightly punching his brother.

'What do you eat anyway?' I ask.

'Wild animals, mostly. But we can stomach raw or lightly-cooked meat.'

'Wild animals? In Hong Kong?'

'Yes, some still exist here you know.'

'You don't eat cat, do you?' I say, as one chases another across a stone path.

Steel laughs heartily. 'No. We worship them. They guard us against ghosts.'

There must be around fifty guests, drinking and eating. *What are we celebrating anyway?* I wonder. The Filipino band ups the tempo and a jazzy song comes to a lively close. The drummer taps one stick against the other then drops them into a quiet drum roll. Which grows. Louder. And louder, until the guitarist stamps his foot and strikes a questioning opening chord, and the lead singer seizes the mike and launches into a jaunty rendition of *Money, Money.*

At the final cadence, all the guests clap and cheer then turn towards the house, as if waiting for a VIP to arrive. My heart sinks when Tiffany emerges from the terrace doors, hips swinging down a red carpet, which leads to a temporary stage on the lawn. The train of her blue satin evening dress flows behind her. Her red-lipsticked lips pout.

Kung and Peach start clapping in rhythm and everyone follows. Tiffany mounts the stage and a bespectacled man with a frilly dress shirt appears from behind the curtain. He's holding a blank placard almost as tall as himself. Tiffany stands opposite him, blinking in the spotlights and smiling vainly. The drummer starts a roll which crescendos into a cymbal clash. The ensuing silence hums.

'Ladies and gentlemen,' squeaks the little man onstage, 'let's raise our glasses to Tiffany Tang.' He turns the placard, displays it horizontally, and I read in big letters: FIFTY-EIGHT MILLION DOLLARS.

There's a burst of applause and a group of photographers surges forwards, cameras flashing. Tiffany shakes the frilly man's hand and nods to Kung and Peach.

'WHAT?' I screech.

'The Mark Six lottery,' Steel says, hands in his pockets. 'Tiffany won the jackpot last Wednesday.'

Did I see right? 'Fifty-eight million dollars? What's she going to do with all that?'

Steel wraps his arms around my waist from behind. 'I dread to think.'

Tiffany descends from the stage, still waving at the crowd.

'She could win every week if Kung let her. I told you she had a gift for numbers. She's an expert of numerological divination.'

'Life isn't fair,' I think angrily, envisaging Ma patiently queuing

up once a week at the Hong Kong Jockey Club to buy a lottery ticket.

'No, it isn't fair, is it?' Steel says.

'Surely she'll get caught one day?'

'Unlikely.'

Steel goes on to tell me that Tiffany also plays the stock market, and the casinos in Macau. Their parents pool her winnings; it supports their family's lifestyle. Kung and Peach have mountains of gold hidden away from previous lives anyway. But they often donate to charity.

I still feel pretty hot and bothered. But Steel quickly becomes bored with my indignation. To distract me, he plucks a fragrant rose from a vase, presents it on lowered knee and asks if I would care to dance.

The band is full on now, ploughing through a set of golden oldies. Around twenty people are jiving on the mosaic dance floor, including Tiffany and a gangling guy in tails. She's doing some complicated footwork. His eyes are wandering around women's cleavages. 'That's Ben,' Steel says. 'Tiffany's boyfriend.'

'Is that his twin?' I ask, pointing at an identical guy on the dance floor. He's dancing with a petite girl in a tight miniskirt, sparkling stiletto heels and fake eyelashes. I notice she's staring at Steel, with longing.

Tiffany swings my way, and sniggers.

Steel grabs my hand and laughs awkwardly. 'You could say so. Ben can bilocate.'

The girl? Is that Janet? It must be Janet.

I feel sick. Not just at the thought of Steel and her together, kissing, making out, but 'cos I'm surrounded by vampires! Vampires who would love to devour me. Vampires with psychic powers. Vampires who can be in two places at the same time.

Steel senses my alarm. 'Come on baby, let's dance,' he says, sliding a long leg between mine and clicking his shoes to the rhythm of the bass guitar. He's a slick dancer. I close my eyes, focus on the beat and try to enjoy the sensation of his body close to mine.

He's dancing with me. Not her, stupid.

The next number is a slow one. My cheek nestles in a comfortable nook on his shoulder while his arm slips around my waist. He squeezes my body towards his. His eyes are closed now and we're swaying in perfect harmony. He breathes deeply. 'Anna, you smell so sweet,' he says.

I push him away, but feel kind of excited.

Steel will take care of me. Whatever happens.

When Kung and Peach retire indoors, the party becomes more riotous. The tempo of the music quickens and we're stomping and romping under the light of a full moon. Clusters of glasses chink as waiters mingle between the suits serving more and more of the red-coloured drink. There are roars of laughter when a group of youths start tossing raw beef steaks and pork chops in the air and catching them in their jaws.

The band takes a break. I'm hand on hips trying to catch my breath. That's when Steel says he wants to show me his room.

It's the coolest room out; I feel like I've entered a tropical jungle. A low king-size bed is draped with a thick batik bedspread of tigers crouching behind fern fronds. Two massage chairs are shaped like elephants with floppy ears. From a giant window, there's an open view of palm trees, bright pink bougainvillaea and sprawling hibiscus. His bathroom has a steam bath and a sauna. One whole wall is stacked with gear – plasma screen TV, speakers, Xboxes, computers – and gazillions of DVDs stretching up to the ceiling. An acoustic guitar is propped up by the side of the bed.

'You play guitar?'

Steel nods, sits down cross-legged on a thick cream carpet and balances the instrument on his lap. 'And I've composed a song for you,' he says shyly.

He strums the strings, whistles softly. The finger pads of his left hand skate across the frets. I look down to avoid embarrassing him as he starts to sing. The song has a haunting melody with a sad lilt. He sings of his yearning for me, his desire.

'That was beautiful,' I say, eyes misting.

Steel puts the guitar down and gently lowers me onto the bed. We sink into his duvet, into an ocean of goose feathers.

'May I kiss you?' Steel says. His lips are red and full. They're so close, I can feel his breath on my cheek. I prise my eyes wide open, with horror. But my heart is still singing his gentle song. It's a delicious mix.

'You … you won't eat me?' I blurt.

'I can control myself tonight. I know I can,' Steel says, as if forcing himself to believe it.

His slim fingers stroke my bare arm gently. The pupils of his eyes are as round and bright as the moon.

I hear footsteps approaching and raised voices. Steel hisses like an angry cat, swears, and we sit up, waiting to be disturbed.

The footsteps stop. The door rattles. 'It's locked,' Steel calls.

'Janet is really upset. You'd better come out.' It's Tiffany.

'Mind your own business,' Steel says.

'But it IS my business,' Tiffany says tartly.

I stand up and re-arrange my bed hair. Shudder.

Steel stands up too, curses, and adjusts the belt on his trousers. 'I'm coming, okay?'

I turn to the mirror to check my face. I look flustered, grim. 'Janet is Miss Stiletto, the one dancing with Ben's clone, isn't she?' I say.

Steel spins me round, suddenly furious. 'Yes. But you are my soulmate. Is that clear?'

'What's the difference?' I say, feeling thoroughly fed up.

Steel drops to his knees. 'Anna, Anna,' he moans. 'Please believe me when I tell you that everything will work out between us. I just need more time.'

'There never seems to be enough,' I say, stomping into the bathroom and locking the door.

I hear Steel leaving the room. The bedroom door slams shut.

I'm dazzled by the bright fluorescent light. I freeze at my reflection in the mirror, and ask myself: *You do like him, don't you?*

Footsteps approach. Voices get louder. Then there's a knock at the bathroom door. I open it a crack.

'Tiffany wants to talk to you,' Steel says. They're both standing outside.

'Hi,' her smarmy voice drawls.

I open the door slowly and, without looking at them, sit on the edge of the bed.

'I'm sorry,' she says icily.

Yeah, right. 'No worries,' I say, as casually as I can, using a finger to trace a tiger cub's whisker on the bedspread.

'There'll be no more nasty surprises, okay?' she says.

'Okay,' I say, raising my eyes to give her a stony stare.

Steel grabs Tiffany's shoulder pad and pushes her towards the door. 'And now you can go and tell Janet to piss off,' he shouts.

Snatches of *Bloodswell* circle round my brain:

> *'Blood swell*
> *Not well*
> *Go to*
> *Hell!'*

CHAPTER 16
Blackmail

Why bother slaving away at exams to land a good job? I ask myself in that mind space between dreaming and waking.

Ma's angry teeth snap back at me: *The money isn't yours, stupid.*

I come round to the sound of my mobile bleeping. It's a message from Steel: **here's my number. not sure if we can meet much this week x**

I reply immediately: **thanks x**

Oh yeah, Max. Too bad.

Oh yeah, Janet. What about her?

Ma has laid out my school uniform at the foot of my bed. 'One slice of ham or two?' she calls gaily from the kitchen.

'One, please,' I say. 'And Ma, I'm old enough to make my own breakfast now.'

Ma peers round my bedroom door. Her breasts sag when she doesn't wear a bra.

'Thanks anyway,' I say, 'but ... I mean ... '

'I just hope you're studying hard for your exams,' she says, brandishing a chopstick as if it were a sword. 'Promise you're not going to Peggy's flat at nights?'

I shake my head. She sure knows how to make me feel guilty.

There's the clammy racket of summer in the air. Tropical trees sprout, bamboo creaks, cicadas buzz. I wish I could say I'm singing with the birds. I dawdle so slowly I almost don't make it to registration on time.

Tiffany's desk is empty. I'm soooooo relieved.

Peggy sleeps on her desk throughout English class. I still can't forgive her for splitting on me. Then a needle inside me pricks my conscience and I start worrying she may be captive to K. Again.

you ok? I text, and watch for her pocket to start vibrating. She heaves herself to her elbows and stabs the keys of her mobile.

ok, comes the answer. Then she slumps back on her desk. She doesn't even bother to look over.

During afternoon break, Wing and Mimi sidle up, say they need to talk. Urgently. While we are walking around the perimeter of the playground, I have to dodge a wayward pass. The guys from our form are in sleeveless shirts playing basketball.

As soon as we're out of earshot, Wing and Mimi start pecking at my brain, like parrots.

'Peggy says she doesn't like you anymore,' Wing says.

'Too bad,' I say. 'I like her.'

'She says you don't visit her place anymore,' Mimi says.

'It's not my fault I'm under house arrest.'

'She says you spend all your free time at Steel's. That you're keeping him a secret from your Ma,' Wing says.

'Of course I am,' I say, giving her a withering look.

'She says you're crazy about him,' Wing continues. 'So we're worried about you. There are rumours, you know. About Steel, and Tiffany. Are they really, you know … '

She daren't voice the word. And I've suddenly had enough. 'We're talking like primary school kids,' I say, raising my voice.

Mimi is smarting behind the thick lenses of her glasses.

I have a quick ogle at Mike (not Jordan) as he hurls himself towards the basket for a dunk. A sliver of his muscular torso sends a shiver up my spine. *Yep, Steel. I'm still crazy about you. Even after last night.*

'Peggy says she's hooked again and you don't care,' Mimi says hoarsely.

'Well, tell her, I do,' I say, putting my hands on my hips, letting them drop. 'And her being back on drugs, explains a lot!'

Wing is opening and shutting her mouth like a goldfish.

I glance at Mike; he's lost his magic. I start walking back to the main building.

Mimi mutters something to Wing.

'You know Steel has a girlfriend, right?' Wing calls.

I stop in my tracks, turn to face them head-on. 'What?'

'Yeah, Tiffany wrote something on her wall.'

'Rubbish.'

The bell is ringing for the end of break. Mike is bouncing the ball back to the games shed and I'm floundering for something to say.

It's not until we're back in the classroom that I can trust my voice. 'You know what?' I say. 'Until the 1950s, Chinese men could have as many wives as they wanted. Like Muslims. Muslims still can, even today.'

I'd trade my iPod to replay Mimi's look of amazement.

'You're condoning Steel?' Wing says.

'Yes,' I lie.

Ten minutes later my phone is vibrating with a text from Mimi: **are you planning to get rid of her?**

yep

how?

the usual

what u mean?

poison. murder

The minute I have a free period – it's the last of the day – I go to the library, get online, and click into Facebook.

Wing was right: STEEL IS TWO-TIMING ANNA WANG, Tiffany's Facebook page declares.

And there's a photo of Steel sitting on a sofa, with Janet. She's practically stuck to his side, like Velcro. They're leaning into each other, tipping heads touching. His fingers are intertwined with hers and their fists are clasped together, on his lap.

How embarrassing! I fling down my schoolbag and throw myself on the desk.

I just want to die.

A few seconds later, my mobile rings. The librarian tut-tuts and wags a finger.

It's Steel. *Gaau choa!* There's some static on the line. 'Sorry, you're breaking up,' I say, cursing my bad luck.

'I'm coming to pick you up from school,' he shouts.

If librarians' looks could kill, I'd be dead.

I make a quick exit.

But what can I tell Ma? I told her I'd come straight home after school. It's her free day. She'll be waiting, wanting to take me clothes shopping. I tap my mobile despondently, then have a brainwave.

I take a deep breath, punch in Ma's number, breathe again.

She picks up.

'Ma,' I say, 'I need to go to a revision class tonight … Yeah … it's free … in the school library … should finish quite late.'

Wa! Steel has turned up in a bright yellow Lamborghini! I plonk into the front seat and sling my schoolbag in the back.

He gives me a knowing smile.

'Chi sin!' I say.

'What?'

'That you can read my thoughts. You know I'm really upset, don't you?'

'I can block you if I want,' he says defensively.

'How about you ask your dear sister to block me on Facebook?' I say, my voice oozing with venom.

Steel hands me a bottle of water. 'Calm down, please Anna. We'll have no more trouble from her soon, I promise.'

'Oh yeah?' I'm crying now. Angry tears sting my cheeks.

'Yes,' he says emphatically, passing me a tissue and accelerating up a hill.

A glimmer of hope shivers up my spine and glows like a light bulb in my head.

'I'm afraid we don't have much time,' Steel says, looking at the clock on the dashboard. 'Kung will kill me if I don't capture Max soon. And I've got a lead.'

I dry my tears.

We're winding our way up Tai Mo Shan mountain on Route Twisk. The busy streets of Tseun Wan drop away behind us. We pass some dingy whitewashed barracks, exercising PLA soldiers, rundown houses and scanty vegetable patches. Then the road narrows and steepens. My ears pop.

Near the summit, Steel slows the car, stops in a lay-by and switches off the engine. He takes out his iPhone, taps to camera mode and levels it at our heads. 'For the memory,' he says. *Click. Click.*

Don't you know it hurts to smile?

We sit in an uncomfortable silence for a while. The slopes below are wreathed in fast-moving clouds. In the distance, clusters of skyscrapers stick out of the mist like bad teeth. I'm overflowing with a gazillion unsaid words.

'I'm going to finish with Janet,' he suddenly says.

'When?' The question just tumbles out.

'Soon.'

I take a sip of water. 'Tell me, is it possible for humans to become vampires?'

Steel doesn't answer immediately. He bangs his head on the headrest, and frowns. 'Yes, of course. But I don't recommend it.'

'How?'

'I don't recommend it,' he says sternly.

'But tell me, how?' I repeat.

Steel bangs his head harder. 'In a turning ceremony. Organised by Taoist priests. By drinking a chalice of vampire blood. Purified vampire blood.'

I meet his eyes, begging for more.

'Female vampires can't reproduce, you know,' he says.

What's that got to do with it? a little voice screams inside.

Steel's lower lip trembles. 'Try to understand my problem,' he says. 'I mean, it won't be a problem because I'm working on it, but ... '

'But?'

'The younger you are as a vampire, the harder it is to control your bloodlust.'

Yeah, I've grasped that.

'Look, I hate being a vampire. But there's nothing we can do about it,' he hisses.

I take another sip of water. 'I believe there is.'

He seems too stuck on his own issues to get my meaning. Clutching the steering wheel, he shouts, 'Bloodlust poisons your thoughts, boils your blood. Bloodlust ravages your desire. Desire becomes a frenzied monster that feeds upon itself.'

'Gothic, or what?' I shout back. He sounds like he has just stepped out of a horror film.

He reaches out for me, clasps my hand to his heart. 'You are my soulmate,' he says. 'But you're human. If I accidentally bite you, I may kill you. If I completely lose control, I'll eat you up.'

I'm suddenly cringing at an image of him making out with

Janet. 'Forget it,' I say.

Steel licks his cracked lips.

A patch of mist clears to reveal a loaded container ship sliding across a pea-green sea. 'The word, soulmate. What, exactly, do you mean by that?' I say. Deliberate-like.

Steel releases my hand, stretches his legs and opens the window for some air. 'A soulmate is someone you've loved in a past life. We have met before, twice. Last time, you were my wife.'

WHAT?! I choke on some water.

Steel solemnly pats my back. 'We met when I was twenty,' he says. 'I was the eldest son of a rich businessman. We manufactured steel.'

Steel? I'm still gulping for air. 'What year are we talking about?' I manage to say.

'Nineteen thirty-seven. You were the beautiful daughter of one of my father's business partners. We were married at a lavish wedding and lived in a mansion in the French Concession area. Nine months later you gave birth to our daughter. We called her Ming Ming,' he says, his voice cracking with emotion.

'Father and I escaped to Hong Kong in late 1938. Leaving you, Ming Ming and the rest of the family behind. Two of my father's plants had been bombed by the Japanese and with the occupation, everything was going from bad to worse. My father planned to rebuild factories in the safe haven of the British colony and reunite the family when things quietened down. But it was not a good time to invest. There was a war in Europe, as well as in China. Rumours abounded about a possible Japanese invasion of Hong Kong. Which happened, in 1941. Conditions were appalling. I missed you terribly. And I never made it back to Shanghai.'

'Why?'

'A Japanese soldier killed me,' he says, looking truly bereft. 'I'd joined the Resistance, become a messenger for a local newspaper. Looking back, it was an impetuous thing to do. But I was so angry that my life had been ruined by the Japanese. One night, in Central, with a secret missive hidden in the sleeve of my gown, I was waiting at some traffic lights to cross the road, when a Japanese soldier hailed me, body-searched me, found the letter and shot me dead on the spot.'

I reach out to hold his hand. It's cold. Dry as a bone.

'My father was devastated. He never really got over my death. Shipping my body back to Shanghai and organising my burial in the family grave was just not feasible. So I was buried, temporarily, in a cemetery in Hong Kong. Soon after, my mother fell seriously ill, and Father lost millions of dollars in a business deal. A Taoist priest told him our family's bad luck was caused by my soul not being at peace, it being so far away from our ancestral home. That's when Father arranged for corpse-walkers to carry me back to Shanghai.'

I'm feeling emo. From sadness or joy, I'm not sure. 'And how do you know that … that I was your wife?'

'The blood-red handprint. Is it still there?'

Something prangs inside me. 'No. It's faded.'

'But you saw it, didn't you?'

I nod.

'The first time soulmates touch each other in another life, that's what happens. It's a manifestation of their everlasting love for one another.'

Now I'm blinking back tears.

Steel grips my hand harder, he forces me to smile.

'We should count ourselves lucky,' I say. 'I mean, our story has a happy ending.'

'That's my dearest wish,' he says, cradling my hand, lifting it to his lips and kissing it.

'It's mine too.'

'So, how about we cheer up?' he says, brushing away a tear.

The atmosphere between us is lighter as we drive back down the mountain. I'm freaked out but feeling much better. A monkey darts across the road. Its mischievous face is caught in the headlights, then disappears in the undergrowth. 'Horrible animals, forever biting and fighting each other,' Steel says. 'And foul to eat.'

'Even their brains?' I ask, remembering that in olden days they used to be served as a delicacy at Chinese banquets; that an emperor loved them so much, he ate one brain a night, served on a golden platter, scooped with a golden spoon.

Raindrops splash on the windscreen. Steel flicks the wipers on. It's already dark. The narrow road snakes towards the colourful neon lights of Tsuen Wan. I lean my head on the fur headrest, enjoying the Cantopop that's blaring out from a back speaker.

We're driving through dense low cloud. Steel switches the headlights on; they tunnel a way forward. I see a white road marker, a luminous traffic sign warning of zigzags ahead, trees mounting darkly on either side. Steel follows the road to the right and something flashes before us in the headlights. My heart seizes up. But it's only a monkey dashing across the road. With a *kung fu* kick of its hind legs, it leaps up a tree.

The road turns sharply to the left and the moon appears in a break between the clouds. Its light is watery and dim. I glance up at its fizzy sheen and when I bring my eyes back to the road, a thick-set man has appeared in the headlights.

'Max,' Steel cries, slamming on the brakes. Max raises his hand; it's a clear gesture to stop. As Max holds his ground, both hands raised now, four other men appear. They're dressed like savages, wearing animal skins, brandishing knives.

Steel presses the accelerator in defiance, swerves sharply, the tires screech. He drives round the gang, the wheel heavy in his hands, and brings the car to an abrupt stop.

'What the hell?' I cry.

Max's face is rugged and savage. He's bare-chested and heavily-tattooed: a fat green snake coils its way around his calf.

Steel gets out of the car and strides towards him. Max's henchmen raise their knives, poised to attack. The two brothers start shouting at one other, so loudly I can hear every word:

'Six hundred thousand dollars in my bank account and I'll come home,' Max yells.

'I can't arrange that.'

'Ask Tiffany.'

I hunch down in the car seat and stare at my bare knees like someone possessed.

'Come home.'

'Dad will revert me.'

'No, he won't. You know he won't. I've told you a hundred times. He's going to give you one last chance.'

'He reverted Jeff.'

'That was different.'

Cautiously, I sneak a look sideways. Three pairs of eyes gleam through my door-side window. The closest face leers at me; its nose dangles from a flap of skin and there are two scabby pulsating holes where its nostrils should be. 'Fresh blood,' it roars.

I scream.

Steel's head swivels round. He leaps.

A henchman lunges a knife at his neck.

Steel takes a swipe at the knife and it clatters onto the tarmac. 'She's mine,' he says hoarsely.

Max susses what's going on. 'Come off it Jack,' he says. 'Anna's his.'

Jack bangs the roof of the Lamborghini heavily, scowls with frustration and shuffles away.

Steel is back in the car. He opens the window. 'I'm coming here tomorrow. To talk properly. I want to see you, alone,' he says.

Max throws his head back and laughs with derision.

My hands are shaking.

We speed away. Steel's hand finds mine. He rests it on my lap. 'I'm really sorry about that,' he says. 'Max is living wild with a coven of delinquent vampires up here.'

'Why didn't you capture him?'

'Impossible. Not with those louts around. No, I need time to reason with him. Alone.'

I suddenly feel tired and very confused. About all the weird things I have experienced over the last few weeks. For deceiving Ma about where I am.

Steel gives me a dejected look.

'Steel, I could have just been eaten,' I say.

'Yes. But you weren't,' he says flatly.

He switches on the radio. There's a crackly old Mandarin love song playing. Gradually, the tension between us dissipates. But I can't help feeling uneasy.

When we arrive at the entrance to my estate, Steel leans over. 'One kiss?' he asks.

'Sorry, no. Not tonight.'

Steel flicks some dust off his jeans. 'I'll always be here for you. If you want me, that is,' he says despondently.

I don't say good-bye.

When I open the front door, Ma is behind it, smiling, holding my slippers. There's a bowl of freshly-boiled *won ton* steaming on the table.

'You deserve a *siu ye,* an evening snack for all your hard work,' she says. She sits down on the chair opposite me with her a-dollar-for-your-thoughts look.

'Thanks,' I say, guiltily, sniffing the delicious soup.

There are two talking heads on the TV screen discussing one-room brothels. 'Most of the prostitutes are lured into the trade because of family debts,' a nerdy man with glasses says.

'I'm dead tired,' I say, finishing the last dumpling, laying the chopsticks across the bowl.

'You must be, my dear. Eat up and then you can enjoy a good night's sleep,' Ma says, her voice humming with affection.

CHAPTER 17
Foot fetish?

I'm alone with Steel. Just him and me.

A tropical sun sears through the window of our whitewashed villa perched on a cliff.

In the distance, an azure sky and a bolt of taut turquoise marbled silk: the South China Sea.

In the garden, lush ferns and leathery palms, moist, growing.

Our world inside the master bedroom is shimmering yellow and white; the colours vibrate harmoniously: the gold brocade of the satin coverlet on our four-poster bed; the yellow blossoming buds of hibiscus flowers hand-painted on the walls.

On the floor, smooth white marble slabs – cool to my bare feet – and our clothes, carelessly strewn.

In the centre of the room, five marble steps spiral up to a throne-like Jacuzzi, and Steel.

He stands up and water droplets sparkle on his naked body. He's as finely chiselled as a Roman statue. Then the walls of the room disappear; there's just him and me, and the sky and the sea. And I'm lying in a long white nightdress and he's floating above me, his eyes wide with desire. I lower the neckline of the elasticated bodice that covers my breasts. They're rosy apples, ripe for picking. Steel jerks his head upwards; the veins in his neck tangle and engorge.

'Look at me,' I demand, grabbing a handful of his rag doll hair.

His eyes lock into mine; his canines sharpen, lengthen. His body hovers above, but it's losing its strength. It's becoming fuzzy, vaporous. 'I'm a vampire,' he moans.

'Take me,' I implore. My breasts morph into volcanoes, seething, molten, ready to blow.

'Vampires drink blood,' he says menacingly.

A plug of rock rips from me. 'Then bite me,' I beg, and my mouth spurts red hot lava. I try to speak between eruptions but my tongue is stuck to a wall of rock.

'No, no. I mustn't,' Steel cries.

I throw my arms around him and – to my horror – he softens, melts, curls at the edges. I can't grip, he's dripping between my fingers, and I'm shouting his name, repeatedly.

I'm dreaming, I think, opening my eyes a second for a snatch of reality, breathing heavily, my sheets damp with sweat.

I'm a lump, of longing and despair. Still half asleep, I find the spot where a delicious pain is throbbing, aching. I press it firmly with my forefinger.

I'm suddenly on a journey which coils upwards, which begs forward motion. I'm the foam of waves, swirling higher and higher, splashing across precipitous rocks, up a cliff, reaching an ecstatic plateau of no return, a panoramic glimpse from the tip of a mountain top.

And then I'm lying, panting, exhausted on my bed.

Eiya! WHAT was that?

There's NO WAY I'm going to school. It's definitely a day to cut class. I need time. Space. To think.

I can't bear the thought of facing Peggy's grumpy face, or

Wing and Mimi's.

At breakfast I tell Ma it's a home-study day.

'How about we go and buy you an interview dress?' she says, still in that you've-been-working-so-hard-you-deserve -a-reward mood.

'Interview for what?'

'A summer job.'

A summer job? As if it's a fruit you can pluck off a tree. An interview dress. As if it's something that will transform me into a little-Miss-Perfect employee.

'Or uni,' Ma says.

Eiya!

Hong Kong: Asia's shopping paradise. I'm spoilt for choice, even in suburban Tsuen Wan. Racks of clothes criss-cross the newly-opened branch of Zara. Skirts and tops and pants are all neatly mixed and matched by colour.

Ma makes a bee-line for the discount corner. She flicks through droopy dresses and baggy trousers and flouncy blouses. A strappy top catches my eye but before I can remove it from the hanger, Ma has already given it a disapproving look. 'Too skimpy,' she says.

'Too skimpy … too low … too long … too tight … too … too … ' She twitters down a list of objections whenever I pick clothes she doesn't approve of.

Eventually, we make a compromise about the length of the 'interview dress'. I choose five acceptable specimens and try them for size. Meanwhile, Ma fusses outside the changing room, and sneakily checks the price tags. I hear her telling the shop assistant how expensive clothes are these days, about where she purchased her (fake) Prada handbag.

Frazzled, I reluctantly agree to the purchase of a plain grey dress with a lace collar that has been marked down thirty per cent.

Ma tells me she's on a day shift; it'll save time if she goes directly to work from the shopping mall. She'll be late home 'cos she needs to go to the pharmacy to buy some medicine for Grandpa. I ask when she'll start allowing me out again, if I can go round to Peg's place tonight.

Ma frowns. 'I suppose so. Just be sensible, okay?'

'I'm an adult now,' I remind her.

'Hmm.'

When I get home, I curl up on my bed, put on some music. I'm shattered. Too much stuff going on. I don't even bother to open the curtains.

It's dark when I awake and a mosquito is buzzing around my room. There's a text on my phone from Peggy: **coming round?**

no, i can't.

It's very clear in my mind what I have to do tonight. I zap off a message to Steel before hitting the toilet: **can we meet?**

He replies immediately: **i'll be outside your place in ten minutes.**

I dither about what to wear – matching black top and pants? A frilly blouse and skirt? *He dresses so kind of traditional.*

There's hardly enough time to brush my teeth and make up

my face.

He's waiting in the Porsche in a line of parked cars outside the main entrance. When he waves, my heart flutters with anticipation.

The Panda Hotel Coffee Shop is my idea of a good place to talk. But when I hint about what I want to say, Steel insists on driving to a bar high up a mountain road near the Chinese border. You can sit on a terrace and drink with the distant lights of Shenzhen and the starry sky as a backdrop, he tells me.

Bad luck. Tonight is overcast. The wind humps bulky clouds across the sky. I order a glass of white wine. Steel recommends the New Zealand Chardonnay. He scans the cocktail list and orders a Virgin Mary. Drinks it, surprisingly. Then another.

There's a vase of fresh red roses on the table. A scented candle flickers in a crystal glass. Steel is restless, fretful. 'It's about Janet, isn't it?' he says.

I take a sip of wine. Of course, there's a telepath in my head. 'It's not just her,' I say, defensively. 'Last night, that was really scary. I was terrified.'

'I'm going to finish with her,' Steel says grimly, enunciating each word.

'And Kung doesn't like me anyway,' I continue.

'*Lap sap*. Rubbish,' he says. 'He supports our relationship. And Peach loves you. She's always asking about you.'

I'm shaking my head. 'My Ma would never agree.'

'Agree to what?'

'To me dating a vampire.'

Steel stares at me. His forehead is furrowed. 'You've just had some nasty surprises recently.'

'A corpse who tried to kill me! A humongous hairy spider! Three vampires who wanted to drink my blood!'

Steel scrapes his neatly combed hair with manicured fingernails.

'Did you capture Max today?' I say, guessing what the answer will be.

Steel's face darkens. 'I tried, I promise. I drove back to where we met him last night. But he wasn't there.'

It's hopeless, I think. 'I'm returning the trinket,' I say, unclasping it.

Steel looks alarmed. 'No, don't do that. Keep it on.'

I pass it to him and he refuses to take it. 'You never know when it's protecting you,' he says.

His intensity frightens me.

A saucer of uneaten peanuts sits on the table. I take a long swig of wine. 'And I'm not sure if I believe in … us,' I say.

'How can you say that? We are soulmates,' Steel says, clutching the edge of the table and staring at me with disbelief. His eyes are fully dilated; I feel myself being sucked into the black holes of his pupils.

'Are you *absolutely* sure?' I say.

'Positive,' he says, plucking a drooping rose petal. 'And when married to you, physical pleasure was a delight of the heart, an ecstasy of the spirit. I have been longing to meet you again ever since.'

I blush.

'Hey, I've got an idea,' he says, lightening up for a moment. 'I know a re-birther. Someone who can regress you into past lives. How about I arrange for you to go and have some sessions with her?'

I let the offer pass, instead taking another swig of wine to harden my resolve. 'So, what about Janet?' *At last, it's out, splat on the table.*

'Ah, yes. I haven't explained clearly,' Steel says, dropping his gaze. 'I tell you what. How about we talk over dinner?'

'What, here?'

'No. I know a better place.'

'Dinner with a vampire. Mmm.'

Steel drives me to this smart restaurant near Langham Place in shop-'til-you-drop, acid-throwing Mongkok. You sit on high stools around a large oval-shaped counter with hundreds of sushi and sashimi dishes spinning round on conveyer belts. In the middle of the counter, Japanese chefs prepare slices of raw seafood – tuna, salmon, swordfish, yellowtail, lobster, crab – which they press on to bite-size slabs of freshly-cooked rice.

'Pick what you want,' Steel says.

He has already unwrapped my chopsticks and poured me some green tea. I forage for a California roll covered in fish roe.

'Try some *uni,* sea urchin,' Steel says, giving me a wedge of sushi topped by orange mush wrapped in seaweed. His plate is piled with sashimi.

I mix too much wasabi with the soya sauce and it burns my nose.

'You know what goes really well with sushi?' he says.

I shake my head, my nose still tingling.

'Sake.'

Before I can stop him, he's ordered a jug of the stuff. It's clear as water, warm as tea, and served in mini porcelain bowls.

'Jam bui, cheers to you and me,' Steel says, lifting his cup and clinking it against mine.

'To us,' I say.

He smiles happily.

'So you can drink?'

'In small amounts on special occasions,' he says, with a twinkle in his eye.

He suggests I sample the green tea ice-cream and *mochi.* The sake is delicious. It complements the desserts and tastes as fresh as lemon water. The more I drink, the less gloomy I feel.

'Don't be deceived,' Steel says. 'Sake is very alcoholic.'

But the liquid that slides down my throat gives me the confidence to ask the question that's really burning me up:

'Do you still have sex with Janet?'

Steel's long eyelashes flicker. 'Yes … no … I mean, I don't love her or anything.'

I drink another cup of sake. *Jam bui.* Bottoms up.

Steel lets out a long breath, the kind that means bad news is coming. 'You have to understand that if I didn't, I'd be a real danger to you.'

'So you use her, like a kind of prostitute?' I ask, trying to make myself feel better.

He looks round the small restaurant. Five other couples are perched on stools, shoulder to shoulder. None of them are within earshot.

'It's really dangerous for Chinese vampires to make love to mortals. We find it almost impossible to control our bloodlust. If we totally lose it, we could eat you up. Even if we just bite you a little bit, you may turn into a vampire.'

I swig another cup of sake. "You've told me that before.'

'What I'm going to tell you now is even more embarrassing,' Steel says. 'You might think I'm a bit of a pervert.'

'Okay,' I say, leading him on. Inside thinking: *eiya!*

'To help vampires stay in control, Taoist priests have written a treatise about having sex with mortals. The key is that male vampires don't ejaculate.'

I cringe at the 'e' word. I've never heard it said out loud, only read it online.

'The treatise is based on an ancient Taoist technique.'

I'm blushing.

Steel laughs, but his eyes are soft. 'If I can control myself, I'm much less likely to kill you. I will retain my vital juice, my *qi,* and bring greater satisfaction to you.'

I nod, not quite sure what he's going on about.

'And I'm studying a method right now.'

'Studying?'

'Yes, with Kung.'

'I just can't believe you talk to him about this stuff.' I say. The words just slip out. There's no way I would talk to my Ma about sex. Ever.

Steel sniffs a piece of tuna and pops it into his mouth.

I suddenly twig something. 'So, 'cos Janet is a vampire, you can beat her, bite her, completely let rip, and it doesn't matter. Right?'

'That's right,' Steel says, his eyes levelling with mine.

The uneaten sashimi on my plate look like lumps of flesh and I push them away. The revolving belts and blobs of food are making me feel dizzy. If I fix my eyes on the menu list attached to the opposite wall, it swings like a pendulum.

My resolve is as strong as rock. But then I can't remember what I was fighting against and the walls surrounding my fortress collapse, become rubble at my feet. And a voice echoes around the turret that is my mouth: 'Kiss me, please kiss me,' I say.

'Better not in public,' Steel says, grinning. His eyes dart around the restaurant.

I moisten my lips.

He settles the bill, helps me put on my cardigan. I reach for his proffered arm, hold it with both hands.

Together, we are indestructible.

Love hotels. I've heard about these pay-by-the-hour places, noticed the purple neon signs, but never been inside one. Cheaper ones are often advertised as foot massage joints in commercial buildings; up-market ones, like the one Steel has brought me to, are in posh residential areas behind tall garden walls.

A turbaned guard quickly closes the wrought-iron gate behind us and covers the registration plate of the Porsche. Another guard escorts us inside the building, where, accompanied by soothing piped music, we follow an amah along a maze of corridors with erotic pictures, vases of plastic flowers, and closed doors. The room the amah leads us into is equipped for one purpose only: sex. The sheets on the bed are neatly folded at the corners. There's a TV for titillation, an air-con for cool air. Blankets, towels and slippers are wrapped in cellophane bags. On a tray, two bottles of water, beakers, combs, and condoms.

Steel signs a chit; the amah bows her head and slips out of the room. We are alone.

'Come here,' Steel says. He's standing stiffly with his back to the bed. I pad across the carpet and stand opposite him. He raises his hands. His long tapering fingers are straight, slightly spread, ivory white.

'Let's start with a heart salutation,' he says.

Clumsily, I lurch towards him.

Steel takes a step back, chuckles. 'No, like this.'

He aligns his feet, stands tall and presses his palms together, as if about to pray.

I copy him. Our eyes meet. The black holes of his pupils are ocean deep.

He speaks, tells me to repeat: 'With my body, I honour you.'

'With my b-b-body, I honour you,' I say.

Steel bows.

A sweet smell of frangipani flowers floats around the room.

Steel steps forward and extends his arms – palms open, fingers spread – in front of me. His shoulders are square, his eyes are closed. 'Touch me,' he says hoarsely.

As my hands move to join his, I feel a rush of heat. When our fingertips meet, Steel takes a sharp intake of breath and his chin jerks forwards, as if tweaked by a puppet string.

I gently push my palms into his and they melt; a heavenly surge of energy flows up my arms.

He laughs, joyously. 'I love you too,' he says. His cheeks are pink, his teeth straight and white.

I'm glowing now, from a molten core that's becoming familiar. I sway closer to him, longing to kiss. Abruptly, he steps back and releases his hands, short-circuiting the flow.

'Slowly,' he says. 'We have plenty of time.'

I regain my balance.

He smiles. Relaxes his shoulders. 'Please lie down.'

He dims the lights, stands at the foot of the bed, loosens the top button of his shirt and unbuckles his belt.

I'm lying on top of the cool white sheet. Arms open wide. A human sacrifice. A complicit human sacrifice, not caring if I perish.

Steel curls his upper lip. The air-con blows.

'You're mine,' he says. He kneels at my feet, legs apart, and gently removes my flip-flops.

My toes are pink and plump.

Steel brings my foot up to his lips, his nostrils quiver, his eyes gleam.

A lump in the pit of my stomach is red and raw.

'Beautiful. Beautiful toes,' he whispers, kissing them one-by-one, tip-by-tip.

My other foot is crying out for attention and Steel gives a deep throaty laugh. He's more impatient this time: after kissing my toes, he licks them. Breathing thick and fast, he sniffs between them, sucks them two-by-two. Then he gnaws my big toe like a dog with a bone; the jagged points of his canines skate across its pudgy pad.

'Take me,' a tremulous voice sings inside.

Steel raises his head, as if listening. He gently lowers my leg to the mattress and lies on his back beside me. 'Wonderful, wonderful,' he says, panting, and punching the air.

I'm breathing heavily. I close my eyes, to savour his joy.

'You've drunk too much, my darling,' he says.

My darling, he said. A snatch of melody swirls around my brain.

He puts his arms around me, draws me close.

You've drunk too much, the melody sings. That's true. In complete denial, I rock my head from side to side.

'And that's probably enough nooky, for tonight anyway.'

I feel a laugh coming up from deep inside me.

It's contagious: Steel is laughing too. A deep hearty laugh, and we're laughing and laughing, laughing until tears drip down my cheeks and my stomach aches.

'I was hoping ... for a kiss ... on the lips,' I say, between guffaws.

Steel stops to catch his breath, then roars with mirth, blinking away drops of blood that fall from the corner of his eyes.

CHAPTER 18

A screening in Cheung Chau

'He took you to a love hotel?' Peggy says, slurping from a can of Diet Coke. We're sitting in the school canteen with Wing and Mimi. Tiffany is absent. Again.

It's one of those swelteringly hot humid days where you'd rather be in a dark air-conned room watching DVDs. Especially if you've had too much to drink the night before.

'Yeah,' I say airily. 'There were triple-X movies on demand. But we didn't watch any.'

Mimi and Wing's heads are down, noisily sucking their drinks through straws. Mimi's eyes are as wide as saucers. 'Any lesbian movies?' she says.

Peggy sneers. 'Gross.'

'I told you. We didn't switch the TV on,' I say.

None of them dare ask what went on between Steel and me. I decide there and then, if they did, I wouldn't tell.

Later, I'm snoozing through English class when Principal Lee's secretary comes knocking at our classroom door. Peggy nudges my elbow, I quickly lift my head, sit straight, and – *chi sin* – the secretary has a this-is-an-emergency look and is staring at me. 'Anna Wang, please report to Principal Lee's office,' she says.

A few classmates titter, I make a can't-think-why face and reluctantly follow the secretary out of the door.

Principal Lee peers down his thick-rimmed glasses. On his

desk, there's a mountain of papers. His bookshelves heave with leather-bound books. 'Someone by the name of Miss So called to say that she needs to speak to you as a matter of urgency. Here's the number,' he says, passing me a scribbled note.

I study the number but don't recognise it, thank the principal politely, then almost trip over a loose floorboard in my haste to get out of his pokey little room.

There's a coin-box telephone in the basement outside the sports changing rooms. I run downstairs and phone the number right away. *Hope it's nothing to do with Ma.*

'Why didn't you answer my text?' a rough female voice says.

'I didn't receive one. My phone is out of battery. Who is this?'

'Well, let me tell you, Janet is really upset. Actually, she's suicidal. Last night she tried to bleed herself to death. I know I told my brother that I wouldn't harm you again. I promised him. But we vampires aren't very good at keeping promises.'

Tiffany. Again. Harassing me. Turning me into a psycho.

'I'm going to hang up,' I say. But don't.

'You know too much about my family anyway,' she snarls. 'And I don't like the rumours either.'

'What are you talking about?'

Tiffany doesn't answer my question. 'You know what? I'm going to kill you. Devour your flesh and spit out the bones. Next time, it won't be a corpse. It'll be Janet and me, crazy with bloodlust,' she says, laughing menacingly, before hanging up.

Anxiety shoots through me like a physical injury. I can almost feel my body hair bristling. I twirl around, breathing heavily.

There's no one there. Just rows and rows of lockers along a long grey corridor. And the smell of sweat and toilets.

I figure the safest place to be is back in class. I start running; I'm turning the corner into the stairwell, heart pumping, and bang into … Steel. He's wearing sunglasses and a baseball cap. 'Steel,' I shout, amazed and relieved.

'You're in danger. I need to get you out of here,' he says, grabbing my hand.

After Tiffany's latest threat, I'm not taking any chances.

Rajaram is driving the BMW SUV. Steel is trying to flatten my goosebumps. And we're speeding down the Tsuen Wan highway, weaving between heavy traffic, like sharks. Dull light filters through the sun shades on the windows; we're swimming under murky waters. But with Steel by my side, I'm prepared to attack.

'What a nerve Tiffany has to call school directly,' I say. 'I could get her into serious trouble.'

Steel takes off his sunglasses. He seems strangely animated. Something has changed but I can't put my finger on what it is.

'I've something to tell you,' he whispers.

I take a sharp intake of breath. 'Go on.'

His golden eyes zoom into mine. 'Tiffany is so very mad at you, because … '

I'm hanging on to every word.

' … because I finished with Janet last night. She's history.'

I'm singing. His words are music to my ears.

He snaps his glasses case shut.

'Thanks,' I murmur, a weird combination of excitement and fear rushing through me.

Steel leans forward and his lips melt into mine. The kiss seems to last forever.

'Thanks,' I say again. I glance at Rajaram. His eyes are on the road.

'As long as I can control myself with you, I don't need her,' Steel says.

I'm so thrilled. So scared. *Drip drop, Stitch clot,* I sing. Inside. 'What's the worst Tiffany could do?' I say.

'Drink you dry, eat up the evidence.'

I feel blood draining from my face.

'We mustn't underestimate her. She's a spiteful bitch.'

I lean back on the leather headrest; its sweet smell reminds me of the books in Principal Lee's office. I stare out of the window, watch nameless buildings whizzing by. 'She really scares me,' I say, shivering at the memory of her high-pitched laugh echoing down the phone.

'She's full of vengeance. Because of her past.'

Feel the power, taste my glory. I give Steel a questioning look.

'She was the first wife of the Tang dynasty emperor, Emperor Daizong. Although she gave birth to a male heir, the emperor preferred his favourite concubine's son. The concubine schemed with the emperor's second wife to have Tiffany and her child murdered.'

'That's terrible,' I say, but can't help feeling gleeful for a second.

'They got the eunuchs to throw Tiffany down a well in the palace. The child was never found.'

I roll my eyes.

'The Emperor went on to have literally hundreds of concubines and nineteen more sons,' Steel says pensively.

'Phew!'

Steel goes back to the subject of Tiffany, the modern-day Telephone Fiend. 'I was on my way to a screening when I sensed that she was harassing you,' he says.

I raise an enquiring eyebrow. 'What?'

'At Yuk Bui temple.'

'Where's that?'

'Cheung Chau.'

An island. Dumb-bell shaped. About half an hour's ferry ride from Central. Famous for its cheap hotels, seafood restaurants and sandy beaches.

'And now you're coming with me,' he says.

I'm totally unprepared.

'It's too dangerous to leave you alone at school. Actually, the temple's a bit risky too. But I'll be there to protect you.'

'From what?'

'Corpses,' he says. 'Tens of them. In the last week alone, we have received a guy who was murdered in the Philippines, a suicide from Bangkok and five sisters burnt to death in Indonesia.'

I imagine charred blackened bodies, and cringe.

'The temple is the most sacred in Hong Kong to us. The sea

god, Pak Tai, formerly a prince of the Shang Dynasty, cured hundreds of locals from the plague in the 1770s. Later, under an order of the Jade Emperor, he killed an evil ghost king and became the Supreme Emperor of the Northern Heaven. We worship him for his power and courage. He guards the corpses for us when they arrive at the temple.'

I sigh, really not feeling up to all this. 'Why do you sound more and more like a history book?' I say.

Steel smirks. 'Sorry. I am pretty ancient.'

The SUV swerves round the corner of the Western corridor highway. When I raise my window screen, the bustling harbour and office towers of Hong Kong Island sweep into view. It's clear enough to see the Peak Tram crawling ant-like up the steep mountainside to the Peak.

Then we change direction. The sun's rays bounce off the metallic buildings and I quickly lower the screen to cut the glare. The highway drops underground and we're travelling through the Cross Harbour Tunnel to Hong Kong side, where Rajaram successfully navigates through noodles of intersecting roads to reach the centre of town.

Steel lifts my fingers to his mouth and kisses them. 'By the way,' he says, 'don't tell my parents about Tiffany. They've got enough to worry about at the moment.'

We arrive at Central pier. Pleasure junks jostle for space in the choppy waters, their weighty wooden hulks creak in the wind. Sunburned sailors wave and shout to attract the attention of groups of people who are congregating on the pier to be picked up. Steel points to a luxury yacht floating on the water like a three-tiered wedding cake. A uniformed captain is standing by the gangplank. As the SUV approaches, he clicks his heels and salutes us.

A crew member gives me a hand on board. I follow Steel along the gangway, holding a rail for support. We walk down to a lower deck, into a darkened gym, full of sports equipment. Peach is working out in there. She's wearing a pink tracksuit; her lush long hair is plaited and wound round her head like a crown. She pauses on the treadmill, steps off it and glides towards me. 'How lovely to see you,' she says.

Kung is sitting in a lotus position on a sheepskin mat at the far side of the gym. He's ringing a chime and quietly chanting a liturgical text. 'Where's Tiffany?' he asks, emerging from a kind of trance.

'She said she would make her own way,' Steel says.

'Then give the order to set sail, son,' Kung says.

Steel leaves the cabin. Peach offers me a cup of water from a drinks dispenser. 'I believe you may be coming to stay with us in Lantau this weekend?' she says.

This weekend? I'd really like to, but how can I persuade my Ma? I think.

Kung nods authoritatively. 'Yes, it's time we all got to know each other better.'

'Thanks!' I say, gulping the water down.

Steel steps back through the teak door, closes it, and gives me a sheepish grin. We sit on a slatted wooden bench together and look out of a porthole. Peach climbs on a step machine, and plugs herself back into her music. Kung turns a page of his tome and resumes chanting.

The yacht ploughs through the harbour. It gathers speed, overtaking bobbing fishing boats, bulky ferries and a spiky police launch. A jetfoil laden with gamblers races past us on its way to Macau.

Kung suddenly snaps his book shut and glances at his gold Rolex watch. 'We'll arrive at Cheung Chau in twenty minutes,' he says. 'It's time to give Anna her robe.'

Peach pulls out a long black garment from a cubbyhole. 'The headdress will hide your identity, so don't worry. As long as you don't open your mouth, no one will suspect that you're human,' she says.

'Won't they smell her blood?' Steel asks anxiously.

Kung has taken off his tunic, revealing a hairless chest. 'Yes, of course they will. It's your responsibility to protect her.'

I blink away a bead of sweat. Peach wipes my forehead with her towel. 'You really shouldn't worry, dear,' she says. 'I know you'll be safe.'

Cheung Chau harbour is a hive of activity. Trawlers with snub-nosed bows are moored in the typhoon shelter with today's catch and there's a steady stream of coolies loading sacks of fish on dinghies. Fishermen spread nets leeward to check for rips. The seafood restaurants that line the shore are buzzing with customers, who choose lunch from banks of aquariums squirming with colourful fish and crustaceans.

At the pier, hawker women wearing wide-brimmed hats barter fishy snacks and mementoes. As we dock, I peer through the gauze that masks my face to see, moving towards us, four red palanquins carried by a team of bare-chested men. Lifting the folds of my gown, I alight from the yacht to the stares of a crowd of curious onlookers. Steel, keeping hold of my hand to accompany me to the last carriage, guides me into its dark interior. Four carriers lift the bamboo yoke onto their shoulders, bearing me along the busy promenade. I peep out of the curtained window, see families of day-trippers, careless young lovers linking hands and licking drippy ice-creams. *Eiya! Everything looks so normal!*

We start climbing and I'm flung backwards as my carriage is propelled up some steps. As we enter a building, our arrival is announced by the clash of gongs and the beating of a drum. It's dark as pitch and there's the acrid smell of incense. We must be inside the temple.

But my palanquin doesn't stop. We're going down and down even farther and there's a musty smell of dampness and decay. *Where are we going?*

'Steel?' I call out.

'Nearly there,' I hear him reply, in a muffled voice.

What's that scrabbling sound?

At last the bearers lower my palanquin and someone swings back the curtain.

'Steel,' I cry with relief. His pallid face is lit up by the hurricane lamp he's holding.

A bald priest leads us down a narrow passageway. The walls are dripping with water and I can't help shivering. Something flits past, scraping the top of my head. 'Aargh!'

'Sshhh,' Steel says. 'It's only a bat.'

He leads me into a prison-like observation room. Good thing I'm not claustrophobic.

'I'm here, right by your side,' Steel says. 'But remember: stay silent, *whatever* you see.' He shines the lamp onto the ancient brick wall in front of us.

There's a peep-hole; it overlooks a long gloomy hall lit by candlelight. Wooden pillars embossed with dragons support a low-hanging ceiling. Close by, there's a large iron cauldron and a long stone trestle table.

A line of darkly-robed priests march in procession towards us. The head priest is bearing a golden sceptre. When he reaches the cauldron, he strikes a gigantic bronze bell that is hanging from the rafters of the ceiling. As it tolls, the priests assemble along the opposite side of the stone table. Their faces are hooded. When the last one is in position, the priest strikes the bronze bell with a final flourish and utters a brief command. The other priests answer with a resounding *'Hai'*.

I'm on tiptoes to watch what happens next. Kung emerges from a side door. Followed by … Tiffany, looking proud and powerful. *Does she know I'm here?* Both are wearing silk gowns embroidered with golden thread. Their long sleeves have elaborate cuffs: *yin yang* medallions dangle from their square hats. The priests freeze in respectful silence.

After a pause, Kung starts reciting the only lines I know from *Dao De Jing:*

*'The Way that can be described is not the true Way
The Name that can be named is not the constant
Name.'*

With another strike of the gong, a column of ragged corpses are led through a fortified door at the darkest end of the hall. Their rigid arms are tied with chains attached to a long metal pole which is supported at both ends by two priests. There are young corpses and decrepit ones, males and females. Others with missing legs, eyes and noses. All have a ghastly greenish hue. I cover my eyes in shock. Steel puts his arm around my shoulders.

Kung moves away from the table. He lifts a heavy metal scabbard from the cauldron and with a swift upward thrust, unleashes a sword. Its silver blade quivers with energy.

'The hilt is encrusted with precious stones. It was wrought in the Song dynasty,' Steel whispers to me.

Tiffany is sitting at the head of the table. Beside her, a priest brandishes an ink brush, eager to inscribe a bulky leather-bound tome that is open in front of him. Another priest is arranging sheaves of yellow papers into two piles. Two priests shuffle the first corpse to where Kung is standing.

'Name?' says Kung.

'Yung Wai Ki.'

'Place and date of death?'

'Vietnam. Eighteenth of May.'

'Age at death?'

'Twenty-four.'

'Cause of death?'

'Brawl.'

'Perpetrator or victim?'

'Perpetrator.'

Kung lifts the sword, then slowly lowers its tip to touch the corpse's shoulder. 'To the morgue.'

The corpse is walked to where Tiffany and the priests are sitting. One priest slaps a piece of yellow paper on its forehead, the other scrawls a Chinese character in the tome. Tiffany stands. She presses an intricate golden seal on an ink-pad and officially chops the page. Then the corpse is carried through one of the two ancient doors that lead off from the main area.

A second corpse is shuffled forward. There's a bloody mess of gore where half its face should be.

'Name?' Kung says.

'Suky Lee.'

'Place and date of death?'

Twenty-fourth of May, the Philippines.'

'Age at death?'

'Forty-nine.'

'Cause of death?'

'Suicide.'

'The reason?'

'Infidelity of husband.'

'Do you wish to be converted into a vampire?'

'Yes.'

Kung lifts the sword, lowers the tip to the corpse's shoulder: 'To the Vampire Chamber.'

'Dad sifts out the good souls from the evil ones,' Steel says. 'He offers the good ones a second chance.'

'Like her, Suky Lee?'

'Yes. After six months' training, her soul will be converted into a vampire. Meanwhile, her body will be put into a coffin and sent to the Luen Institute for burial arrangements.'

'So her vampire will be the same age as the age when she died?'

'Yes.'

'What happens if someone recognises her?'

Steel smiles. 'There's little chance of that. She's forbidden to return to where she died for fifty years. The greater risk is someone noticing that she's not ageing.'

'What can she do about that?'

'Move. Every five years or so.'

The last of the corpses is kneeling before Kung. He's arguing that he deserves to be a vampire.

'I admit I was careless,' he pleads in a deep rasping voice. 'My car was a write-off. But I didn't kill anyone.'

'You were drinking and driving,' Kung says imperiously. 'TO THE MORGUE.' The corpse lets out a roar which echoes round the temple as he's dragged off by two priests.

'What will happen to him?' I ask.

'He will be sent to the Luen Institute, made comatose and placed in a sealed coffin. Then his relatives will be notified that his body is ready for burial.'

Kung intones an incantation to bless the sword. Tiffany closes the tome and approaches Kung, followed by the priests. They all kneel before him and chant a long prayer while Kung taps them one-by-one with the sword.

'It's a ritual to keep them loyal,' Steel says.

'Why is Tiffany working with your Dad, not you?'

'You have to be a member of the Taoist Vampire Council. She is. I'm not. You can't join the Council until you've been a vampire for at least one hundred years.'

I'm shivering with cold, and creepiness. Crossing my arms over my chest, I accidentally touch a spider's web. 'I don't like it here', I say.

'Let's get you out into some fresh air,' Steel says, taking my hand.

We're back in the SUV, stuck behind a double-decker bus in a traffic jam. Steel is restless and I think I know why: 'cos of what is going on in my mind. He takes out a packet of wet wipes from a glove compartment and offers me one.

I decline it.

He switches on the TV that's affixed to the back of the driver's seat. An advertisement for package holidays to Phuket flips up. He watches it for a few seconds, sighs, then depresses the off switch.

'So you know what I'm thinking, right?' I say, hyper-aware that it's probably going to cause trouble between us.

He gives me a withering smile.

'So … Can Kung turn humans into vampires?'

Lines of anger etch across his forehead. 'Stop it, will you?'

A surge of emotion courses through my veins. 'Then we'd be together forever. I wouldn't grow old. We'd never have to worry about you losing control,' I say.

'No, no, no,' he shouts, running his hands through his hair. 'I want you as a human. Kung would never agree. Your life as a vampire would be full of danger. Vampires have so many enemies.'

'In more danger than I am now?' I ask. Staggered.

'Yes, of course.' He covers his face with his hands.

I've blown my bridges now. The only direction is forwards. 'I'm not afraid,' I say lightly.'

Steel grabs me by the chin, turns my face to his and stares at me: he's furious.

At that moment I have a vision. From another place. Another time. I'm looking at us from above. I see Steel's hand crook my chin sharply upwards. My neck veins arch, engorged, like tangled stems. Then he raises his head, as if to summon a magical power, cries out, lunges towards me, greedily sinks his teeth into my throat. The taut skin punctures immediately. Blood spurts, like a fountain.

Rajaram's anxious eyes appear in the rear-view mirror. 'Steady on there, master,' he says.

Steel pushes me away roughly. 'I want to give you a good life,' he says, his voice cracking with emotion.

'You do?' I say.

'I want to marry you. Father a child with you,' he says.

A surge of joy, then terror, zaps me. 'A half-vampire child?'

Steel is taken aback, for a moment. 'No. If you are human, our child will be human too.'

The dollar drops. My throat feels dry. 'And if I'm a vampire?'

'You will not even be able to conceive. Female vampires are infertile.'

We sit in silence for a while. The temperature drops. Disappointment sags and dulls my mind.

'Anna, don't even think about it, I beg you,' Steel suddenly says. 'Kung wouldn't let you. I mean, what about your Ma? You wouldn't want to leave her completely alone in this world, would you?'

I sigh. *Why are things so complicated? I don't do complicated.*

CHAPTER 19
Eternal love

'Rebirthing works well in remote places. In forests, on mountains, by waterfalls. Sai King country park is ideal,' Steel says.

It's a bright sunny day and the countryside is green. Tropical green. We're driving through the rural north-eastern part of Hong Kong, passing sleepy villages, yacht anchorages, rolling hills and desolate beaches.

We stop at a gate entrance where city cars can't go any farther and open the windows for some fresh air. Sprawling trees and ferns and flowering bushes spring from the hillsides. Busy insects buzz the day away.

Susie, the re-birther, arrives. She's a middle-aged woman in dungarees with untidy curly hair pulled off her forehead by a hair band. Steel says he'll wait for me in a car park nearby.

'Follow me,' Susie says, smiling beatifically. We meander through old paddy fields along an overgrown path to reach her house. A friendly golden Labrador greets us in the porch.

'Don't be afraid of Poppy,' Susie says, patting the dog's rump.

Cheerful patchwork quilts decorate divans and the sofas look spongy. An antique Chinese chest has sprouted a stone forest of crystals and amethysts. We drink peppermint tea on rattan chairs.

'Unconsciously, we are forever searching for our soulmates.

The lucky ones find them,' she says.

Susie draws the curtains and turns the lights off. She commands me to lie on an exercise mat on the floor: knees up, eyes closed, breathing deeply. Her bones crack as she sits cross-legged on a cushion beside me and massages my arms and shoulders. Then she starts to speak in a hushed monotone:

'Breathe in. Breathe out. Slow-ly. Link those breaths. Transform them – they've become a golden ring of energy. See that ring? Hovering above you? It's a halo of energy. Your karma. A karma crown. Floating above your head.'

My elbows are hurting from being rubbed against the floor tiles. Poppy tries to lick my face with her sloppy tongue. Susie shoos her away. There's the croaking of cicadas and the mewling of a cat. But no karma crown.

'Your ring of karma. Your ring of power. Glowing. Pulsating. Like an orb,' Susie intones huskily. 'It's the karma of your past lives.'

Gradually, my limbs feel heavy. The sandalwood oil smells sweet. I feel time slowing down to the rhythm of her voice. My voice.

I'm a lady,
An ancient lady.
I'm cradling a baby,
A son.
I'm alone,
In a wood-panelled room.

A stiff qipao collar rubs my neck.
Tortoiseshell hairpins adorn my hair.
My skin is pale.
My waist is slim.

The walls are thick.
The tea in the pot is cold.
From a latticed window,
I see footprints on snow.

Beyond a padlocked gate,
A dark and brooding sky.
Skeletal trees.
Dry leaves.

Heavy thoughts.
My husband is at war.
My son is crying.
The embers in the hearth are black.

I must have come round for a few moments, 'cos next thing I see is Susie's moon face shining over me. She's holding my hand, squeezing it, reassuring me that everything will be okay.

I used to have a baby!

Who was my husband?

'Breathe in. Breathe out. Slow-ly. Link those breaths,' Susie intones.

I close my eyes again and effortlessly slip back into the dream.

A sour maid.
Starched white blouse,
Baggy black trousers.
Her face is pinched and lined,
Her hair screwed tight in a bun.
She gloats over my sadness.

*'He **will** come back,' I say.*
'Yes, Ma'am,' she drawls.

A distant gunshot pierces the gloom.
My baby stirs.
The maid takes him.
Leaves the room.
It's deathly quiet.
I do not dare speak,
For fear of waking ghosts.

Time stands still. Then I feel myself, as in a lift shaft, descending another level.

Chattering monkeys, night fall.
Barren hills above the northern wall.
White water, winding east,
To the single spot, where we meet.

I drift towards him.
I kneel at his grave.
Passing clouds echo my prayers.
The winter wind knows how bitter I feel.
The willow tree will never again be green.

'There, there,' Susie says, gently patting my shoulders. 'It's all right. Just keep breathing.'

Fat water droplets drip down my cheeks and into a frigid sea.

'Look for hope. Look for redemption. Look to your next life.'

Susie's face laps against my shore.

The next dream feels closer, sharper.

I stand up.
Shooting pains,
Up my legs.
Crippling,
Heart-stopping pains.
One step is agony.
I scream.

I lift my gown –
Two dainty pointed slippered feet.
Fox fairy's feet.

Exquisitely obscene festering broken feet.
Putrid purple warped toes,
Hanging, like grapes,
Pointing to hell.
Marking my mortality.

A living room.
A rosy fire, glowing embers.
Intricate pieces of jade.
Happy voices.
Crabs boiling in the pot.
Galloping horses.

A warm, cosy bed.
Silk sheets.
A baby, my daughter,
Wrapped in an embroidered shawl.

A Chinese scroll –
I reach for it.
The ivory rollers are smooth.
The ink smells fresh.
Some characters are blotted with tears.
It's dated July 1937,
Shanghai.

Steel plunges a brush in a porcelain inkpot.
Shiny black ink slithers down the silk.
His bold calligraphy bursts with energy.
The ink smells fresh.
A flock of birds swoops –
Plump, red-chested lovebirds.
They roost on the canvas,
Pecking at juicy plums.

I'm a heavenly spirit, floating weightless on pregnant clouds. 'Beautiful,' I murmur, warmed by the fire and the leaping delight of unrolling the scroll still further.

I hear Susie's voice drifting through the eons of time. 'Go back, go back,' she moans.

'Yes,' I say, sighing with pleasure and sinking back into the swirling memories.

But something has changed.

I see his fingers grasping the bars.
He's on the other side, waving.
My heart feels thick as mud.

I have a key to a padlock,
Hidden in a locket,
Close to my chest.

'Ming Ming?

Where are you, Ming Ming?'

'You're coming round,' I hear Susie say. She's shaking my shoulders, rigid shoulders thick with bone.

I'm crying, as if there's no tomorrow: knees to chest, like a foetus, covered in snot.

Where's my baby?

'There, there,' Susie says, stroking my hair. 'Welcome back to your present life.'

I'm panting, pushing away strands of hair that are pasted to my cheeks.

I used to have bound feet!

Susie gently massages my shoulders, passes me another tissue to dry my tears.

'Where is she?' I cry.

'I'll just go and put the kettle on,' Susie says.

'Do you believe me now?' Steel asks.

We're in a log cabin surrounded by trees in the country park. My silk stocking tea lies untouched. His cold fingers are entwined with mine and he's asking lots of questions and I'm gazing into his eyes, never wanting to leave them again. They're ablaze. Dripping with love.

'What did you see in our living room?'

The image is crystal clear. 'A jade cup, shaped like a gourd, on the mantelpiece. Framed calligraphy on the walls. A watercolour painting of soldiers waving flags on galloping horses … '

As I reel off the objects, Steel nods enthusiastically. 'Did you see the shawl we swaddled Ming Ming in?'

I can see it clear as a bell. 'Bright yellow, hand-made, with butterflies drinking the nectar of sprays of flowers.'

'My mother embroidered it,' Steel says softly.

'And your lovely calligraphy. Do you write poetry?'

'Yes, I love poetry.'

'What were you writing?'

'I'm not sure,' he says. 'I wrote so many poems, always about you.'

I nod, to the excited trill of a lovebird.

Steel grips my hand ardently. 'It sounds like you saw me inscribing the scroll I wrote for you the night before I left Shanghai.'

His eyes are round, his pupils deep as the night sky.

'And I had bound feet,' I say, suddenly trembling.

Steel's eyes moisten. His long eyelashes flutter with agitation. He suddenly looks in acute pain. 'My darling,' he says, 'I'm afraid you did. It was the custom then. Your parents crunched your feet into three-inch golden lilies for the delectation of a rich husband.'

A wave of nausea brings bile to my throat. 'It was sooooo painful. And so frustrating, not being able to walk properly, I mean. I felt imprisoned, like a singing bird in a golden cage. It was … '

Steel grabs handfuls of his hair and howls. Fortunately, we're the only ones left in the cabin.

When he speaks again, his voice is choked. 'That's why I love your feet so much now,' he says. 'Your perfect little toes, your smooth heels, your noble arches. That's why I'm so happy to find you again in your present life. I want to liberate you from previous lifetimes of physical pain, of suffering. I want you to share my future, our future, our destiny, forever.'

CHAPTER 20

Apparitions

'Please stop talking about it.' Steel accelerates so quickly into the fast lane that my head bangs against the headrest.

I've brought up the subject again. You see, I never want to be without him. Not after yesterday. Not ever. 'If I'm a vampire, we can always be together,' I plead.

'So what?' he shouts, yanking the steering wheel. 'We wouldn't be happy.'

'How do you know?'

'You never believe what I say, do you? I told you we were soulmates and you didn't believe me. Now you do.'

'That's not the point,' I say.

We've never argued before and it doesn't feel good.

'You just don't trust me,' he says, with a grimace.

'I do.'

'Bah.' He brakes so sharply to avoid hitting the back of a taxi that I'm straining against my seat belt.

We're in a Lexus on the way to the Luen Institute to find a spell. Steel was dead against the idea; it took ages to persuade him. He's obviously having second thoughts.

I'd better try and compromise, I s'pose. 'I know for sure we're soulmates now,' I say, my voice quavering, 'but … '

'But I'm a vampire, right?' Steel says angrily.

'But if I stay human, what happens if I have an accident? If I'm run over by a bus?'

Steel grits his teeth. 'I'm not arguing anymore,' he says. 'Let's just find that spell. One glimpse into the fifth dimension should put you off forever.'

We race up the hill to the Luen Institute. Luckily, there's a vacant parking space at the top. The imposing stone archway of the Institute towers above us. The temples are decorated with colourful prayer flags and bustling with people. There's a queue of visitors who have come to have their fortunes told. Others are delivering packages of goodies to their ancestors, seeking names for newborn children, buying lucky charms for new homes, receiving blessings from priests.

Steel is wearing a simple grey Taoist robe, a peaked hat, white leggings, and sunglasses. He leads me into the complex via a side entrance. We pass smoking chimneys of burning incense and jaunty pagodas with vermilion columns and yellow-tiled roofs. Crouching near a shrine, a gnarled old woman sticks pins in a photograph of an old man and mutters curses of revenge.

One temple, set apart, smaller than the rest, with hexagonal stained-glass windows, is hidden behind a row of cypress trees. It's dark and empty inside, apart from an ancient wooden chest set on a pedestal in the middle of the chamber. The chest is engraved with Chinese characters and embossed with *yin yang* symbols. It reminds me of the ones you see in historical dramas on TV.

'I trust you to expunge all memory of this when you next see Kung, okay?' Steel says. His voice echoes around the dome.

I nod.

He teases out a loose brick from the stone wall above the chest and extracts a cloisonné box. From the box, under a hidden drawer, he extracts a rusty key.

The lock of the chest turns easily. Carefully, we lower its heavy lid to the floor. Inside, there's a collection of dusty wood-bound books. Steel lifts the topmost tome, brushes away the cobwebs and opens it. The parchment is musty and browned with age. I sneeze.

'I know it's in here somewhere,' Steel says, closing the book, passing it to me, lifting another.

I pile them high, one by one.

'Got it,' he whispers excitedly.

I shiver with excitement. And trepidation.

The book cover is blank. Steel turns to the index page and scans a finger down to the spell he's looking for. I hold down the crinkled page while he carefully copies the weird Chinese characters into a notebook.

'I'll enchant you tonight,' he says. 'Then let's see how you feel about being a vampire.'

'No hurry,' I say. As my stomach turns.

There's no hurry 'cos I've booked a session at China Chicks at nine. Wing and Mimi made me feel really guilty about not getting round to it earlier.

Steel insists on coming too: For My Safety.

I tell him to bring ear-plugs.

So tonight is on me. 'Haven't seen you for a while,' Charlie says, as I sign in at the reception.

I notice a new poster on the wall behind Charlie's desk. There's a knocked-over bottle, spilled pills, an outstretched hand, a bowed head and a mop of greasy hair. The caption reads: 'NEVER DONE DRUGS. NEVER HAVE. NEVER WILL. DRUGS KILL.'

Poor Peg. I try to block her cute dimples from my mind.

Steel sits on a stool and hides in the corner of the room. Being invisible is one skill he hasn't mastered yet. I set up the video camera, check the mike.

'Oh! Hi Steel,' Wing says, in her didn't-expect-to-see-you-here voice. Her lycra bodysuit is black-cat tight.

He gives her an uncomfortable nod.

'How are you?' I say. 'Cool shoes.' Platforms. She's hung up about being so short.

She smirks, takes the bass out of its case, twiddles the pegs and strums the strings. Normally, we'd already be goofing around.

Mimi comes dashing in, and freezes with surprise. 'Steel!' she says, straightening her glasses.

'Just ignore me,' he says, running a hand through his hair.

'Steel plays real guitar,' I say.

Mimi gives him a blank stare then looks around for his guitar case.

'Not today,' Steel says.

'Cool,' Mimi says. Sarcastic-like.

The room is icebox cold. Steel goes to ask Charlie to turn the air-con down.

'What's he doing here, anyway?' Wing hisses, as soon as he's out of earshot.

'Just this once,' I say.

Wing plucks some bum notes on the guitar.

You know what? I don't care what you both think.

I flick through the song list, turn on the spotlights, and put *Bloodswell* first up. *Bloodswell* always gets us in the groove.

Then we go through our other bookmarked numbers: *Strip Club, Tears and Fears, Everlasting Lovers.*

Wing has mastered a mean new riff and Mimi shows off a complicated drumstick technique. But with Steel in the room, we're lousy soft ball rockers. It feels so different when there's someone watching.

We're just picking our way through *Winner Takes All* when there's the sound of raised voices, moving furniture and the splintering of glass.

Steel jumps to the door and presses his ear against it. His eyes dart from side to side. I could swear his hair is standing on end. 'It's only Peggy,' he says.

I groan, throw down the mike.

Wing throws me an accusing look. 'She's not doing too well without you, you know,' she says.

I hear Peggy's slurred tones: 'I know she's *shin* here,' and the voices of people trying to calm her down.

'Sorry guys,' I say, switching off the projector.

Steel opens the studio door.

Peggy is staggering along the corridor. Her hair is dishevelled and she stinks of alcohol. She's hanging on to a butch girl wearing army boots, leather gear and heavy metal jewellery.

Ah! This must be Jane.

Steel and I prop them on our shoulders, lead them into the studio and sit them on stools.

'Peg, what's up?' I say, with my heart in my mouth.

My voice arouses her. She looks up at me, sees Steel and moans. 'I just wanna hear you sing,' she says. 'Sing a song for me.' Her eyeballs are webbed with red lines.

'Okay,' I say. I walk back to centre stage and flick back to the lyrics of her favourite number.

Peggy's head flops to her chest.

'How much has she taken?' I ask.

Jane's face is dead pale too. 'Dunno,' she says. 'And I feel sick. Really sick.'

They're both completely wasted.

Metal jangles as Jane stands and lurches dangerously towards the door. Her legs buckle as she crumples in a heap on the floor. She lands heavily, seems winded, and then passes out.

Steel dashes out to get help.

'What's happening?' Peggy says, coming alive.

'999,' I say.

Mimi and Wing shake Jane, call her name. When she starts vomiting, we know she'll be okay.

Peggy's eyes search for mine. Her skin is pasty, pudgy. It's the texture of a *cha siu* bun.

'I wanna go home,' she says. 'Just me and you. Like old times.'

Steel takes Peggy's arm. 'Let's drive you,' he says.

He seems concerned about her. Light bulb moment: he cares for her, 'cos I do.

Wing packs the guitar.

Mimi says she'll look after Jane until the ambulance comes.

Steel and I apologise to Charlie, pay him for the broken beer glass and drag Peg to the car.

Nathan Road is overflowing with people late-night shopping, eating, dating, smoking, hurrying to catch a movie. Peggy is completely out of it. A dribble of saliva slithers down the side of her mouth and she mumbles nonsense.

Steel drives carefully. He rounds the corners slowly.

I call Ken, Peggy's brother. There's some loud rock music thumping in the background. He says he's working late, won't be back until after midnight. I tell him I'll watch over Peggy until he gets back.

Their flat feels unclean, unloved. Clothes are strewn across the floor. Dishes fester on the table. The family shrine looks untended: a muddle of burnt incense sticks and mouldy fruit. We carry Peg to her bed, mop her brow and loosen her trousers. She falls immediately into a deep sleep. Too deep. For my liking.

Steel sits on a chair by her desk, twiddling his car keys. 'She should be okay,' he says.

'I feel bad,' I say.

Steel taps his foot impatiently. 'There's little you can do to help. It's up to her, what she wants to make of her life, ultimately.'

'But I'm her best friend,' I say. I suddenly long to see her laugh, to pinch her dimples, to dance to Lady Gaga in our bras and panties.

Steel shrugs his shoulders. 'She needs time. She'll grow up, discover who she really is,' he says.

My brain starts to question what he's on about. I wonder what he would do if she stopped breathing. Does it matter, if he only cares about her 'cos I do?

Steel sighs, takes his hands out of his pockets, checks Peg's pulse, then walks out of the bedroom. I follow.

It's sooooo humid. I turn the air-con up and help myself to a can of Sarsae from the fridge. Steel sits on the sofa and switches on the TV.

Peggy stirs.

I'm fed up. Steel's restlessness is catching. *This is not what we were supposed to be doing tonight.*

There's a creak, like wooden furniture, only louder.

Steel jumps to his feet, stiffens, listens. 'It's a hungry ghost,' he says. 'It's feeding off Peggy's sadness.'

I look around furtively, just see peeling wallpaper, and damp stains on the ceiling.

'I've got an idea,' Steel says excitedly, pulling his notebook out of his back pocket. 'I'll use the spell to enchant you here. I'll show you what I can see, right now.'

He sits straight, asks me to kneel in front of him and look into his eyes. Their intensity frightens me. He clears his throat and starts reciting the spell. No sooner has he uttered the last word when a clammy, ghostly mass rears between us. It swirls around me, shrinks into a ghastly torso, a stinking mouth, and grasping fingers. It seeps into my pores and up my nostrils. It's suffocating me. 'Get off,' I scream, flailing my arms. I fall onto the floor, kicking wildly.

Steel pulls me up, jerks my chin and beseeches me to open my eyes, to look at nothing but him. Shaking my arms, he cries out another spell.

The apparition disappears. But my screams have woken Peggy. She sits up with a start, sees Steel and gasps with surprise.

We rush to her side. She's drenched in sweat.

'Anna? What happened?' she says.

I lower her back onto the bed, mop her brow.

'What are you doing here?' she says, sitting up again.

Steel goes back into the front room.

'Everything will be okay,' I say, still trembling.

'Switch on the lights. I'm scared.'

'Just sleep now. Ken will be back soon.'

Peggy stays sitting. She purses her pale lips. Her dimples have disappeared. 'How can I sleep, with you around?' she says.

'Lie down.'

Her bloodshot eyes stare at me longingly. 'I miss you so much,' she says.

CHAPTER 21
Bauhinia Lodge

From the air, the many islands of Hong Kong look like handfuls of opals scattered on a swathe of crisp turquoise silk.

I'm strapped in the backseat behind the pilot wearing earmuffs to dull the sound of the helicopter engine. 'Amazing,' I mouth to Steel, who's sitting next to me. He squeezes my hand.

The Tang family and I, plus Sport, are on our way to their homestead, tucked behind the Po Lin monastery on Lantau.

It's too noisy to talk. But I can still text. **10 minutes to landing,** I write to Peg.

She texts back immediately: **watch your jugular.**

I reply: **if ma calls, tell her i'm in the library and i'll call her back.**

I can't believe my luck, although I feel a bit worried about Grandpa. When Ma came back from work yesterday, she told me that he's in hospital. He's got a blood clot in his leg and needs an emergency operation. It's money first in Chinese hospitals and Grandma doesn't have enough. So Ma flew to Hunan first thing this morning with the dosh. Leaving me to study for my exams. Not.

The helicopter is flying over the south side of Lantau Island. I see palm-fringed beaches, wooded slopes and the green slab of a reservoir. The engine grinds as we gain height to skirt round Lantau Peak. The Big Buddha sits impassively on a lotus leaf below us.

'There's the landing,' Steel shouts, pointing to a concrete spot in the middle of a wooded plateau.

The heli lowers itself like a hen roosting on an egg and Bauhinia Lodge comes into focus. It's a rambling country house with gardens, stables and a swimming pool. A line of servants has formed to greet us on the verandah: housemaids, cooks, grooms and gardeners. And cats, an army of cats, frolicking on the grass.

In the house, there are so many rooms I fear I'll get lost on my way to dinner. Peach shows me to a cosy bedroom with low wooden beams and an ensuite bathroom.

'Make yourself at home,' she says gaily, switching on a ceiling fan. The fragrance of a fresh bunch of ginger flowers permeates the room.

A thought takes my guts and twists them into worms: *so this is the place Steel and I will make love for the first time.*

Peach, smiling, motions to leave.

'I'll just unpack my things,' I say airily.

An animal skin is hanging on the wall. Buffalo? I'm just getting my mobile out to take a photo when Steel is beside me.

'Found you,' he says.

'You frightened me,' I say shrilly. Secretly delighted.

Steel pushes me to the bed, rolls me over and lays his head on my shoulder. I feel his body tighten. Then he sighs deeply, forces himself to relax. He's washed and changed. 'Ready to go downstairs and be sociable,' he says.

Kung, Peach, Tiffany and Freddy are having a late afternoon snack in the dining room. Hungry cats are sitting expectantly underneath their chairs. Sport is stretched out on a rug by the fireplace.

'I hope you're not squeamish,' Steel says, passing me a pair of chopsticks.

There are plates and plates of offal on the table: stringy intestines, strips of cow's stomach, sliced kidneys, livers and hearts.

'Bought fresh from a hawker this morning,' Peach says, popping a pig's ovary into her mouth.

From the corner of my eye, I catch Tiffany throwing me a hateful stare. If looks could kill, I'd be dead.

Will I ever get away from here? I suddenly think, and quiver with fear.

Kung is sitting at the head of the table. Pensive. His hair is neatly tied in a ponytail and, for once, he's wearing casual clothes. He notices that I'm looking at him. 'Anna,' he says, 'At last, we have an opportunity to spend some time together.'

He raises a hand and puts three fingers to his forehead. *Is he blessing me?* I wonder.

'Try some kidney,' Peach says. 'It's delicious dipped in soya sauce.'

'Thanks,' I say, suppressing the urge to retch.

Freddy greedily sucks up a bowl of intestines as if they were soba noodles.

'We usually come here at weekends,' Kung says. 'We find it

makes a pleasant change from the city.'

And gives you an opportunity to hunt, I think.

'Yes, that too,' Kung says.

I flick my fringe forward, trying to hide my face. Tiffany titters.

The chair next to Peach is empty. A waiter comes up to remove it. Peach holds on to the back, says there's no need.

Tiffany shakes her head and sucks on her chopsticks noisily. 'He won't come,' she says.

Peach lowers her head.

'That was quite unnecessary,' Kung scolds.

There's an awkward silence. Steel serves me some cooked duck's wings.

I reach for some soya sauce and notice that, to my horror, tears are spilling down Peach's face.

Steel notices too. 'Don't cry, Mum,' he says, offering her a clean serviette. 'I'm sure he'll come home one day.'

Tiffany scowls at Steel.

'Max will come back one day, Mummy. I know it,' Freddy says, climbing on to her knee.

'I love you all so much,' Peach says softly. 'How could he abandon us?'

Kung clears his throat and straightens his back. 'Max's problem is that he wasn't loved as a human being,' he says. 'Vampires who were unloved when human are the ones most likely to turn evil.'

That kind of makes sense. 'What happened?' I ask Steel.

He sighs. 'Max was an orphan. He never knew his parents. In the 1850s, he was sold into slavery in Hong Kong and worked as a miner in a silver mine, until it went bust. Then he went to Canton and became an Anti-Qing gangster.'

'And was killed in a brawl,' Kung says.

Freddy is bored with the conversation. 'I want to go outside,' he says, scrambling off Peach's knee. Sport pricks up his ears.

'Let's go and watch the sunset. It's spectacular from the patio,' Kung says.

'What a good idea,' Peach says, giving her nose a final blow.

'I'm going upstairs to change for the hunt,' Tiffany says, and stalks out of the room.

My heart skips a beat.

The patio is on the first floor and overlooks the stables and the garden. Peach reclines on a sunbed. Kung swings on a rocking chair. Steel and I share a two-seater with two tabbies. 'Brothers,' Steel says, when one starts licking the other. We watch Freddy chasing Sport around the lawn, then picking up some kittens and wheeling them in a wheelbarrow.

A herd of cows grazes in a distant meadow. The air starts to feel cooler. The sun slowly sinks behind the mountain and frogs strike up an evening chorus.

'Can we sleep together tonight?' Steel whispers down my ear.

'Yes,' I say, setting the word free before I register what I've said.

Steel licks his lips. In anticipation of what, I'm not sure.

Kung says it's time to change, and Peach and Steel stand up.

I'm left alone on the patio.

It's twilight. Night is crouching in the trees. An evening breeze is rustling through the leaves and insects fuss around a stable light. Grooms have been busy preparing the horses, which are all tacked up and ready to go.

'You'll be quite safe here,' Peach says, appearing from the front door in her jodhpurs. 'And you can keep Freddy company while we're away.'

Freddy is behind her, his hands laden with rocks. 'Ma, I'm hungry. Bring me back a leg.'

Tiffany emerges from the house and, slapping her whip against her riding boots, walks towards the horses tethered outside the stables. She's dressed in full riding gear: velvet hat, tweed jacket, and spurs.

A bat flits past and disappears in the forest.

Eiya. Where's Steel?

He appears from the front door with Kung; they give me a wave. 'Come down and say hello to Red Hare,' Steel calls.

'He looks more like a horse to me,' I say, then remember Red Hare is the name of Lu Bu's horse in *Three Kingdoms.*

Freddy is feeding Peach's horse a carrot. Tiffany has already mounted. Peach and Kung are checking their horses' girths. Steel chuckles. 'Come on down. He doesn't bite.'

'Are you sure?' I say. A tad wary.

Ignoring Tiffany's glares, I walk down the stairs.

Red Hare's muzzle is as smooth as silk. He smells of freshly mown grass. 'I've never stroked a horse before,' I say.

Steel smiles happily. 'He's a good hunter.'

'What do you hunt anyway?'

'Cows, buffalo, barking deer, boar.'

'Ah, wild animals.'

'Yes, they still exist here.'

Red Hare paws the ground and I step backwards.

'He's just excited,' Steel says.

Kung mounts his horse. Balancing a hunting horn on his horse's rump, he adjusts his stirrups.

'Let's go,' Tiffany says impatiently, swinging her prancing horse in the direction of the forest.

Kung blows the horn and the horses' ears flick forwards. There's a flurry of swishing tails, the clack of shod hooves, and they're off.

Peach waves. Steel blows me a kiss.

I feel at a bit of a loss without Steel. A Filipina maid offers to cook me some noodles but I'm not feeling very hungry. She takes Freddy upstairs for a shower instead. I switch on the TV and flick through the channels.

Beside the sofa is a rack of magazines. I take out a booklet that attracts my attention. It has a red spine and a laminated cover. I read the title: *Memoirs of Peach Tang, the Beautiful but Barren Han Princess.* The Chinese characters are embellished with paintings of peach trees, prancing horses and taloned birds of prey. Tentatively, I open the first page:

> My father, the emperor, talked about nothing but war. The futility of war. He told me that he had been

fighting for over fifty years, and he was weary.

Our main enemy was the Xiongnu tribe. Their empire stretched right across the steppes of eastern Asia to the north. The Xiongnu were fearless warriors who were bent on conquering China.

The military campaigns continued. I rarely saw my father. My mother complained bitterly in his absence. My brothers became unruly. With so much discontent in the palace, I cannot say I had a happy childhood.

I scan through the pages to reach the time when Peach was my age.

My life changed forever in the thirty-fourth year of my father's reign. That was the year that our army lost an important battle. Father came back home wounded and dispirited. He forbade banqueting and disbanded the musicians. After a few weeks, rumours started spinning around the palace. When courtiers saw me, they would look away. Even my dear mother avoided me. Father would spend days locked in his chambers.

In the end, I couldn't bear it any longer. I just had to find out what was going on. I demanded to see my father.

I remember being shocked by his appearance. His beard had grown wispy and grey. His skin was sallow and his eyes seemed to have sunk into their sockets. I noted that, in order to receive me, he sat on his throne. But when he saw me, he leaned forward and took my hand. His eyes were full of tears. Speaking softly, he told me the details of his negotiations for a peace settlement with the Xiongnu: I was to be sent to

Mongolia to be the chieftain's bride.

I was eighteen when I left my beloved home city of Chang'an forever. It was the only time I saw my father weep in public. The entourage of horses and carriages bearing gifts of precious treasure, tea, liquor and rice stretched as far as the eye could see. We travelled for over three thousand *li* and the journey took many months. How I missed my parents, my brothers and sisters! Only one of my ladies-in-waiting was permitted to travel with me, and she died of dysentery in the mountains.

The first thing I disliked about my husband-to-be was his hairy arms and legs! He had a rough face but he smiled as I alighted from my carriage. He didn't speak a word of Chinese, of course, but he gestured to a large tent that would become my private quarters.

Inside, the yurt was much more comfortable than I imagined. It was furnished with exotic carpets and divans. Slaves were on call night and day to serve me food and water. A fire burned on the hearth.

It was shortly after I was settling in that I heard that we would be relocating. Little did I know that the Xiongnu were nomadic and I would spend the rest of my life on the move, following sheep and horses across the plains. These animals provided us with food, clothing, milk and medicine.

In those early days, my life was tolerable. I was wed with great fanfare and the marriage started well. I enjoyed so many luxuries. I even ate off solid gold plates. My loyal slaves attended to my every need. I even had my own band of musicians who serenaded me after meals.

As I turn the page, I can almost hear a drum beating through time.

At first, my husband loved me very much. The bell outside my yurt – the one that summoned me to his bedchamber – rang every night. Its ring would be the cue for my handmaidens to prepare a hot tub for me. They would undress me, wash me with freshly-ground aphrodisiacs, smooth soothing balms over my body and comb my thick long hair. Then they would roll me, quite naked, inside a silk carpet and carry me to my husband's yurt.

But two years later, I was still not with child and my husband began to lose patience. He started shouting at me. Once he was so angry he cut me with his knife. Regarding the lack of an heir, all the fingers of blame were pointed at me. Then I heard a rumour that my husband had taken another bride. She produced a son within a year. My husband never called me to his bedchamber again.

My heart feels sore at the remembrance of Peach's tears in the dining room.

I tried to make the best of my fate. I became an excellent horsewoman. I trained falcons to hunt birds, which my cook would roast and serve my husband as a delicacy. Against his wishes, I even learned to read and write the Hun language. But I was lonely, very lonely. And I died never having experienced the joy of raising my own children or taking care of grandchildren.

'Anna?' A voice jolts me back into the present. It's Freddy, at the door. 'Come and play with me.'

'Okay,' I say, quickly turning to the last page:

> I died at the age of fifty-two and my body was buried in Mongolia. A hundred years later, to celebrate my centenary, corpse-walkers carried me back to Chang'an.

How interesting! I close the booklet, put it back on the rack and resolve to read the bits I skipped later on.

CHAPTER 22
Two firsts

'That's alkali feldspar – pink granite, to you,' Freddy says. kneeling in front of a pile of rocks that we're taking turns to stack in the playroom.

Sure enough, the underside of the coarse-grained stone I've picked up is fleshy pink.

I balance it on the uppermost rock, let go, it wobbles, and the stack tumbles down. Freddy stands up and starts kicking the rocks around the room.

'Let's make a pyramid,' I say.

'I'm bored,' he says.

A Filipina maid comes rushing in with a brush and pan.

'How about a game of tag?' I say. *Surely I'm able to outrun an eight-year-old vampire kid.*

The maid takes off Freddy's hat in readiness. It's square and tiered, with two feathers pointing out at right angles above his ears. It's the kind of ancient emperor's hat that is painted on a board for joke photos at Chinese theme parks. You can stick your head through a hole underneath it and look stupid.

'No, it's babyish to play games,' he says.

'How about dressing up?'

'Nah.'

'Hide and seek?'

'I'm hungry,' he says, baring his teeth at me.

'That's rude, Freddy,' his maid says.

'Your parents will be back soon,' I say. *With a cute little Bambi deer for you to eat,* I think. And my stomach turns.

'How about you show Anna the music room?' the maid says.

'Good idea,' Freddy says, and jumps to his feet.

We go up to the top floor. It's been converted into one large room. There's a collection of band equipment on a stage – guitars, a drum kit, percussion, synthesisers, a collection of wind instruments. Even a double bass.

Freddy sits at the drum kit, picks up some drumsticks and taps out a funky rhythm.

'Hey, you're good.'

He gives me a haughty look.

'Freddy the Fabulous,' I say.

'No. I don't like that name. How about, 'Duanzong the Dashing'?' he says, hitting a cymbal.

'You're weird.'

'Off with her head,' he cries, slicing the air with a drumstick.

'*Gaau choa!* Don't frighten me.'

'Don't tell me what to do. I was an emperor, you know, a Song dynasty emperor. When I was human,' he says. His dark curly hair bobs to the rhythm of the march he's beating.

Hence the hat, I think. 'Well, you're dead now,' I say.

'Undead,' he says, stressing the first syllable, and hitting the cymbal so loudly I have to cover my ears. 'Do you wanna hear a rap?'

'Sure.' Anything to stop those cymbal crashes.

Tum-tee TUM, tum-tee TUM. He has started:

> 'Mongols here,
> Mongols there,
> Mongols everywhere. (TUM TUM)
> From Ling An,
> To Canton.
> On a boat,
> Moving south,
> TO HONG KONG. (CRASH)
>
>
> (Tum-tee TUM, tum-tee TUM)
>
>
> 'Typhoon here,
> Typhoon there,
> Typhoon everywhere. (TUM TUM)
> Sinking boat,
> Can't keep afloat.
> THIS IS WHERE I DIED.' (LONG DRUM ROLL)

'Where?' I ask.

'Lantau.'

'There's a Song dynasty emperor, you, buried on Lantau?'

'Don't you study Chinese History at school?'

'I don't believe you.'

'Then you're dumb,' he says, and flings the drumsticks on the floor.

'Hey, temper, temper,' I say. *What an annoying little kid.*

Freddy stands up. 'When the Mongols captured Canton in 1279, they launched a naval attack and drove us farther out to sea. Our boat sunk in a typhoon. I would have drowned if it were not for Uncle Hau Wong. But unfortunately I died of my injuries a few days later. My uncle buried me on Lantau. There are three temples in Hong Kong to commemorate his bravery,' he says imperiously.

I shrug my shoulders. I'm fed up with entertaining Freddy. I'd rather be having a shower, making myself beautiful for Steel. It's already dark outside. Coal black. A full moon has risen high in the sky.

'I can prove it to you,' Freddy says mischievously. 'Come and see my grave. It's not far away from here.'

'Yes, no – I mean, are you allowed?

'Of course.'

'How about we phone your Mum?'

'No network,' Freddy says. 'It happens sometimes.' He picks up the drumsticks and puts them back in their case.

I check my phone. He's right. There's no signal.

'It's in a secret place,' he says coyly. 'You'd be the first human since Hau Wong to see it.'

'Okay,' I say, persuaded.

Freddy runs towards me and hugs me. 'You smell so fresh,' he says.

It's a warm clear night and the sky is full of stars. Crazy or what? I'm going to ride a pony with Freddy. In the forest. To see his grave. Wow, maybe I'll become famous.

Our steed – brown and white with a black mane and tail – nuzzles me with wet nostrils. She's called Harlequin. The groom gives me a leg up and I'm gripping the saddle behind Freddy.

'Squeeze with your thighs,' Freddy says, 'and hold me tight.'

The moonlight splashes through the canopy of trees. Low-hanging branches slap my legs as Harlequin jogs along a mud track. Sport pads faithfully behind. Freddy's chatter interrupts hooting owls as we go deeper and deeper into the forest.

There's a rustling in the undergrowth and something flits out of a tree. SPOO-KY. 'Hey, you said it wasn't far,' I say.

'Scared of the dark, are you?'

Precocious little twit.

We drop down into a bushy area with a steep ravine and crashing waves below. Freddy passes me a torch. 'My grave has the best *feng shui* in southern Lantau,' he brags, leaping from the saddle. He pulls a reluctant Harlequin closer towards the edge of the cliff and tethers her to a tree.

'Dismount, Anna,' he orders. 'Help me clear the weeds.'

Keeping one foot in a stirrup, I carefully lower myself down. 'How about I just watch with Harlequin?' I say, miffed that a kid is bossing me around, and secretly scared of snakes.

Freddy is on his hands and knees, tearing long tendrils of weed off a grey slab of stone. He shines his torch on it. That's when I realise it's a gravestone. The inscription reads:

SONG DYNASTY
HERE LIES EMPEROR DUANZONG
ELDEST SON OF EMPEROR DUZONG

'Cool,' I say. Genuinely impressed.

For a while, the two of us stand there under a bright moon, with the pounding of the surf below. Then, something – *a bird?* – brushes my leg. I cry out and knock it off. Sport growls and raises his hackles.

Freddy laughs. 'It's just a ghost.'

Thank God I can't see it. 'Let's go back,' I say.

Harlequin pricks her ears as we mount. When Freddy kicks her sides, she starts trotting, happy to be heading home and I'm bouncing all over the place. 'Slow down,' I cry.

'Dad says I can join the hunt soon,' Freddy says, turning round and baring his teeth at me.

There's an unpleasant smell – *rotting meat?* – as we pass a derelict outhouse. I cover my nose. I didn't notice it on the way.

'That's where we burn carcasses,' Freddy says brightly.

Chi sin!

It seems an age before Steel comes back. When I hear approaching footsteps and the sound of my bedroom door being unlocked, my heart pounds. 'It's me.' he whispers.

I switch on the bedside light, rub my eyes. The satin sheets I'm lying between are smooth and glossy.

At last, we're alone.

Steel shuts the door and leans against it. He's wearing a pair of dark blue silk pyjamas.

'How I've longed for this moment,' he says. Standing firm.

I raise an arm, entreat him to join me.

'What are you wearing?' he asks, a little nervously.

'The white cotton night shirt Peach gave me.'

Steel bows his head.

I raise my other arm, longing to be enfolded in his. But he steps back and covers his face with his hands.

'A dollar for your thoughts,' I say.

'I don't know if I can do this,' he blurts.

I sit up, my arms still extended. 'But you've just eaten, Steel.'

'Not a lot.'

I hug my knees.

'You smell so sweet,' he says. 'Even from here.'

He stands motionless. Rooted as a tree.

My eyes mist. I blink away a solitary tear.

'I'm not scared,' I say. Firmly.

Firmly. Deliberate-like.

Steel slaps his thigh.

I stand up. Walk towards him, walk until I'm a breath away from him. Take his hands in mine.

My lips edge closer. I can see his unblemished skin, can smell his blood. He's breathing heavily. His fingers grip mine. My hair brushes against his cheeks.

'One kiss?' I say.

'Just one,' he says.

He dips his head towards mine. His eyelashes flutter. My lips rush to meet his and I implode, disappear into our embrace.

His lips are soft. His tongue is furtive. His teeth are pearly smooth. And I'm lost somewhere inside his mouth.

Time stops still. Blood swells.

Gently, our lips part and we are two again.

And then he's kissing me lightly all over my face – the tip of my nose, my cheekbones, my forehead – like a lovebird, drinking dew drops, from a red flower.

Hibiscus.

My lips are blurry. I can't tell where they begin and end. My cheeks burn.

His lips range over my ears. He nips my earlobes, skates down my neck. 'You're mine. All mine,' he murmurs.

'Yes. I am,' I say, arching my neck, hoping he'll kiss me some more.

CHAPTER 23

Ancient love

Sunlight peeps from the sides of the curtains. I'm lying with one arm across my forehead, confused by a fragment of a dream that is struggling to break through. I roll over, hoping to sleep some more. And then The Kiss floods back into my memory.

I open my eyes. Blink. A digital clock is flashing eleven thirty. Where's Steel? I sit up so fast my head spins.

'You look lovely when you're asleep,' he says, from a shadowy corner. He's reclining on a sofa, wearing a pair of Y-fronts, one leg carelessly slung over the other.

'There you are!' I say, leaping up and running across the room into his lap. Then my thoughts catch up with my actions and I freeze, shocked by my forwardness.

Steel, although startled, is obviously pleased. 'Would you like a good morning kiss?' he says. His hand strokes my back.

I cautiously lay my head on his shoulder and rub against his smooth chest. 'For a horrible moment, I thought I was dreaming,' I say.

Steel chuckles. Next second, he has flown us both across the room and we're rolling on the bed and he's kissing me again and again. His hungry lips drop down my windpipe, along a collarbone, inching down …

'Hang on,' I say, feeling his body tense. He rolls off, lies on his back and laughs. 'You smell so good,' he says. I'm beginning to hear that a lot.

'Good enough to eat?' *Poor joke.*

He feigns gnawing my arm. 'Which reminds me, you need some breakfast.'

'I need the bathroom first,' I say, sitting up. My feet feel under the bed for slippers.

'I'll be downstairs in the kitchen.'

'You cook?'

'For you, yes.'

I look at myself in the bathroom mirror. My hair resembles a bird's nest. My cheeks are flushed. My tongue is slimy. But my eyes are sparkling.

Someone has laid out my facecloth, my toothbrush and a tube of toothpaste. Hurriedly, I clean myself and brush my hair into an acceptable style. Then I'm stuck on what to wear: *skirt? strappy top? jeans?* With so many vampires around, should I cover myself up? If it's baking hot outside, are we going to stay inside? What are we going to do all day anyway?

I've tried on at least four different outfits when there's a knock at the door. It's Steel, asking me what kind of tea I would like to drink with my *dim sum* breakfast.

Downstairs, the blinds are closed and everyone is assembled at the dining table. Kung is at the head, stroking his beard, lost in thought. Peach is chatting with Tiffany, who is wearing a body-hugging leotard.

'These are for you,' Steel says, pointing to a stack of bamboo steamers. *Cha siu* buns, shrimp dumplings, chickens' feet and radish cake. *Delicious!*

A waiter pours me a cup of green tea.

'Did you sleep well?' Peach says, dipping her chopsticks into a plate of neatly-sliced raw beef.

Tiffany gives me a hateful stare and commands the waiter to bring her another juice.

'Very well, thank you,' I say politely.

Freddy crams his mouth with fish balls. Peach frowns. 'Table manners please,' she says.

Steel is looking thoughtful. 'We usually have a jamming session on Saturday mornings. Would you like to join us?'

'What do you play, Anna?' Peach asks.

'I sing. But I haven't got much of a voice.'

'That's not true,' Steel says, refilling my tea cup.

Kung lays down his chopsticks. 'I'm afraid we'll have to postpone. I need to finish a report for the Department of the Environment this morning.'

'The one about biodiversity in Lantau?' Steel says.

Kung nods.

'What are your recommendations this year?' Peach asks.

Kung takes out a list from his pocket. 'To preserve the boundaries of the country parks. To plant more native trees in the forest. To clean up the South China Sea. To maintain the moratorium on fishing. And to protect the remaining indigenous animals.' of course.

'Good luck,' Tiffany says tartly, reaching over to take the last prawn.

'Indigenous animals?' I say.

'Yes. There aren't many left these days. There used to be wild pigs, otters, foxes, leopard cats. Even tigers,' Kung replies.

'Tigers?' *Eiya!*

'You'll be relieved to know that the last one was killed in the 1960s,' Steel tells me.

'Game used to be plentiful too: snipe, quail, partridge, wild duck,' Kung adds.

I notice that all the vampires are listening attentively. Freddy is licking his lips.

'Due to their depletion and extinction – by man – vampires are finding it increasingly difficult to hunt,' Kung continues.

'Dad says that until the 1950s, there were thousands of barking deer roaming on the island,' Steel says, with a touch of longing in his voice.

I'm surprised. 'What happened to them?'

Kung folds his arms. 'Most were captured and eaten. Mainly around Luk Tei Tong where they used to come down from the forest to drink.'

'Locals even killed pregnant females and their young,' Tiffany says.

'We never do that,' Peach says softly.

The empty plates have red splodges on them. I've lost my appetite. Freddy wipes his mouth and his serviette is smeared with blood.

'How about we listen to some music in my room?' Steel says to me.

'What kind of music do you like, Anna?' Peach asks. They're both trying to divert my attention from Freddy's serviette.

'All sorts,' I say. 'But there's nothing like the old Canto classics – Teresa Teng, Leslie Cheung, Roman Tam.'

'I guessed you were a romantic at heart,' Peach says warmly.

We're being rocked and kneaded on massage chairs in his bedroom while listening to Mandarin love songs. *And then you touched me,* a throaty voice sings.

'Pleasure palaces have existed since ancient times,' Steel says dreamily. 'Even now, in China, there are whole buildings where you can have your body massaged and your back scrubbed and your feet manicured and your ears cleaned. I must take you to one someday.'

I smile mysteriously.

'And that reminds me,' Steel says.

He switches off his massage chair, saunters over to the bookshelf and plucks out a book with a well-worn cover: *The Art of the Bedchamber.* 'This is the treatise I was telling you about.'

'Uh-oh.'

'Read the caution,' he says roguishly, placing the heavy tome on a sheepskin rug at the foot of his bed.

I turn to the first page and read: 'Sex is a vital component to romantic love. However, Taoism emphasises the need for self-control and moderation.'

'What do you think?' Steel asks playfully.

'Quite right,' I say. Not knowing what I'm talking about.

'The Chinese perfected the art of lovemaking long before any other culture,' Steel says happily.

I raise a quizzical eyebrow.

'While Westerners were beating each other up in battles, Chinese were in bed 'making clouds and rain'.'

'Clouds and rain?' I pretend to look disgusted.

On his knees, Steel flicks through pages and pages of nude bodies in compromising poses. 'Look, here are the illustrations of the nine basic positions,' he says enthusiastically.

I recite their names with deliberation, surreptitiously glancing at the graphics as I read: 'somersaulting dragons, stepping tigers, wrestling monkeys, clinging cicadas, mounting turtles, soaring phoenix, licking rabbits, nibbling fishes, entwined cranes.'

Nine descriptions with explicit images of juicy-thighed women wrapped around their men. Men wearing nothing but slippers, their long hair tied in buns.

Steel jumps up and reaches for another tome. 'Here's the Tang dynasty classic, *The Mystic Master of the Grotto.*'

'Grotto?'

Steel is laughing excitedly. 'You can't guess what it is?'

I feel myself blushing.

He reads out the subtitle: *Sexual Secrets for Chinese Lovers.*

My heart skips a beat.

'It was written by a doctor, the director of the Imperial School of Medicine, in the ninth century,' Steel says, his finger scanning the contents page.

I shake my head in disbelief. 'That's when Tiffany was alive,' I say. Why, I've no idea.

'It's one book of many.'

The bushy tails of 'wild horses leaping' catch my attention.

'Yes, that's a good one,' Steel says eagerly. 'And what about 'spider trapped in its own web'?'

A woman is tied to a bed, open arms and straddled legs strapped down with silk scarves.

'Gaau choa!' I say, blushing bright red.

Steel turns to me, notices my colour and guffaws. 'Anna, don't be so prudish.'

'How many positions are there, anyway?'

'What, in this book?'

I nod.

'Thirty.'

'Thirty!'

'One for each day of the month, with an occasional night off.'

I'm speechless.

Steel has found what he was looking for. 'My favourite,' he says, and points to a page entitled 'stepping tigers'.

A woman is on all-fours, breasts hanging loose. The man's long hair flows down his back. I can just about decipher the ancient Chinese script: *the man kneels behind her and clasps her belly. He inserts his jade stalk and pierces the innermost cave of her grotto. They advance and retreat in mutual attacks.*

EIYA!

Steel leans back on the massage chair and beams. The music has stopped. Clumsily, I get on my feet, sit in the massage chair and click on a 'de-stress' programme.

Steel watches my face intently. I rearrange it into an expression he recognises. 'Any questions?' he asks teasingly.

The silence grows heavy.

A cat jumps off the bed and scampers out of the room.

Steel changes the playlist to shuffle.

'Come on,' he says. 'You can ask me anything.' The back of his massage chair whirrs as he lowers it.

'Okay,' I say, taking a deep breath. 'There's something I don't understand. It's about … ' My voice trails off.

'About why it's good for a girl if a guy can last long?' Steel says lightly.

How I hate that he can read my thoughts. Sometimes.

Steel lowers his head on the back of his massage chair. 'When a guy is aroused, he can climax in a few seconds. It usually takes a girl longer. Which can leave her dissatisfied.'

'Does that matter?' I ask. Genuinely curious.

'Anna,' he says, in a throaty voice. 'Good lovers satisfy their partner. Good lovers don't just score.'

I flick my fringe forwards, examine my fingernails.

When I look up, Steel's face has changed. His brow is furrowed. He looks agitated but stops short of saying why.

'What's wrong?'

'I should tell you … Dad has taught me a new way of

controlling myself.'

Relieved that he's the one who is feeling embarrassed now, I laugh out loud. 'How?'

'You really want to know?'

I nod.

Steel opens his mouth and lifts his chin. Crooking his neck to the ceiling, he presses the tip of his tongue to the roof of his mouth.

'Kung taught you *that?*' I say, incredulous.

Steel laughs. 'Weird, right? Until you remember that Kung is a certified Master of the Bedchamber.'

No wonder Peach always has a smile on her face.

'And there's another way,' Steel says.

'Too much information,' I shout, blocking my ears.

'Hey, what's the big deal? If you can't talk openly about sex with your girlfriend, when can you?'

I unblock my ears. I close the book.

Steel checks I put it back in the right place on the bookshelf. 'Sex is one of the greatest pleasures known to man. Stupid to deny it,' he says grumpily.

I close *The Art of the Bedchamber* too.

Steel has jumped to the window. His back is to me. When he turns, his face has transformed into one of pain and distress. His canines have dropped and his gums are blood red. 'How I long for you,' he moans.

I grapple for some words that will calm him down. 'You're

just hungry,' I say.

'I'm just hungry,' he repeats.

Inexplicably, I feel a twinge of excitement.

'Let's wait until I get back from hunting tonight,' he says.

Half my mouth smiles. The half that wants to be eaten by Steel.

CHAPTER 24

Love frustrated

I'm woken in the depths of the night by Steel switching on the bedside light. It takes a few seconds to work out where I am. He paces around the room, still dressed in jodhpurs. His shirt is streaked with mud.

'Are you alright?' I say.

'No.' Abrupt. Angry.

'What's wrong?'

'Janet is here.' He glares.

I sit up. Wide awake. 'What?'

'Janet. Tiffany invited her for a sleepover. She joined us on the hunt.'

A wave of disappointment knocks me flat. 'And?'

'And, nothing,' he says. 'I didn't touch her or anything. I didn't even talk to her.'

He plonks himself on the bed. I search for his eyes.

'You don't believe me, do you?' he says, aggressively.

'Yes, I do,' I say softly.

I hug my legs, hook my chin over my bony knees.

Steel walks over to the dressing table.

I suddenly feel reckless. 'Have a shower and come to bed.'

He's using a mirror to peer inside his mouth. 'I have fur between my teeth,' he rasps.

I have an image of a mangled bloody deer. Torn skin, a spurt of gore. Steel and Janet ripping its body apart.

'How can you love me?' Steel moans, hitting the top of the dressing table, rattling the perfume bottles.

'Steel, what's wrong? Tell me, honestly.'

He puts his head in his hands. His voice is shaky. 'I can't do it.'

'Do what?'

He swings round and stares at me with troubled eyes. 'What do you think?'

With Janet under the same roof, I'm not one hundred per cent sure. 'Tell me,' I say.

'Make love to you.'

I lie back on the pillow. Look at the ceiling. Look back at him.

Steel grabs a handful of his hair, pulls at it. 'You don't trust me, that's the problem,' he says.

I kick the covers off, walk over to him, grip his arms and shake him. 'Steel. That's so not true.'

'Sorry. I shouldn't have said that. It's all my fault.'

'It doesn't matter,' I say. Knowing it does.

Steel suddenly shoves me aside and I bang the funny bone of my elbow on the corner of the dressing table. 'Ow! That really hurt.'

The moment it happens, he's full of concern. 'Anna, are you okay? How could I do that? I'm so sorry,' he says.

He puts his arms around me and draws me towards him. He smells of horse sweat.

'Clean up. You stink,' I say.

He smirks, drops his head, gently kisses my throat. 'I should have changed first.'

I lie down on the bed while he showers. Close my eyes. Try to empty my mind.

Steel comes out of the bathroom wearing a T-shirt and boxer shorts. He walks away from me, towards the door.

'Where are you going?'

He smiles sardonically. 'There's something I have to do,' he says. He clicks on all the light switches. We blink under the strip lights. *Like deer. Dazzled deer. Road kill.*

He walks towards a velvet green curtain at the far side of the room and, with a flourish, draws it. I'd assumed it covered a large window, but there's an alcove and a metal cage, a huge empty cage.

'Get out of bed,' Steel says. His face is grave, his manner stern.

I sit up.

A hinge squeaks as he opens the cage door. His hair is shaggy, still wet.

'What are you doing?' A surge of adrenaline courses through my body.

'Come over here. Please.'

With spindly legs, I gambol towards him.

'Lock me in, with this,' he says, unhooking a heart-shaped padlock from a bar and thrusting it into my hands. The padlock is soldered to a thick chain, which almost slips out of my grasp.

He slams the steel door shut and rattles the cage impatiently. I wrap the chain around the bars and fumble to close the padlock. *Click.*

'Put the key under your pillow,' Steel says.

I do. The cage is now as secure as an HSBC bank vault.

Steel's hands grip the bars. Before my eyes, they stiffen and sprout claws. With a yowl, he drops his canines.

Oh my God! His arms, chest, legs are stiffening.

'Come forward, about six feet away,' he says hoarsely.

I do. Spindly legs shaking.

He jiggles the metal bars, pokes a snout between them and puckers his engorged lips. 'STEEL?'

'Take your top off,' he says. Cold wolf eyes gleaming.

'What?'

'You heard me.'

He says it again.

I straighten my pants, then reach under my T-shirt for the seam under the armpit. My nipple is hard and my breast feels full. I pull the sleeve down and slip my elbow through, gradually dropping my free arm.

'And the other side,' Steel says.

I turn round to look at him. Saliva is dripping from his mouth.

'Go on,' he commands.

I reach for the other sleeve. Pull it down. Release my arm. Wriggle the T-shirt to my elbows.

Steel is breathing heavily; he's almost panting.

With trembling fingers, I hold the neckline, then slowly lift the top up and over my head. The T-shirt drops to my feet. And I stand there, half naked. Shy virgin breasts peaking.

Steel leaps halfway up the cage and, wrapping his clawed feet around the bars, howls pitifully.

'Calm down,' I say.

'You're beautiful,' he moans, wiping foam from his jaw.

I swing back, my throat dry, my ears ringing.

It seems an age that I'm standing there while he throws himself around. His fiery eyes seem fixated on my breasts and he's howling with ... with what? *Pleasure? Pain? Love? Hate?*

Gradually, his breath steadies. Mine too.

He's standing on two feet, at last. I realise I've lost the compulsion to cover myself up.

'They're exquisite,' he says. His voice is back to normal.

Instinctively, I cross my arms over my chest.

'One day I WILL make love to you,' he says.

I've got goosebumps.

Suddenly Steel starts pacing around the cage again, to and fro like a trapped beast. Faster and faster, until – *wham!* – he lunges towards me and lands awkwardly above the door. Hanging on all fours, he rattles the cage furiously.

'What is it, Steel?' I say. My heart is beating wildly.

'Take your pants off,' he hisses. Spittle slobbers down his jowls.

I give him a long, hard stare. A long defiant stare.

'Please?' he moans.

I see the pain in his tortured eyes. I see a virgin forest, and a deer rigid with fear, its dewy eyes, its quivering nose, its belly full of fresh blood.

'A quick flash?' His voice cracks with misery.

Slowly, freely, I lower the elasticated waist over my hips. When my pants drop to the floor, I step out of them, and confront Steel, head on.

He snatches a look. Then another. He shakes the bars with such force, I fear they're going to buckle. He collapses onto the floor, writhing in apparent agony.

'You're so beautiful,' he howls.

I can't help laughing, with relief and embarrassment.

'One day I WILL satisfy you,' he cries.

'I know. I know. Of course you will,' I say, turning away from him.

'Don't leave me,' he wails.

I pick up my clothes. Put them back on. Sit cross-legged on the floor.

He curls his back, knees to chin, and shudders.

'I won't,' I say. 'Leave you, I mean.'

His body gradually loosens, relaxes.

My eyes are hurting. 'Can I switch the main lights off?'

He wipes his mouth clean, smoothes tufts of hair. 'Wait,' he says.

I watch, astonished, as, with a strange sucking sound, his body shrinks back to its human form.

The tension between us ebbs; it lets go of my stomach.

Steel rocks his head from side to side, smiles bashfully. 'You're cold, my darling,' he says.

'I am, a little.'

'Turn the air con off.'

I do. I switch off the strip lights too, and stumble back to bed. 'Are you staying there all night?' I say.

'Yes,' Steel says faintly, and slumps in the middle of the cage.

I snuggle under the covers. Safe. Warm.

Steel sniggers. 'Keep the bedside light on.'

'You wanna watch me?'

'Yes. It'll be a test.'

I'm past caring. It must be nearly dawn. The early birds are singing.

'Sleep,' he says.

The truth is, living on vampire time, I do feel a bit tired.

'Let me out when you wake up.'

'Yes,' I say, patting the pillow where the key is.

He sighs. 'Everything will be okay.'

'I know it will,' I say, as a sudden fear whips through me at the thought of meeting Janet at the breakfast table tomorrow.

Later, when I get up for a pee, I see Steel curled up in a corner of the cage. Fast asleep.

CHAPTER 25
The murderer

Steel bangs a gong downstairs: breakfast is ready.

I had let him out of the cage mid-morning when we both woke up. He came out repentant and apologetic, saying a gazillion times that he hoped he didn't scare me, that he wouldn't ask me again, not in a cage anyway, that I was the most beautiful girl in the whole wide world. We lay in bed together, shared the earphones of his iPad, drifted in and out of sleep. 'Would you like an English style brunch?' he'd asked, before he went downstairs.

'What's that?'

'Fried eggs, bacon, tomatoes.'

'Sounds good.'

> *'Blood's well,*
> *All's well,*
> *Ding dong*
> *Bell.'*

No time to wash my hair. At least I showered last night.

On the way down, I close the bedroom door to prevent cats from entering. The smell of fried bacon floats along the first-floor landing and my stomach juices churn.

I notice that one of the doors is ajar – Tiffany's bedroom. I lighten my step, sneak closer, drawn towards two voices.

'I have a copy of the keys,' Tiffany is saying excitedly.

'Are you sure he's going to be caught?' *Gaau choa!* I guess that's Janet.

'Positive. Probably today, according to my Mum,' Tiffany says.

'Why should he help us?'

Tiffany laughs cruelly. 'I'll make it worth his while.'

I tiptoe closer, crane my neck forwards. 'What if your Dad finds out?'

It's quiet for a few seconds. All I can hear is my thumping heart. Then footsteps creak across the parquet floor towards me and I seize up with fear, until they move away from where I'm standing.

'Won't he punish us?' Janet says.

'I think it's worth the risk,' Tiffany snarls.

The footsteps pace towards me again. With my heart in my mouth, I slink past the door and quickly go down the stairs, gripping the banister for support.

Eiya! What are they scheming?

Steel is cooking at the stove, apron around his waist, spatula in hand, seemingly oblivious. Two eggs sizzle in the wok. Rashers of bacon and fried tomatoes are already neatly displayed on a plate.

He smiles ruefully at me as I sit down at the kitchen table. I'm shaking. The landline rings. Steel turns the gas down, frowns, listens intently, looks concerned. 'Bad news,' he says, putting the phone back on its stand. 'I've got to go out.'

'What? Now?' I look at the kitchen clock: it's eleven forty-five.

'With Kung. I've got to go, right now.'

'Steel,' I say. 'I've just heard … '

But Steel is busy transferring the fried eggs to the plate. He gets a knife and fork out of a drawer and lays them on the table. 'Sorry, Anna,' he says. 'I really haven't got time to talk now.'

'How long will you be?'

Steel gives me a doleful look.

'I've just heard Tiffany … ' I begin.

He raises his hand. 'As long as Peach is around, she wouldn't dare to hurt you,' he says, and presents me with a plate of perfectly-cooked food.

'Thanks,' I say. Not. Food is the last thing I feel like.

'Eat up, then go back to the room,' Steel says. 'I'll be back as soon as I can, I promise.'

He kisses me lightly on the cheek.

The kitchen is eerily quiet without him. In the corner, a line of cats are eating from a row of bowls. I dip the toast – cold now – in the egg yolk and force myself to eat. The cats lick their paws, jump up to a cat flap and go outside. It's only when I walk over to wash my plate that I hear someone sobbing. A female, in the room next door.

I knock. The sobbing stops. Someone clears her throat and calls, 'Come in.'

It's Peach. She's wearing a silk dressing gown embroidered with butterflies. Holding a tissue over her nose, she leans forwards and clicks the TV off with a remote. 'Sit down,' she says.

'What's wrong?' I say. Genuinely concerned.

Peach blows her nose, smiles faintly at me. Her eyes don't

match her smile. 'Where do I begin?' she says.

I sit opposite her on a cream leather sofa. *At the beginning?* Feeling awkward, I stroke a tabby that's curled up fast asleep on a cushion.

Peach blows her nose again. 'Yes, I am going to tell you,' she says. 'Because you're a woman too.'

Uh-oh.

But her eyes look so sad. 'You know, there's no love like mother's love,' she says.

I nod my head guiltily.

Just at that moment, there's the pitter patter of footsteps and Freddy comes bounding in the room dressed in a muddy football kit. Sport follows close behind, wagging his tail enthusiastically. 'Mum,' he says. 'Will you play dinosaurs with me?'

'I'm just talking to Anna.'

'Mummm!'

'Never mind,' I say. 'We can talk later.'

Peach seems to appreciate my offer. 'Yes, I suppose we can,' she says softly. 'There's plenty of time.'

I slip upstairs, praying I don't bump into Tiffany and Janet. Fortunately, their door is closed. My bed has already been made.

There's a text on my mobile screen, it's from Ma: **hope the revising is going well.**

Shame! My exams are less than three weeks away. But at this moment in time, school seems on another planet.

yes. love you. I reply, and make a resolution to start revising as soon as I'm back in Tsuen Wan.

I send a text to Steel while I'm at it: **i'm in my room now.**

No reply. Then I remember that the network is erratic. But I check my message, and it's sent.

There's no other way to describe it: I'm shit scared. This place is spooky. I check that my door is locked.

Bottles of expensive shampoos and conditioners adorn the shower rack. They're way more upmarket than what I can afford. Trying to allay a sense of doom, I seize the moment to wash my hair before Steel comes back. I sniff and squeeze, rub and lather, try to enjoy the warm water splashing down my back and the squeakiness of my hair.

In the top drawer of the dressing table there are some electrical hair straighteners and three different types of hair dryers. I sit on a puffed velvet cushion and check out my profile with the help of a hand-mirror. *Anna, you're okay,* I tell my face.

Before plugging in the hairdryer, I walk over to pick up the remote and switch the TV on.

I'm not really concentrating what the top news story is 'cos I'm brushing in some hair treatment. But when I glance up, there's a reporter on the screen, standing in front of a tenement building.

'A neighbour heard screams and alerted the police. It is alleged that the victim was a single woman who lived alone. Her mutilated body was found on the bed in the flat. At this stage, the police are unable to identify the woman due to the extent of her wounds.'

Another prostitute, I think, idly imagining how disgusting it must feel to have sex with complete strangers.

'Wanchai is renowned for its one-room brothels,' the reporter

continues. *'A section of Hennessey Road has been cordoned off because it is believed that the killer is still at large.'*

A couple of policemen pass by, jabbering into walkie-talkies. The reporter turns to an inspector who was waiting off-camera.

'It's possible that the perpetrator of the crime is the same person who recently killed prostitutes in Tai Po, Mongkok and Tsuen Wan,' the inspector says. *'Certain details at the crime scene are similar.'*

There's some disturbance, some breaking news. The reporter presses his earphone to his ear, then looks up to face the camera excitedly.

'We're hearing that an arrest has been made on the floor where the killing took place. A young man was acting suspiciously and the police believe he may be linked to the crime.'

I've switched the hair dryer off by now; I'm glued to the TV screen.

In the stairwell behind the reporter, I see a group of three men. One is handcuffed and chained to two policemen. They're coming down the stairs of the tenement building. The person who has been arrested is short and thick-set. He's wearing a stiff black hood with eye-holes. There's something about him that's familiar. I feel a shiver down my spine. It's the tattoo, that's what it is. A snake twirling up a leg ...

Max! Is Max the one who has been killing the prostitutes?

So where is Steel?

I watch with amazement as the two policemen shove Max into a waiting van. Cameras flash and the sliding door of the van is snapped shut. The van is being driven away and reporters are running after it.

There's a knock at my door and I'm paralysed with terror. I unlock the door and Peach comes in, followed by three cats. She's sobbing her heart out. 'So now you know,' she says, throwing herself on the sofa. 'Isn't it terrible? Kung and Steel didn't get there in time to stop him.'

I'm still holding on to the hairdryer. Surprised. Confused. Petrified. I rummage for some tissues to give to Peach – when Tiffany marches in. Her face is hard. Stony. She smells of bonfires. 'So it's back to the morgue for him. Is that right?' she snarls.

Peach gulps with emotion, sobs some more. A cat jumps on her lap.

'Where's Steel?' I ask.

'Worried about your darling boyfriend, are you?' Tiffany says, with a crooked smile.

Her body stiffens. Her long painted fingernails flick forwards. *Is she going to attack me?*

Peach's eyes dilate.

Tiffany jerks away. Hisses.

'Tiffany,' Peach says. 'How dare you.'

Ignoring her, Tiffany swivels her head round to meet mine. 'I told you to keep out of our family business.'

'Tiffany! Stop it. Now,' Peach shouts.

Tiffany laughs haughtily, before turning her back on us.

Trembling, I pass Peach the box of tissues.

'Poor, poor Max.' Peach is snivelling again. The other two cats jump on her lap.

Tiffany has deflated. Her body is back to normal. But she's still really mad. 'So what are we going to do about him?' she says.

Peach doesn't answer.

'Mum?'

'I need to discuss something, with Anna,' Peach says coldly.

I blink with surprise.

Tiffany hisses. 'Well, I'm going to the morgue, to make preparations,' she says.

Peach blows her nose. 'Okay,' she says sadly, stroking a tabby.

Without a backward glance, Tiffany stomps out of the room and slams the door.

Peach turns her eyes on me. 'She's just jealous, you know.'

I can't stop blinking. 'What?'

'Jealous. Of you.'

'Of me?'

Peach nods.

Freddy is knocking at the door, asking if he can come in.

'Give us a minute,' Peach calls.

She looks curiously animated. 'First things first,' she whispers to me. 'It's up to you and me now. Together we must execute Plan B.'

CHAPTER 26
Reversion

I'm hurtling through the night in the black SUV, with Peach. Ishvar is driving. He smells of curry. The North Lantau highway is busy with trucks and tourist buses, taxis and cars. Even at this hour.

'I don't think I can do this,' I say.

Peach gives my thigh a reassuring squeeze. 'Of course you can. They won't suspect a thing.'

As we streak towards the colourful neon lights of Kowloon, I cool my mind by going through the facts one more time: one, Max murdered the prostitute; two, Kung and Steel didn't arrive in time to stop him; three, Max has the psychic skill of transvection – he can fly. *So Peggy wasn't hallucinating.* But this time, in his haste, Max failed to notice that the prostitute's room didn't have a window. By the time he'd battered her door down, the police were ready to ambush him. He was arrested and put into custody. Kung and Steel have tracked him down to a cell in Victoria Prison.

Peach smiles sadly at me. 'Even if Max appeals for clemency, I don't think Kung would grant it,' she says.

'Will Steel be punished too?'

'No. In the circumstances, he did well.'

'Why can't Max just be tried, like a human, and sent to prison?'

Peach's eyes start watering.

'He wouldn't get the death penalty, would he?' I ask.

Peach gives me a withering look. 'No, this isn't mainland China.'

I blush at my ignorance but persist. 'Then he would serve a life sentence, and just wait to be released.'

Peach shakes her head. 'No, Kung would never allow that. Vampires don't age, as you know. Over time, the wardens would discover that Max is paranormal. The publicity would be huge. And as he has murdered a string of innocent women, humans would hate us even more. It would ruin all Kung's efforts to change common attitudes about us. And lessen the chance of our coming out in society someday.'

Wa! They want to come out of the closet. Like gays.

Peach sighs. Her arms droop lifelessly on her lap. 'But I feel quite suicidal at the thought of Max's fate,' she says.

I nod my head sympathetically. So even vampires want to kill themselves sometimes.

'I love Max. Despite what he's done,' she says vehemently.

Ishvar's dark eyes appear in the rear-view mirror. 'A mother's dilemma, if you don't mind me saying so, Ma'am.'

Peach smiles through her tears. 'I love all my children. Maybe to a fault. But I have to forgive myself. We all have to forgive ourselves sometimes.'

After reading her memoirs, I feel a pang of compassion for her. But even more confused about what to think about Max's case.

The SUV climbs up Cotton Tree Drive. Ishvar takes a sharp right turn then drives alongside the high walls of the Botanical Gardens and Government House. Then we drop down towards Victoria Prison. When we reach its south perimeter wall, he turns the van into a narrow street and parks. The stone wall towers above us, dark and foreboding. It must be around thirty feet high and is topped by barbed wire.

'When everyone is in position, you will walk down to the police station via Old Bailey Street,' Peach says. 'Come straight back here when you're done.' My heart thumps.

She punches some numbers into her mobile. A male voice answers and she listens attentively.

'Okay,' she says to me. 'Off you go. Good luck.'

Central Police Station – an old colonial building with a heavy grey façade – abuts the northern wall of the prison. It looks angular. Imposing. *What if I get arrested?* I ask myself, as I leg it down the steep street. The stone steps are slippery. The air is humid and the distant neon signs fuzz. It's around 3 am but late-night revellers are still spilling out of bars on Hollywood Road.

Inside the reporting centre, there's a long counter with scattered folders and flasks of tea. From a wall shrine, the fierce black-faced ghost-busting god Zhong Kui brandishes a sword. A middle-aged policewoman is gazing sleepily at a computer screen. She raises her heavy head at the sound of the squeaky swing door and gestures towards a rattan chair, which screeches as I pull it across the floor.

'I've been robbed,' I say. 'My purse, my money, my ID card, everything.'

The policewoman yawns, moves her computer keyboard to the side, reaches for a pen and a sheaf of lined paper. 'Name? ID number? Address? When? Where? Amount?'

My voice gradually stops quavering. I notice that her computer screen shows images from CCTV cameras in nine places around the prison. Every ten seconds or so, the angle of the images changes.

The policewoman lowers her head to take notes. Her permed hair is streaked with grey. From the corner of my eye, something moves on her computer screen. I see Steel on the wall, balancing on top of the barbed wire. With supernatural effort he throws up a rope, which hooks on to an overhang of the prison roof.

'*Wa!*' I say.

Abruptly, the policewoman looks up. 'Have you been injured?' she says.

'No, no,' I say breezily. 'Just … just remembered that I had a thousand dollar note in my purse.'

'One thou-sand dol-lar note,' the policewoman records on the statement. As she's writing, Steel, clinging to the rope, takes a gigantic leap, lands safely, and starts scaling the sheer prison wall.

'And my house keys,' I say quickly. As Steel, suspended in mid-air, stops at a small window, rips off its metal mesh and starts bending a grille of iron bars apart with his bare hands.

The policewoman takes a sip of tea while glancing up at the

computer screen. In that millisecond, I cough loudly and she looks at me instead. It seems an age before the image changes to another section of the prison wall. Phew!

'You need to read and sign this statement,' she says, handing me the form.

'Okay,' I say nervously.

The policewoman swings round on her chair to place her flask back on the table. Just then, Max's head and shoulders appear from between the warped bars. Steel grabs him, wrenches him forward and Max jumps onto Steel's back.

'Sorry, what's that word?' I say, pointing to a handwritten word on the form.

'Which one?'

'This one.'

The policewoman slides her glasses back up her nose. 'Your surname,' she says, and gives me a pitying look.

'Sorry,' I say, resisting the urge to make a run for it.

A wall alarm starts to flash red. Silently, at first. Then there's the wail of a siren. The policewoman blinks, registers mild surprise. She reaches for her walkie-talkie, which is now crackling and mumbling. She picks it up, barks, '1257,' then puts it back down on the table.

I quickly scribble my fake signature on the document.

In one of the CCTV images, a rapidly accelerating police car flits by. I can hear the roar of its engine from the street outside. I watch two police motorbikes pass with their blue lights flashing.

The policewoman yawns and hands me a slip of paper. 'Here

is your case number: G138709. I suggest you call the credit card company to cancel your card as soon as possible.'

'Is that all?' I say, standing up as a couple of red-faced policemen burst through an internal door.

The policewoman nods mechanically and turns to her colleagues. 'Anything wrong?' she says.

Kung, Steel, Freddy and Sport are waiting at the gates of the Luen Institute. Kung and Steel are dressed in their Taoist garb. It's dark and deathly still.

'What's Freddy doing here?' Peach says, aghast, as she alights from the van.

'The sooner he learns the consequence of violating our laws, the better,' Kung says.

Freddy runs to Peach and hugs her legs. 'Quartz, tremolite, wolframite.'

Kung cocks an eyebrow in disapproval. 'This is a serious matter, son,' he says gruffly.

Steel gives me a weak smile. I flash back to the time he and Kung visited Peg's place.

'Sorry about all this,' he says to me.

Peach takes Freddy's hand and follows Kung to the side entrance of the temple complex. Sport faithfully pads behind.

'Take my arm,' Steel says, lifting up a lantern to cast some light.

We make our way past pagodas and incense burners to a sheer wall of rock. An ancient door leads to the catacombs below.

I hunch forwards to squeeze through the narrow passageway, feeling more and more apprehensive the deeper we go. Drips of condensation slide off the craggy rock and drop into pools.

The passageway opens out into a main chamber where a row of identical coffins stretch out as far as the eye can see.

My heart races when I see Tiffany. She's also dressed in full Taoist robes. She's standing in a kind of ceremonial area, at the foot of a coffin which is set apart from the others, chanting from a weighty tome that's perched on a lectern.

On the walls, there are paintings of trigrams and *yin yang* symbols. In alcoves, there are models of heaven and hell.

Steel's gown swishes against the stone paving. He takes my hand to steady me as I climb up a narrow staircase hewn from the rock. It leads to a gallery which overlooks a stone trestle table that's been placed parallel to the coffin.

Peach, Freddy and I sit down on a stone bench. Below us, Steel takes a place next to Kung at the head of the coffin. Sport sits to heel tethered to a column behind them. He's panting, his long purple tongue pulsates between jagged white canines.

'This won't take long,' Peach says, seeking to reassure me.

I shiver with anticipation.

Tiffany strikes a gong. Kung starts intoning a prayer. Two priests approach him and lift the coffin lid. Inside, there's a corpse wearing a Qing dynasty gown and black boots. Headless. Decapitated, by the look of it – straggly bits squiggle from where the neck should be. Freddy gasps and hides his head on Peach's lap.

Another two priests dressed in black stand guard at a tall metal gate at the far end of the chamber. When Tiffany strikes the gong again, they slide a latch, lift a heavy lever and the gate creaks open. A heavily-shackled Max is escorted in by two priests who are holding the ends of a clanking chain that's wrapped around the prisoner's neck. Only Max's mouth and nose are visible from the hooded black gown. Sport strains at the lead. Steel restrains him. Peach puts her arm round Freddy.

Max is led to a dock opposite us, on the far side of the coffin. One of the priests unhoods him. He's filthy dirty. Unshaven. His hair is long and matted. His manacled hands clench into fists as he takes a sharp intake of breath. Then he relents, and slowly drops his head.

Kung reads from a tome in a low measured tone. 'Maximilian Thomas Montague Tang, are you guilty of the murders of Qian Wen, Wu An Yi, Choy Na Sun, Sri Wulandari and Mabel Alfonso?' he says.

Max's voice echoes around the chamber: 'Yes.'

'Do you confess that you killed the victims for the purpose of consumption?'

'Yes.'

'Are you aware that this is a violation of Article 7 Section 2.2 of the Molestation of Humans Act?'

'Yes.' Max's voice is fainter now.

'And that the punishment is reversion?'

'Yes.' In a whisper.

'Speak up, boy,' Kung shouts.

'YES!'

'Maximilian Thomas Montague Tang, you are guilty as charged,' Kung thunders.

Peach stifles a sob. Freddy wriggles round to comfort her.

Max bangs his shackled arms against the dock.

'Do you have anything to say before the commencement of the reversion?' Kung's voice is less strident now.

Max raises his head and looks directly at the gallery. His eyes are menacing and defiant. 'No.'

Did Tiffany just smirk?

Sport gives a spine-tingling howl, leaps forward, and nearly strangles himself. Steel restrains him.

Kung bangs a large drum and starts chanting. A priest replaces the hood on Max's head and pulls him by the chain to the stone trestle table. Steel and Tiffany assist him in laying Max in a prone position on top of it.

I glance over at Peach. She's covering Freddy's eyes.

Tiffany is staring vacantly ahead.

Steel looks scared.

I look down again. A priest hands Kung an axe. Its blade glints in the candlelight. Kung positions himself at right angles to Max. He raises both arms and aligns the blade. With one fell swoop, he brings the axe down on Max's neck; blood spurts and Max's head is bouncing on the stone floor. I watch with horror as the rest of the body seethes, sizzles, bubbles, congeals into a sticky clotted mass of gore. In the heat, the gown smoulders, ignites, flames.

The priest picks up Max's head – the eyes are bulging – and places it upright on a silver platter. Carefully balancing it on his shoulder, he marches towards Kung. The head, drained of blood, has turned a greenish-white.

Kung ceremoniously lifts the head by the ears, and lowers it towards the headless corpse in the coffin. There's a hissing and steaming as the head fuses with the body.

Kung leans over the body and pastes a yellow prayer paper on the forehead while Tiffany recites a verse.

Kung closes the lid. Tiffany intones a few final words.

Water droplets splash into a puddle.

The bloody mass that remains on the trestle table has hardened and solidified. It's substantial enough to be scraped up and tossed away.

CHAPTER 27

Castles in the sand

'It was disgusting. Revolting,' I say, blubbering into a tissue.

I'm in Steel's car; it's a Ferrari! A blood-red Ferrari! Steel says he's driving it 'cos he wants to cheer me up. It's the fastest one of the fleet.

But I just smell blood.

The black SUV must be way behind us. We're already on the road that bisects Lantau Island from north to south. There's no hint of dawn yet; it's desolate. Windy and remote. And it's pouring with rain.

The windscreen wipers flit to and fro. Steel accelerates up and over the cleft between two mountains. Over the crest, there's a panorama of heaving sea and brooding sky. Boats dotting the far horizon twinkle like spent fireworks. Steel tells me it's the perfect time to catch squid.

'How can you talk about fishing? I say.

Steel pats my leg. 'I know you're really upset. But it's over now. Just don't think about it.'

The flanks of the mountain curve gracefully down to the sea. Down below, the road runs parallel to a long stretch of beach. When we reach it, Steel takes a slip road and parks in a lay-by. He tips his head forwards and rests it on the steering wheel.

A shiver of fear shoots up my spine. *Why has he stopped here?* Raindrops dribble down the windscreen. The branches of palm trees flail in the wind.

Steel slouches back in his seat and turns to me. 'Don't worry,' he says. He looks tired, but relaxed. He smiles mysteriously. 'How about we take a run along the beach?'

'What, in the rain?'

'Why not? We've got to get out of this lousy mood. It's not that cold.'

'Crazy.'

'I bet you've never done it before,' he says, and reaches for my hand.

'I wonder why,' I say, sarcastically.

There's a distant flash of lightning and a grumble of thunder.

'If you catch a cold, I promise I'll cure you,' he says.

That's reassuring.

As we jump down the embankment onto the beach, one of my flip-flops snags on a tree stump. Steel takes his shoes off and digs his heels in the powdery sand. 'It's a great feeling. You should try it,' he says.

I do. The sand is pleasantly abrasive between my toes. The air smells fresh. The rain feels soothing. The waves of the sea sparkle and fizz on the shoreline. There's the glimmer of dawn on the horizon.

'I'll race you to the rock over there,' Steel says, pointing to a boulder in the distance.

We start running, faster and faster, blown by the wind. *Running from the clunk of the axe and a bouncing head. Running from gore and fire and the stench of certain death.*

'Faster,' Steel shouts, ahead of me, and I can feel my heart pounding and the rain spattering my cheeks.

'I'm going to beat you,' I cry, as my feet skim the surf. *Running from vampires and corpses and spiders and ghosts. Running from love and hate and blood and tears.*

Steel lets me win. I tag the rock, panting, laughing. I throw my arms behind my head to catch my breath, and watch Steel's dancing eyes. My sodden T-shirt is plastered to my chest. My nipples show. Two pointed tips.

Steel cruises up to me, clasps my hands and swings me round and round like a spinning top until I'm begging for mercy. I collapse in a heap of laughter and he jumps on top of me, spreadeagles my body. His wet hair is glued to his scalp; sand chafes my skin. He licks my snot-smeared face. 'And now I'm going to kiss every pore of your body,' he says.

His lips are right there, waiting for mine.

I give a murmur of assent.

We kiss deeply; his lips are salty. He kisses me again and again, kisses me until all I can feel is the wetness of his hungry tongue.

His lips move downwards, down my neck, down to my collarbone. His breath is warm, fragmented. He raises a bleary head, smiles, then lifts my T-shirt and buries his head underneath it. His tongue slides up from my tummy button to the underside of my breasts, and hovers. I feel his body tense, and relax. He bites my nipple gently. Then he slides to the other one and bites again. My whole body aches for his love.

'I want this to last forever,' I say.

Steel withdraws his head and rests it on my stomach.

'For. Ever,' I say.

'Please, not now,' Steel says. 'No talking. Let's just enjoy the present moment.'

I sit up. 'I mean it,' I say.

The rain clouds have swept away. Early birds chatter. We sit side by side, burrowing our toes in the sand.

The edges of the waves are tinged a luminous blue. At first I think I'm seeing ghosts.

'No,' Steel says. 'They're tiny sea creatures. Only visible for a few days each year.'

The waves are dancing, frothing with phosphorescence.

'Like champagne,' I say. 'Fountains of champagne.'

A crack of light appears on the horizon. Sunlight.

It floods my head and my thoughts leap like a bird, soaring, speeding, singing: he *does* want us to be together forever. He will let me turn one day. But I still have stuff to do in my human life. And he's putting that above his own wishes. For now. I can suddenly see that really clearly. 'I love you,' I say.

Which seems to take Steel completely by surprise.

'You do?' he says. He leaps to his feet, cartwheels across the beach. 'I love you too,' he shouts, picking up a branch from among the shingle and scrawling our names in the sand.

I run over and trace the characters with my index finger.

'And I'm going to build you a castle,' he cries. He drops to his knees and starts digging.

I sit on a boulder – it's rough with barnacles – while Steel scoops great handfuls of sand. *I will be your princess,* I think.

I taste the salt on my lips as I watch him beavering away. Crabs scuttle down sand holes.

'Collect some more shells,' he calls.

White scallops, mother-of-pearl, clams, winkles – there are hundreds of them scattered between ocean-smoothed stones.

Together, we decorate our castle and turn it into something rich and strange. Imperishable as the whorls of weed that wreath its turrets. Indestructible as the rounded granite pebble that Steel stamps on the keep.

'My mason's mark,' he says.

'It's majestic.'

'Then allow me to accompany you across the drawbridge.'

He takes my wrist and walks my fingers across a piece of driftwood towards the gatehouse. Water swirls around the moat.

He lifts an imaginary portcullis. 'Permit me to escort you to your throne room,' he says, and walks my fingers to the great hall.

I close my eyes. A sad lump clogs my throat.

'My princess is resting,' Steel whispers. He kisses my eyelids, one by one.

We lie side by side and listen to the waves. When I open my eyes again, pink clouds flush the sky, like candyfloss.

Steel looks at me, long and hard. His body is coated in sand, his eyes are hard as flint. 'Anna, you are human. You have free will. I will always respect that.'

I suddenly want to cry.

'You don't want me to turn, do you,' I say.

'I just want to you to be happy,' he replies.

'But … '

'No buts. Not now.'

'Okay.'

The waves inch towards us. They lap the sides of our castle. The sky has turned blue.

'Steel, shouldn't we be going?'

'One day I'll build you a real palace,' he says wistfully.

CHAPTER 28
Emergency

When we arrive at Bauhinia Lodge, Kung and Peach are standing outside the front porch. It's an indelible scene etched in my memory – the vibrant green grass after rain, the rush of the river, the tightness of Peach's lips.

'There's something wrong,' Steel says, quickening his pace.

His parents hurry along the garden path towards us and we meet halfway.

'Why didn't you answer your phone?' Peach says.

Steel clutches his pocket as if to remedy the situation. 'Sorry.'

Kung's face is grave. He's dressed in his Taoist garb. But his hair is hanging loose. 'There's been an accident,' he says.

They're all looking at me. *WHAT?*

'It's your mother. She's in danger,' Peach says.

'My mother? Where?' Oh my God, her plane must have crashed. She's due back in Hong Kong today. *What was the arrival time?* My mouth is dry, my tongue thick in my throat.

'She's still in Hunan,' Kung says. 'As far as we know.'

He starts walking back towards the house and we follow him.

'So what's happened?' Steel says.

'I think Tiffany is planning to … hurt her,' Peach says.

'Tiffany?' I blurt.

'She's disappeared. Max's coffin is empty. Somehow, he's escaped,' Kung says.

'Is Ma okay?' I screech. My heart is knocking against my ribs like a drum.

No answer.

'It's worth the risk.' I hear Tiffany's voice saying. The overheard conversation in the bedroom will come back to haunt me for the rest of my life.

'I heard her,' I say.

'Who?'

'Tiffany.'

'What did she say?' Peach asks anxiously.

'That she had a copy … of the keys.'

'To the morgue,' Kung confirms.

'How could she?' Peach says, looking accusingly at Kung.

Kung's bushy eyebrows contract into a V. He looks deeply perturbed.

'Well, what can we do?' Steel says impatiently.

'And why my mother?' I say, dreading their answer.

Again, three sets of solid gold eyes stare at me. Worry is written all over their faces.

Peach speaks first: 'You know I'm clairvoyant. This morning, in the peace and quiet of my spirit room, looking into my crystal ball, I caught a glimpse of Tiffany carrying Max's corpse across the border to China. With Janet. At great speed. Full of revenge. They're heading north.'

'I don't understand,' I say, my voice cracking with emotion.

'The bitch!' Steel shouts.

Peach bites her lip.

'We've got to leave. Now,' Kung says.

My heart is thumping in my ears. 'Yes,' I say. *But how? Where?*

'We'll leave in ten minutes,' Kung says, looking at his watch.

'Faster,' Kung says, and Rajaram puts his foot down. We're in the black SUV racing along the airport road and my mind is flapping around like a gutted fish at the wet market.

We whizz past the Departures exit and along a road running parallel to a runway. Parked aeroplanes peer over me like a flock of giant birds. A high metal gate looms in front of us and the car slows.

'There,' Steel says, pointing to a small plane; its lights are flashing. A stairway leads up to an open cabin door. At the top, a uniformed man is ticking a checklist.

Eiya! They own a private plane.

The electronic gate swings open and a guard salutes. The clouds have cleared and the sun is beating down. Steel and I scuttle behind Kung on the tarmac, under the shade of an umbrella. There's a roar of a commercial plane taking off on another runway.

The cockpit door is open. We mount the flimsy steps. A pilot waves to us from a cave of switches and blinking lights. The cabin resembles an old-fashioned living room, with armchairs and wooden tables, walnut panels and pleated lampshades.

'Buckle up,' Steel says.

The plane taxies to the take-off point. *Just flimsy metal between me and the ground,* I think. *How fragile life is.* The whine of the engine increases in pitch and volume as we gather speed and height. Soon, all I can see are container ships dotting the vast expanse of the South China Sea.

'Peach will be tracking Max and Tiffany's movements from Bauhinia Lodge,' Kung says. 'With her prescience, I think we will be able to find your mother before Tiffany does.'

'Really?' I say, wishing I knew what prescience means. Kung's serious expression discourages me from asking. I watch him as, deep in thought, he changes the SIM card of his mobile telephone. Then he says he's going to lie down, and disappears behind a curtain at the back of the plane.

'You should drink something,' Steel says to me, opening a fridge. He persuades me to sip some water; my mouth is dry as a bone.

'Why use Max?' I ask, putting the half-empty glass down. 'I mean, surely Tiffany and Janet could … could harm a human themselves.'

'Max knows his way around Hunan, Tiffany doesn't. When we lived there, she wasn't yet part of our family. Besides, there's no way she would want to risk being reverted, if … if … '

I hold up my hand to stop him going any further.

Then I'm crying. Tears pour down my face. I haven't cried for ages. Not like this.

'I'll kill her,' Steel says, his eyes blazing with revenge.

We hit some turbulence. It makes me want to vomit. At least the shocking thoughts that are racing around my brain are stilled as I concentrate on controlling the rise and fall of nausea.

'Why does Tiffany hate me so much?' I ask.

'Many reasons. She's full of bitterness. About you, about me, about her past. She's a complicated person. She's caused nothing but trouble since Kung and Peach adopted her.'

'When was that?'

'About a year ago.'

'Where?'

'In Hong Kong. She killed her former vampire father in a fit of rage. Kung took pity on her 'cos her father was molesting her. He agreed to adopt her on condition that she got an education and kept away from her former friends.'

'Like Janet?'

Steel grimaces. 'No, Janet is actually her blood relative. She was Tiffany's human sister in the Tang dynasty. It's not common knowledge because Janet was adopted by another vampire family and her parents don't like her spending time with Tiffany. They think she's a bad influence. But Janet is screwed up too. She also had a tough human life.'

A nasty part of me gloats. 'Really?'

'She was sold as a child bride to a corrupt official who beat her up so badly that she committed suicide.'

The plane's engine has finally settled into a steady hum. Steel is looking out of the window at a carpet of clouds beneath us. He's reflecting on something. For once, I don't care if he's re-living a sexy moment with Janet. That's 'cos anxiety is hitting me face-smack hard as I'm imagining what could be happening to Ma. 'Where is Ma now, anyway?'

Steel takes my hand. 'Peach will tell Kung her exact whereabouts when we're closer to Hunan. If she can see it, that is.'

I start getting really emo. 'My poor Ma,' I say. 'Why should she suffer? Why didn't Tiffany just try and kill me?'

'She didn't dare,' Steel says, clenching his fist.

'She just wants to punish me, doesn't she?'

'You and me. Tiffany is really jealous of both of us.'

I nod miserably.

'And it's not just us. She's envious that you're human and your Ma loves you so much. She's mad that Peach has taken such a liking to you. Peach has already told her that if you turn into a vampire, she wants to adopt you.'

'Really?' *That's news to me.*

'And of course Tiffany hates it that you know so much about our family.'

'There's no love like mother's love.' Peach's voice rings in my ears.

I like Peach. But she's not my Ma, I think. *I want my Ma!* And suddenly I want to shout out my love for her. I see her contented smile as she watches me finish the last grain of rice in my bowl. The stoic tilt of her chin as she leaves for work. Her earnest eyes begging me to study. I cover my eyes and grit my teeth. How selfish I have been.

Steel raises his eyebrows, then decides against speaking.

I feel more tears coming.

'Don't cry. Dad's coming back,' Steel says.

Sure enough, the doorknob of the compartment Kung was resting in is turning.

'It's time to robe, son,' Kung says. He's already fully dressed.

Steel jumps to his feet and goes to the back of the plane. Kung sits down opposite me. As soon it's just him and me, I feel awkward.

'Did Steel tell you that we lived in Hunan before coming to Hong Kong?' he says.

'Yes, he mentioned it,' I reply.

'I'm afraid I have many enemies there. As Chairman of the Taoist Vampire Society, I spent five years trying to clean up the province.'

'From what?' I ask.

'Evil ghosts, deviant corpses, delinquent vampires, corrupt priests.'

I blink with astonishment. 'Is my Ma going to be alright?' I say.

Kung raises his chin, rubs his beard, breathes deeply. 'I will do my best to rescue her,' he says. 'But we must all be vigilant. And there's one precaution I need you to take.'

'What's that?' Steel says, closing the panelled door behind him.

Kung takes a charm out from his sleeve. It's a chain with a *yin yang* medallion. Behind his back, Steel waves at me, puts a finger to his lips to entreat my silence.

'This is a simple spell that will enable you to see ghosts,' Kung says.

A surge of adrenaline shoots up my spine.

'Don't worry. You're in good company. Steel and I should be able to deal with any threats. But three pairs of eyes are better than two.'

I nod. Blood pumps round my veins. I drop down to my knees, look into Kung's eyes and listen to the incantation. It's familiar 'cos it's the same one that Steel used at Peg's place.

'Prepare for landing.' The pilot's voice comes over the intercom system and the three of us put our seat belts on. My ears pop as the plane descends into a mountain of clouds. Kung rests his hands on a weighty tome on his lap. Then it's like the engine has cut out 'cos there's silence, just rain streaming down the window and the blinking of landing lights.

'Changsha airport,' Steel says, peering down. Through the clouds, I catch a watery glimpse of stationary aeroplanes and a control tower.

There's a jolt; my head hits the headrest. The engine roars, I'm tipped backwards, the front of the plane pitches skyward and the upward thrust is terrifying.

This is it, I think.

Steel takes my hand. I swallow some bile.

At last, the plane levels. The engine drops to a hum.

Steel looks at me anxiously. 'Are you okay?'

'Yes,' I say faintly.

His hand is a rock. Kung's eyes are closed. He inhales deeply, muttering to himself.

The cockpit door flips open. 'Sorry about that,' the pilot calls. 'Aborted landing. I'll do a loop and have another go.'

I'm still not breathing normally. My stomach has been left a thousand feet below.

'Windshear,' Steel says. 'It's quite common at this time of year.'

Wa!

The engine changes its tune. It skims along a carpet of bumpy clouds and we're buffeted around like shaken dice. I reach for a vomit bag. Seconds pass like hours. Time is suspended.

Kung studies his book intensely. I cling to Steel's hand, feeling like a stranded bird on a cliff edge.

When the plane descends a second time, I take a deep breath and prepare for the worst. I see a meandering river, rice paddies, half-built highways, streetlights, toy cars. The runway is below us. *Eiya! We're going to overshoot.*

The wheels hit the tarmac; Steel releases his white-knuckle grip. The plane slows, the rain heaves and my arm is numb.

'Welcome to Changsha,' Steel says.

I turn to look at Kung: his eyes are closed, and his palms are together. Deep in prayer. The book rests on his lap.

'Look at your face,' Steel says.

I change my phone screen to mirror function. *Gaau choa!* Too much dramarama. I've got panda eyes.

CHAPTER 29

Dangerous times

Changsha city is chock-a-block with half-built buildings and cranes. The roads are busy and grey. Most residential blocks have caged balconies and windows. They remind me of Victoria prison.

We drive farther and farther west along a recently-finished highway. Apart from the occasional road-rage truck-driver, the journey is surprisingly smooth. After a toll gate, we travel along a dimly-lit road which is empty apart from a few sodden motorcyclists and the occasional tractor. On either side, clusters of shabby dwellings and peasants with wide hats and mackintoshes work in the fields.

An unpleasant stench of low-grade diesel and garlic pervades the taxi. The unshaven driver's tea flask jiggles in the compartment between him and Kung, who is deep in thought.

The windscreen wipers mark time. I alternate between feeling an overwhelming need to sleep and panicking about Ma. I realise that I've been so obsessed about Steel lately, she has hardly impinged on my consciousness. She's just been a stooge who feeds me and washes my clothes, an annoyance when I've wanted the flat to myself. When she nagged me about exams, I ignored her. When she banned me from going to Peg's place, I disobeyed her. I never even thanked her properly for my new 'interview' dress.

And suddenly I can't imagine life without her. She's the only family I've got, apart from my relatives here in Hunan. All I want now is to see her again.

The car turns off the tarmac and bumps down a mud track. The rain has stopped but there are puddles everywhere, puddles which hide potholes. Every time the car wheels hit one, my stomach churns and the driver swears.

Steel is nervous about something. His body stiffens, his canines extend. *What's wrong with him?* I turn to see what has caught his attention: it's just a wooded hill.

I lean forward to look at Kung. His eyebrows are knotted and his head is twitching like a compass needle. He's focusing on the wooded hill too.

I squeeze my eyes shut and open them again, hoping to see what they can.

'Stop the car,' Kung calls suddenly. The two of them leap out. I follow.

It's barely perceptible, but the ground is trembling. I sense a chill passing over me.

'What's happening?' I say.

Before either of them can answer, there's the blast of a horn, a blood-curdling cry and the sound of thundering hooves. Hundreds of horses are streaking towards us. They're ridden by ghastly phantasmagorical shapes: ghosts with missing limbs, ropes wrapped round their necks, knives stuck in their bodies, headless torsos.

'Steel!' I yell.

'Get back in the car,' he snarls, and I twirl round to see that he and Kung have transformed. Their quadruped bodies look tough as rhinos, their canines sharp as razors. Their eyes flash like drawn daggers.

I dither, terrified for Steel's safety. 'Get back in, NOW,' he roars. He picks me up and throws me through the taxi's open door.

The driver's dirty fingers grip the steering wheel. I don't say anything to him 'cos I have no breath to speak. Ghosts circle the car, whooping and cheering as if preparing for a head-on attack. There's a tremendous thump above me – I think the car roof is going to cave in – but it's Kung and Steel, who have jumped on it. With a piercing cry, Steel leaps on top of a mounted soldier, wrenches the reins from his hands, tears his feet out of the stirrups and hurls him to the ground.

'Zha!' shouts a leader and there's the scuffle of action as the army charges forward. Through a cloud of dust and swirling leaves, I hear the swishing of swords and the clashing of metal. A ghost looms, swinging spiked metal balls on a chain above his head. Another one shoots a thicket of arrows. Then there's hand-to-hand combat with bayonets and battle-axes, and shrieks and yells of pain.

The taxi driver revs the car engine. 'Get out of my car, I'm leaving,' he shouts.

'No! Stop!' I cry, gripping the door handle in case I have to jump out.

'My car will be ruined.'

That's when I realise he can't see what's really happening. 'Wait a minute,' I say. 'My friends ... are practising *kung fu.'*

We're both distracted by a fan of wild flames which is fast engulfing Kung. Like a typhoon wind, Steel swoops from a tree top and whisks Kung out of danger. The driver presses the accelerator and the car starts moving. 'Please,' I shout. 'They'll finish soon.'

Sure enough, Kung and Steel seem to be gaining the upper hand. Riderless horses flee from the battle scene, trampling on fallen ghosts who are writhing and moaning on the ground.

The blast of a horn suddenly cuts through the chaos. The ghosts swirl and divide like waves of a parting sea to allow a magnificent silvery grey horse to canter towards us. Astride, there's a fully-armoured ghostly figure wielding a magnificent sword. Two black dogs with slavering mouths and glistening coats snap at the horse's fetlocks.

Steel transforms back to his human shape and retreats into the car. I slam the door behind him. He's bleeding from an open gash on his forehead and panting from exertion. The sleeves of his gown are covered with mud. The taxi driver takes one look and covers his eyes.

'Here's a tissue,' I say. It's the only thing I have to mop the blood.

'Did I hurt you when I threw you?' Steel says solicitously, applying pressure to his wound.

My reply is masked by an ear-splitting blast of a horn. The ghost king has halted in front of Kung, who has flown onto a stone wall. Swords, daggers, clubs and cudgels drop away. Apart from the occasional whinny and cry of pain, there's a terrifying hush.

'King Gong is an arch enemy of Kung,' Steel whispers. 'He was one of the eunuchs who killed Dad in the Ming dynasty.'

The two titans out-stare each other for what seems an age. The taxi driver whimpers. Then, King Gong flips open his helmet and clears his throat. 'We meet again,' he says in a deep resounding voice.

Kung's human body seems to expand and fill a stage. 'Peace be with you.'

A laugh, loud and insincere, echoes around the hills.

Kung straightens his back and raises his chin. 'Despite defeating your army, I have no intention of giving you the pleasure of being exterminated.'

A decapitated ghost raises his torso from the mud, groans and collapses back into a heap.

'You know you are not welcome in our territory,' King Gong says. Clouds of vapour swirl around his horse's magnificent neck.

'But I come on a private matter,' Kung says imperiously.

King Gong raises his chin and howls with laughter. His two dogs start yapping; he yells at them to shut up. 'Ah, your son,' he says, wiping his beard with a silk cloth.

Kung bristles with anger. 'I know my son is easy bait,' he says, 'but he's mine. He belongs to me.'

'Too true. He's small fry,' King Gong says, unperturbed by Kung's show of emotion. 'Not nearly as clever as the deviant corpses I already have in my servitude.'

Kung raises his chin defiantly.

'Unfortunately,' King Gong continues, 'we failed to capture your pretty daughter and her sister. Their revengeful natures and evil minds would be more useful to us.'

I feel Steel shudder beside me.

I'm suddenly aware that time is ticking by. That I still don't know what's happening to Ma. *Ma! Where are you?*

'Destroy the seeds of evil, or they will grow to be your ruin,' Kung shouts.

'Bah!' says King Gong, wheeling his horse round on its hind legs. 'And by the way, you can rest assured that your beloved son is about to inflict the damage you came to prevent.'

Laughing scornfully, he gathers his reins and spurs his horse's belly. The horse rears on its hind legs, plunges forwards and bolts back to the woods. Flurries of ghosts scurry like dry leaves along its trail up the hill.

'What did he mean?' I shriek, pulling apart the words I'd just heard and putting them back together again.

Steel's eyes are dark and brooding.

Kung flies down to the taxi and wrenches the door open. 'There's not a second to waste,' he shouts. The beleaguered taxi driver protests but is quickly over-ruled.

We tear down muddy tracks, past donkeys pulling rickety carts, peasants hunched beneath sacks, noisy tuk-tuks and over-laden bicycles. *Faster. Faster,* I scream inside.

'Why hasn't Peach called?' Steel asks.

Kung checks his telephone for missed calls. There aren't any.

I'm beyond panic. The journey seems endless. There's just field after field of rice paddies and vegetables and ducks and fish-farms. *Why don't I recognise anywhere?* It seems ludicrous that Ma is here somewhere. Impossible. And that I was in Hong Kong only a few hours ago. That while I was racing along the beach in the rain with Steel, something horrific was happening here. To my mother.

Kung's phone rings. It's Peach. He blocks his other ear to hear better. I feel a sickening lurch. It must be bad news.

'Yes. Yes. No. Oh, thank goodness,' Kung says.

'What?' I cry.

Kung covers the phone. 'Your mother has been attacked. In your grandparents' barn. But she's alive. Badly injured. But alive.'

'How much longer to get there?'

'About fifteen minutes.'

At last, the low tiled roofs of Ma's village appear ahead. My Aunty Lan staggers through the mud towards us as the taxi stops on the track nearest to Grandpa and Grandma's house. She's all frizzy hair and blood-stained clothes. 'We're waiting for the emergency services,' she shouts, eye-balling Kung and Steel through a wound-down window.

'Is she still alive?' I yell. My chest is so tight I can hardly breathe.

When Aunty sees it's me, she can't speak for sobs.

'Is she?' I repeat, springing out of the car.

'I think so,' she manages to say.

'Where is the injured party?' Kung says, indicating to the taxi driver to stay put. Steel carries the medical kit.

We squelch through a muddy field with Aunty, towards local villagers who are crowding round Grandpa's barn.

'These are the Taoist priests I told you about,' I say.

Aunty nods her head mechanically, too preoccupied with Ma's condition to question their presence. 'She got up early to wash the lotus roots,' she says breathlessly, her words tumbling over each other in her haste to tell me what happened. 'A few minutes later, Grandma heard the screams. She rushed out with the dogs. Whatever it was burst through the window to escape.'

Uncle To's head pokes out of the barn door. His hair is dishevelled and his shirt blotched with blood. 'We need some help to carry her to the hospital,' he shouts.

Four burly men raise their hands and move towards the entrance.

'Wait a minute,' Kung says, pushing the volunteers aside. 'I would like to assess her first.' Steel and I follow.

The villagers mutter to themselves as Uncle To shuts the barn door behind us.

I gasp in horror, cover my mouth in disbelief. Nothing could have prepared me for what I see inside.

Savaged. Like after an animal kill. One of Ma's arms is hanging from her elbow. There's a jagged bite mark on her thigh, a stick-like bone that's protruding. Blood everywhere, matting the straw where she's lying, with her head on Grandma's lap.

And her face, her face …

'Anna,' Grandma wails, when she sees me. She rocks back on her heels, strands of wispy hair sticking to her scalp, bloody hands supporting Ma's squashed tomato of a face.

'Ma,' I cry. I drop to the ground and clutch her lifeless hand. She doesn't respond. *We're too late,* my brain shouts.

'We need to stop the blood or she'll bleed to death,' Kung says.

Steel's body is stiffening. As it hardens, his nostrils dilate and his eyes pulsate beneath closed eyelids. Four canines shoot from his gums.

Grandma and Aunty Lan shrink back in horror. 'What's going on?' Aunty Lan shouts.

'Take your mother out of the barn,' Kung says, ordering Aunty Lan.

Grandma's body goes limp. She has fainted. Kung scoops Ma's head in his hands.

'Brother, big brother, help!' Aunty Lan shouts.

Uncle To, alarmed, comes rushing in. Together, they lift Grandma out of the barn, glancing back anxiously at me.

'I'm okay,' I shout.

Kung has a charm and is swinging it above Ma's head. He starts intoning an incantation.

I lean against a wall to get my balance. My knees are shaking; I can smell the blood. *My Ma is bleeding to death.*

Steel seems paralysed. His fists are clenched as if he's about to attack an enemy.

The incantation stops. 'Son, you can do it. You will do it. You WILL save the life of Anna's mother.' Kung's voice is stern, non-negotiable.

Suddenly I understand: *Ma's blood. Ma smells like me. Steel can't control his bloodlust.*

Steel whirls round to face me, his eyes are fixed in a demonic stare. 'How dare you think that?' he snarls.

I feel the blood drain from my face. My fingers spread like talons against the wall.

Steel grasps Ma's good arm. With mouth agape – forked tongue, tiger shark's teeth – he howls dreadfully. Straw chaff scatters. Then he plunges at her head, ranges over it, sucks it, cleans it.

Like a diver coming up for air, he surfaces, takes a sharp breath – his lips are bruised, his chin dripping with bloody saliva – then bears down on Ma's forearm. He quickly moves to her thigh, back up to her cheeks, along her forehead. Salivating, staunching, sealing, healing. The blood flows lessen to dribbles. Ma's body flushes. Her arms and legs start to twitch.

Ma's chest inflates. She's breathing, her cheeks are pink. 'Ma,' I yell, and rush to her side.

Her eyelids flutter. 'Anna?' she says, as if in a dream, then sinks back into unconsciousness.

Kung resumes the incantation. His voice is softer now.

Steel lies crumpled on the lotus roots. Shrunken, shrivelled, shattered. His hair is matted, with Ma's blood. 'Kiss me Anna,' he says.

I kiss his swollen bloody mouth. It's warm and slippery. I taste the sharp metallic tang of my mother's blood.

'You need to clean your face again,' he says weakly.

Kung is checking Ma's pulse. 'She's much stronger now,' he says. He takes out a roll of bandage from the medical kit. 'Anna, go and tell the taxi driver to standby.'

He starts tying a tourniquet around Ma's forearm.

'Phone the pilot to tell him to prepare to fly back to Hong Kong,' Steel says weakly.

To the three of us.

CHAPTER 30

Unravelling

'Ma, it's me,' I say, blinking under the garish fluorescent lights of the ward.

Her small frame is strapped to a mass of wires, her mouth distorted by an oxygen mask. Cold white walls, tight white sheets, the smell of antiseptic, and Ma's small frame strapped to a mass of wires, her mouth distorted by an oxygen mask. Machines whirr, monitors bleep. A careworn doctor paces between the beds, a stethoscope flapping against his white gown.

Ma has been in hospital for two weeks. She lies supine, hands folded on her stomach, hair fluffed on a pillow. No movement. No response. The surgeon has told me to be patient; Ma's wounds are mending remarkably well. Especially her face. She'll wake up from the coma soon, she said.

A wrinkled old lady sleeps in the adjacent bed. You wouldn't know she was alive but for the occasional twitch of her upper lip. At visiting times, her husband – always first in the queue to get into the ward – ratchets her bed so she's sitting up, and places a stool beside her. He opens a tub of *congee*, adds a sprinkle of dried scallop, dips a spoon in, blows on it, and shoves it into her gaping mouth. Feeds her. Like a baby. After each spoonful, he closes her jaw and orders her to swallow. And she does.

One day, a nurse came by to record the reading of Ma's blood pressure monitor. 'Your mother knows you're here,' she said. 'Just talk to her.'

So I do. Day after day. With her scrawny little hand in mine, I've told her that the flat is clean and yes, I am eating properly and studying hard for my exams.

I've told her how much I miss her home-made Shanghai *won-ton* dumplings.

I've told her that Windy called to say Ma mustn't worry about losing her job 'cos she's covering her shifts.

I've told her that Aunty Lan phoned to say that Grandpa is out of hospital, that Grandma is off the sedatives. They're back working in the fields, threshing the rice.

I've given her daily updates of the Ming dynasty TV serial she loves to watch, omitting the episode in which Concubine Lily dies. Of a neglected heart.

'How about you tell your Ma what's happening in your life?' Steel suggested yesterday.

So, this afternoon I'm telling her how worried I am about Peggy. About how it all started when we were approached by a drug pusher in form three. About how I fear that, despite our pact, she's addicted again. But I'm not. And I never will be. I'm trying to help her quit once and for all. Even though she's mad at me. Even though she doesn't want to be my best friend anymore. 'Cos she's jealous, she says.

Yes. I do have a boyfriend. He's very caring. He's someone really … special. He wants me to study. He's rich and generous. I've even met his family.

I suddenly feel angry: if Ma could really hear me, like the

nurse said, surely she'd be shaking a fist by now?

Then I tell Ma I can't help feeling guilty that she's been so badly injured. That it's all my fault. That I do care. That if she dies, I'll never forgive myself.

I make a deal with her: if I go to uni and get a well-paid job, would she please get better?

A nurse taps me on the shoulder to tell me that the visiting hour is over.

I'm flopped on my desk. At school. In recovery mode. When Wing taps me on my shoulder and passes a handwritten note. 'Can we chill? From Peg,' it says. I turn round, give Peggy the thumbs up.

'My place?' she says, as we walk out of the school gates. No BMW SUV cruising the street anymore. Tiffany has quit school. It's official. Due to a 'private family matter', according to Teacher Pang.

'Okay,' I say, not planning to stay too long.

Peg grunts.

'And where's your phone?'

'Lost.' she says.

As usual, Ken isn't home. The flat is as messy as ever: dirty floor, unwashed dishes, overflowing ashtrays. An ominous smell floats out of the fridge.

Peggy says she needs a shower, emerges hot and red. I notice she has a new metal ring in her belly button.

'How's Jane?'

'Fine,' says Peg, shaking her spiky hair like a wet dog.

'By the way, where did you first meet?' I try to keep my voice neutral.

'In the snooker parlour. Why?'

'She looks … kind of … tough.'

Peggy exhales sharply through her nose. She turns on her computer, shows me her new wallpaper and tells me she wants to teach me how to play snooker online. We sip from cans of cream soda pretending everything is fine. But it's not. She's never even thanked me for looking after her when she turned up stoned at China Chicks.

During the long hours sitting in the hospital, I've sussed out what's wrong with her: she's only interested in her own miserable life.

And I've been asking myself: why she's soooo anti Steel.

I don't want to lose her as a friend, I really don't. I mean, we've been through so much together. Deep down I know I care a lot.

'Ready to play?' she says, clicking the 'enter' box on screen. Noisy snooker balls rush down a shute and assemble themselves on the table.

The events of the last few weeks suddenly surround me. They're tight around my chest and throat. I want Peg to know my secrets. I want to share everything with her. Why shouldn't I? What are best friends for?

'Don't you want to know what's really been happening in my life?' I say.

Peg fingers the tail of her dragon tattoo, wobbles her head from side to side like an Indian.

'But you must promise not to blab, like last time,' I say.

Peggy scrunches her eyebrows, lights a cigarette and puts on some hip hop. 'Okay,' she says, a little too flippantly for my liking.

I take a deep breath and begin. I tell her that the serial killer was a vampire: Max, Steel's adopted brother. He murdered prostitutes, including the one in Jane's block. So it WAS Max she saw flying. That Kung reverted him into a corpse as a punishment.

I tell her how Tiffany seduced a Taoist priest, unlocked the morgue and carried Max's corpse to Hunan to kill my Ma. How Max would have succeeded were it not for my Grandma hearing Ma's screams and setting her dogs on him.

Peggy flares her nostrils and nods mechanically. 'I had my suspicions,' she says.

I can't believe she's so nonplussed. Nothing fazes her anymore. It's as if she's been reading too many vampire novels.

'Where's Tiffany now?' she asks.

'Hiding somewhere in Guangzhou, with Janet.'

'So Steel's ex-lovebird is finally out of your hair.'

'You could say that.' *Yeah.*

'And Max?'

'He's still in Hunan. He's joined a coven of delinquent corpses.'

'Wow!' She lights another cigarette. 'Thanks for telling me everything,' she says, eventually.

We sit in a charged silence. *Does she feel a tiny bit of sympathy for me?* Her eyes are hard and uncompromising.

She stubs out the cigarette and clicks into a video of the latest Lady Gaga song. Gaga's haunting voice sends a shiver up my spine. I could cry. Will Peg and I ever share happy times again?

'Really, thanks,' Peggy says. Confirming she doesn't want to hear any more.

Maybe I shouldn't burden her with Ma's condition; Ma has come out of her coma, after all. But the doctors fear her arm may not fully recover, that it will need intensive physiotherapy. Her leg is still in plaster.

Peggy is expecting sympathy from you, a little voice tells me. After all, she's the one who says she's depressed. I've been her sounding-board for years.

She's just stressed out about her exams.

Well I am too.

Peggy lights another cigarette. 'I want to know more about Steel. You and Steel. Together. You know what I mean,' she says.

I swallow. Notice how stocky her legs have grown. Swallow again. There's no way I'm going to tell her about what Steel and I get up to. 'Is that all you care about?' I say. 'Sex?'

Peg cringes, covers her ears.

'What about my poor old Ma?' I say, suddenly feeling annoyed.

'Well, if you will get mixed up with the paranormal.'

'You mean it's my fault?' I say, hackles rising.

Peggy smirks. 'I'm hungry,' she says.

'Go on, is it?'

She shrugs nonchalantly, looks at her watch. She takes a slow drag of her fag and blows smoke in my direction.

That's when I lose it. Like I've never lost it with her before. 'Look, she was nearly killed. And Steel saved her life. She would have died,' I yell.

Peggy turns the music up.

I jump to my feet and stalk towards the front door. 'That's it. I'm out of here,' I shout. 'All you care about is yourself.'

'It's just as well I do,' she shouts back. 'Because you don't.'

'Why should I?' I scream, and slam the bottle gate shut.

I don't know how long I stomp the streets like a deranged dog. Up and down the crowded main drag, past the Secret Garden, across the park where Skinny tried to escape, past the garage repair shop, ignoring the ogling of oily workers.

What about Steel, anyway? Do I REALLY want to be involved with someone who snarls like a tiger, bends metal bars, transforms into a killing machine? Someone who could accidentally eat me up? I mean, he saved Ma's life, but if he wasn't a vampire, the attack wouldn't have happened in the first place.

And do I REALLY want to be turned into a vampire? I felt so sure about it before. YES, I DO, I think and high-five with an imaginary Steel. But then I see Ma's ravaged body on bloody straw, hear Peggy's plaintive voice saying: *I miss you so much.* And my stomach squirms with guilt.

I curse, using the worst swear word in the dictionary. I soooo hate myself for being a ditherer. When will I EVER make a decision and fricking stick with it?

My mobile rings: 'private caller'. It must be Steel.

'Hi,' I say weakly.

'Are you okay?' he says. Knowing I'm not.

And suddenly, inexplicably, I love him again. 'It's Peggy,' I say. 'She's really winding me up.'

Steel chuckles.

My temper flares. 'You think it's a laughing matter?'

'Calm down, crazy girl.'

I kick an empty beer can.

'Have you worked out what Peggy's real problem is yet? What's really bugging her?'

'No?' I say. Surprised.

'I'll tell you later.'

'No, tell me now.'

'Really?'

'Yes.'

Steel sniffs. 'She's confused.'

'What do you mean?'

'Not sure if she's a boy or a girl.'

I stop in my tracks. 'What?' In my mind, I hear Peggy hit a triangle of snooker balls and the *click-click-click* as they jostle for the pocket.

'She thinks she might be gay.'

Peg pots the black ball; it slides along a clean green table and plops into the net.

'*Eiya!* Really? How do you know?'

'Anna, I've seen a lot in the years I've spent on this planet,' Steel says. And chuckles again.

'Are you sure?'

'Very sure. Think it over.'

Yeah, I certainly will. That could explain a lot.

'Anyway, you should be studying,' Steel says, bringing me back to the present.

'I know.'

'Well?'

'There's so much going on.'

'So?'

'You're positive, about Peggy I mean?'

'Defo.'

I feel shaky, disoriented. It reminds me of the sensation of being tossed around in the storm clouds above Hunan.

'How's Peach?' I say, wanting the security of his voice for a little longer.

'She's okay. She obviously appreciates me staying around for her. She should be better in a few days.'

'Yeah,' I say. Still freaked out about Peg.

'Hey, wait a sec,' Steel says.

I can hear Peach talking in the background. I imagine Steel cocking his head as he listens. 'I tell you what,' he says. 'Peach suggests you buy Peggy some dinner, go back to her place and talk some more.'

'What? Now?' I say, feeling angry again. *Gay, or not. Why*

should I forgive her for being so rude to me?

'Hold on,' Steel says. He must be listening to Peach. 'Yes. Peach says try and make up,' he says.

Hmm.

'You can call me back later.'

'Thanks.'

With a sigh, I send Peggy a text: **rice or noodles,** start walking back towards SG.

Five minutes later, she still hasn't texted back. Then I remember that she's lost, or flogged, her mobile. I call her landline instead.

'*Cha siu* rice, and a bun,' she says, and hangs up. What a charmer.

I'm shocked but … but it's okay. She's still my best friend, I think.

There's the homely aroma of freshly-cooked rice in the *siu mei* shop. The cook slaps water on the chopping board and removes a layer of grease with a cleaver. Wiping its blade clean, he unhooks a piece of dripping pork from the display window, and chop chop chops the meat into pieces.

Why should I believe what Steel said? I ask myself. But find myself nodding my head, kind of acknowledging that Peg being gay makes a lot of sense.

When did our friendship start to go wrong?

Slowly, it dawns on me. Since Peg noticed Steel eyeing me up outside the school gates. Since I started obsessing about him. So she's got feelings, deep feelings, special feelings, for me.

The fact that Steel is a vampire has never seemed to bother

her that much, I realise. But she hates the idea of us being in a relationship.

The takeaway is ready; a waitress pops a pair of wooden chopsticks, a tissue and a sachet of sauce to the bag. I pay up and start walking back to Peg's place.

I re-live the twinges of jealousy I feel when I think about Jane. Weird. 'Cos I don't think I'm gay. Or bisexual. I don't care what I am. I'm not homophobic or anything.

What hurts is that Peggy has been so mean to me. *Being gay is no excuse for bad behaviour,* I decide, as I ring her doorbell.

No answer. *Eiya!* Not again. I rattle the metal gate, hear someone padding across the tiles.

Peggy opens the door. Her face is deathly pale. Her eyes are glazed. *Uh-oh.*

'Peggy,' I say. 'Come on. Let's make up. Let me in.'

A neighbour's gate clunks shut.

'Why should I?' she says. Her speech is slurred.

'You need to eat something.'

'Okay,' she whines, and slides the bottle gate open.

She trips over her school shoes lying in the hallway. As I lift her to her feet, I take her in my arms. 'Peg, please be careful,' I say, suddenly overwhelmed with sadness.

She grips her arms like a vice round me.

'What's wrong anyway?' I say.

'I feel bad. Really off.'

'No wonder.'

She stinks of nicotine.

I sit her down at the table, feel in her jacket pocket for her little bag of powder.

'Hands off,' she says. Without resisting.

I dangle the bag in front of her. 'Have you just had some of this?'

She reaches for the *cha sui* rice. I can hear her stomach rumbling.

'Peggy, how can you?'

She picks up the chopsticks and tries to unwrap them.

'Who's supplying you?'

'Brew,' she says, dully.

'One day you're going to get caught. You know that, don't you?'

She opens the lunch box and sniffs the pork. 'After this, I'm going to paint your toenails,' she says.

'Well you can't. We should be studying.'

She gives me a plastic smile.

'Don't smile like that,' I say. 'It freaks me out.'

'Dimples. You want to see my dimples?' she says, pursing her lips grotesquely.

'Peggy, stop it,' I shout. 'I've come back to make up with you. To make sure you eat.'

'Really?'

'Yes. Really.'

She bites into a *cha sui* bun. 'So you do care.'

'Of course I do, even … '

'Of course I do,' she mimics.

Blood rushes to my cheeks. "… even if you … you are … gay.'

Peggy throws her head back as if she has been punched on the nose. It takes her a few seconds to regain her composure. 'Do you think I am?'

'If you don't know, how do I?'

She gags on the bun.

'Peggy, how about we talk things over when you're in a better state?'

She stands up shakily. Her face is white, white.

'Peggy, are you okay?'

The chopsticks go flying as she grabs at the table to keep her balance.

And then she passes out.

CHAPTER 31
The power of love

'My parents have invited us to tea, in Kowloon Tong,' Steel says. It's Monday afternoon and we're still at Bauhinia Lodge.

'Why?'

Steel gives me a withering look, as if to say: *you know, stupid.*

Another two weeks have passed. Ma is still in hospital but should be discharged soon. Exams are over. Arguments about whether or not I should turn into a vampire are not.

I have to face it. I have a problem: it's my one track mind. I'm obsessed with the idea of turning.

I really thought that after saving Ma's life, after tasting her blood, Steel would have the confidence, you know … But he hasn't. And now Ma's not at home, and Steel and I have all the time in the world to get together. We've foreplayed like there's no after. But we still haven't, you know.

So I started fantasizing about being a vampire, again. And he got mad, again. Once, he even cried. Begged me to consider his wish to have kids! Said it'd be a nightmare for him to protect me from hungry ghosts. That I'm selfish not to consider Ma's feelings.

Finally, he agreed to discuss it with Kung and Peach. But he delayed. And delayed. Until yesterday. And now we've been summoned into town.

We skirt along the palm-fringed beaches in the Porsche. The

turquoise sea shimmers under a boiling sun. Happy people splash and surf. Children dig sand with buckets and spades. Steel smiles sardonically as we pass the spot where he built me a sandcastle. Then we're winding our way up Lantau Peak, familiar now, the breathtaking view of distant tropical islands smoothing my frayed nerves.

Steel has one hand on the steering wheel. The other twitches a gear stick. I can't see his eyes 'cos he's wearing sunglasses. I feel lost without his eyes.

'Whatever Kung's decision is, we should respect it,' he says, as Sport lopes out of the house to greet us. I pat his wiry fur. But his lively pink tongue and wagging tail don't dispel my sense of doom.

Sprays of summer flowers bloom. Only the strongest can withstand the heat. The weaker ones have withered and died.

Peach's face appears at the window and she waves us inside. 'Anna, how lovely to see you,' she purrs. I kiss her lightly on the cheek. Her skin is as smooth and delicate as the finest porcelain. She's wearing a floaty gown and smells of vanilla.

The hallway is cool and my princess slippers are waiting. Bunches of bird-of-paradise flowers peck at the cold white marble walls.

Sport follows us into the dimly lit sitting room and flops on a rug. Kung is sitting on the sofa, smoothing his gown across his thighs.

'Jasmine, Pu-Er, or Oolong tea?' Peach asks, forcing a smile. Elegant cups and saucers dot the lace tablecloth, with plates of cucumber sandwiches, biscuits and Japanese sweetmeats. All for me.

Steel stands like a soldier by my side. Peach pours the tea, stirs in a spoonful of sugar, offers me a sweet rice cake with red bean filling.

'Where's Freddy?' I ask.

'On school camp in Pui O,' Peach says, and giggles nervously. 'Fortunately, the principal chose a camp site on Lantau.'

I imagine Freddy slipping out of a tent in the middle of the night to hunt for a midnight snack.

'At that age, you don't miss a chance to be with your friends for anything,' Steel says, sitting down.

Peach sighs. 'It's quite a challenge for him to hide his identity.'

I take a sip of black tea, my stomach aching with a desperate hope that my conviction is wrong.

Kung offers me a home-made biscuit. *Something sweet to ward away the bitterness of what he's going to say,* I think, and give him a rueful grin.

'Vampires have not yet been accepted in human society,' he starts. 'We still have many enemies, I'm afraid. But that won't always be the case.'

Steel gasps.

What? Kung is going to let me?

Kung smiles and shakes his head sadly. 'Who knows what the future holds? One day it may be appropriate for Anna to turn.'

Peach nods.

I'm still on tenterhooks.

Kung looks directly into my eyes. 'Anna, I'm not saying a definite no. I'm just asking you to consider your options very carefully.'

F-U-C-K.

Kung sighs. 'I know it's difficult to understand where I'm coming from. What my reasons are. But I believe that until you fulfil your human responsibilities, your soul will not be peaceful.'

My eyes follow the gentle contours of the lawn to where great twisted branches of bougainvillaea and honeysuckle are wrestling each other up and over the stone wall. A gardener is pinning back their maze of tendrils, hammering them to a trestle.

'We're losing control of our climbers,' Peach says solemnly.

I glance at Steel. He's staring at the carpet.

'Time is the great healer,' Kung continues. His lips are thin and straight.

'But the doctor said three months. Three months is such a long time to wait,' I blurt.

Peach reaches over to take my hand. 'Or as fleeting as the beat of a butterfly's wing.'

'Your mother will eventually recover, from her physical wounds, anyway,' Kung says. 'But have you considered how she would cope if you just disappeared?'

I know. I know.

'Being here for your Mum at this difficult time will bring meaning to your life,' Peach says quietly, trying not to sound too condescending.

I blink away a teardrop. Steel passes me a tissue.

'And as for your relationship with my son,' Kung continues,

'there's no reason why passion should sully it. True love conquers all.'

I feel my face flushing.

Pearl jogs my arm. 'And, by the way, I should tell you that I have had a premonition, about Peggy. She needs you to stay around too.'

I blink with surprise. As does Steel. We both look up expectantly.

'Sorry, I can't tell you anything more at this stage,' Peach says. *Ugh.*

A cat jumps on her lap. 'But I'll be checking my crystal ball,' she says.

The rest of the tea party drags. I drain my teacup, refuse a fill-up. Steel says it's time he should take me to the hospital; visiting hours are short.

Kung and Peach accompany us to the front door. I lock into Peach's arms and she kisses me. 'Remember, if you do ever become a vampire, I'd like to adopt you,' she whispers.

'Thank you so much,' I say, resisting the urge to cry.

Kung hugs me too. I feel his unnatural strength. 'You are a good person. Your goodness will be rewarded,' he says.

'Which car should I drive?' Steel asks, pointing to the row of shiny cars. Rajaram has just finished buffing the blood-red Ferrari and it is gleaming. He has even polished the tires.

'That one,' I say.

By the time we get to my flat, I'm feeling really upset again.

'Please Anna, stop analysing. I don't think what Kung said was a great surprise to you,' Steel says, puncturing the top of a Taiwanese bubble tea for me.

I'm too fed-up to enjoy sucking and chewing the glutinous pearls.

'And I can't tell you how relieved I am that you're staying human,' he says.

'For now,' I say, scowling.

Steel kisses me.

'Even Ma doesn't need me,' I say, pissed that when I'd called to say I was running late, she'd insisted I didn't come to the hospital until tomorrow.

'Of course she does,' Steel says, and kisses me again. He gazes into my eyes, pushes a strand of hair behind my ear.

He looks ... different.

'And it means we can spend more time together now,' he says.

'Big deal.'

'Well, what about it?'

'What about what?'

'You know.'

'Wow!'

He gathers my hands and presses my palms into a heart salutation. Flesh on flesh stirs up some deep connection between us. He inhales sharply, and chuckles. His eyes sparkle.

We go to my bedroom.

We take off our clothes.

We lie on my bed.

His toenails are perfectly manicured. Square feet. Buddha toes. To match my Buddha ears. He turns over onto his stomach. 'Let me touch you first,' he says.

He runs three fingers along my spine and I shiver with pleasure. His fingers slowly slide further down, down my thigh, dawdling a while to trace the crease of my knee, to traverse the rise and fall of my calf muscle. He pinches my ankle bones, then leans down to kiss them, one by one.

'I'm going to sit on you,' he murmurs. He mounts the fleshy throne of my buttocks, leans forwards, and walks his hands along my outstretched arms, his nipples brushing against my shoulders, his face buried in my hair. Then the tip of his nose traces a line down the nape of my neck, along my shoulder blade, under my armpit. 'You smell so lovely,' he says.

I turn over; he sighs. Sweat glistens between my breasts. We kiss; he fills the hollow cave of my mouth with saliva. I swallow.

Then his tongue glides lazily over my glassy eyeballs, it ruffles my eyebrows, digs deep into my earlobes, my nostrils.

I laugh.

He does too. He's breathing more heavily now. 'I love you,' he says.

'I love you too.'

'And I think I am able,' he says softly.

My insides turn to jelly. 'Really?'

He lowers his head. His eyelashes flutter nervously.

'Are you sure?'

'I love you. I love you so much that … that I'll kill myself if I can't control myself.'

Romantic with a capital R. Warmth washes over my brain.

He's suddenly anxious. 'But please, I beg you, don't expect too much,' he says.

Yes. Of course. This was meant to be.

I close my eyes.

I imagine myself, lost in a forest.

I see crystal mountain tips ranging above, rainbow spectrums of sunlight slicing through the trees.

Then the hunt is on. I'm belly-up; Steel has mounted a horse, whipped its rump and he's galloping towards me, drawn inch-by-inch closer to my desire.

My desire is a frightened deer, hiding in a copse, lost in a maze of trees.

But Steel has caught its scent. He knows where I am. He spurs his horse onwards; its thundering hooves ripple the pond and shake the branches where I am cowering.

'You're mine,' Steel trumpets. 'Give yourself to me,' and his hounds whoop for joy, plunge forwards to root their prey.

With a flick of my hind legs, I zigzag between the trees, bound over rocks and streams, streak up the pine-scented mountain.

But Steel is neck-to-neck with me. His horse rips up clods of earth. The path spirals, narrows, as we climb, and the fresh air fills my lungs, it invigorates me, blows my bones clean.

We're swept up, up to a craggy ravine and I'm panting with exhilaration and exhaustion, but I'm careering out of control, forwards, fearless, the peak is laser sharp, I'm on the edge, there's a precipice below, I lunge forwards, fling myself head-on, into Steel's jaws.

WHAT WAS THAT?

I'm laughing hysterically.

Steel is weeping.

Spots of blood festoon my bed sheet.

CHAPTER 32
Disclosures

'Peggy's been arrested.' It's a male voice. In a fug, I'm drawing a blank as to who it belongs to. I sit up in bed, crook the phone between my ear and shoulder and use the top sheet to preserve my modesty.

'Ken. It's Ken,' the voice says.

Yes. Of course.

'Wait a sec. I think Mum's calling me. I'll call you back,' he says, and hangs up.

Steel's limbs are spread across my tousled sheets in complete abandonment. His eyes are closed and he's breathing peacefully.

> *'Taste my glory,*
> *Crossed swords,*
> *Blood love,*
> *What's your story?'*

I sing, inside.

My mobile rings again. 'She's been arrested? When?' I say.

'Yesterday evening.'

Steel stirs, opens his liquid gold eyes and gives me an angelic smile.

I look at the bedside clock. *Eiya!* It's two-twenty in the afternoon.

'What happened?'

'I don't know. I got a call from the fuzz late last night to say she was caught in possession, on the street.'

Steel reaches for my hand.

'Why didn't you call earlier?'

'I did. You didn't pick up.'

Steel, failing to release my grip on the top sheet, makes a foray from underneath. I catch his hand and he stifles a laugh.

'Where is she now?'

'I'm not sure.'

'Well, can't you find out? I mean, I'd like to know.'

'Yeah, sure. The police said something about a hearing in a magistrate's court.'

Wa! 'Call me later, when you get some news.'

'Sure.'

I fumble for the recharger and connect my mobile.

Steel is using his fingers to walk up my thigh.

'Steel, this isn't a joke,' I say.

He leans back, stretches like a cat and flicks a strand of hair out of his eyes. 'So Peach was right. Peggy has got herself into trouble.'

Oh yeah. Fragments of yesterday's conversation drift back into my consciousness. But they seem hazy and unimportant after The Big Event last night.

Steel strokes my hair. 'Anna, you've tried your best to help her. She's just got no self-control.'

'Ha ha, not like you,' I say.

Laughing, he folds me in his arms and nuzzles my neck. 'This is what happiness feels like,' he says.

We kiss. Kiss some more. Make love again.

Later, much later (we're still in bed), and Ken still hasn't called, I start to worry about Peg. Will she go to prison? 'Do you think I should call him?' I say.

'Why not?'

That's when I find out that Peggy hasn't been granted bail. Instead, she has been sent to Tim Lam remand centre on Lantau Island pending a court case.

'Let's visit her tomorrow,' Steel says. 'With Wing and Mimi.'

We're running late, so late we nearly miss the 2 pm fast ferry. Steel took one look at the fierce sun shining through my bedroom curtains this morning and hid under the covers. 'But I'm coming with you. I have a hunch I'll be needed,' he said.

It's hot, hot. Incinerator hot. The windows of the Mui Wo ferry are covered in condensation. Junks and *gaai dous*, fishing boats and ferries are bobbing in the harbour vying for space.

Wing and Mimi are sitting in the row in front sharing bowls of *ho fun* and fish balls. They're wearing matching shorts and sandals. Meanwhile, Steel is dressed in white from head to toe, with a long headdress and dark sunglasses. I phone Ma to warn her I may arrive a little late at the hospital this evening.

'How is she anyway?' Wing asks, screwing her neck round to get my attention.

'Much better, thanks,' I say.

Wing rolls her eyes. 'What exactly happened again?'

'She fell from the top of a barn.' I flick my fringe over my eyes.

'Is she still in a lot of pain?' Mimi asks.

'Yes. But she's taking her pills.'

'What a shitty time for you and your family,' Wing says.

'It hasn't been too bad,' I say, not daring to look at Steel in case we burst out laughing.

He squeezes my hand.

Mimi wraps her arms around her stomach and grimaces. 'I could do with a pill too. I feel a bit travel sick.'

Mui Wo pier is cluttered with bicycles. Street vendors crowd the pavement. They're selling flip-flops, swimming costumes and suntan lotion. A Hakka woman with a wide-brimmed hat and gold fillings in her teeth offers rent-by-the-hour hotel rooms.

'We must spend a weekend here sometime,' Wing says, admiring the long sandy beach of Silvermine Bay.

'It's a great place for a barbecue,' Steel says.

Wing and Mimi look at him suspiciously.

A fiery sun has burnt through the clouds and even I am sweating. Steel is looking distinctly melty. He says he'll wait under a bus shelter while we go to the supermarket to buy some snacks for Peggy. Fortunately, there's no queue at the blue taxi rank.

As we travel along the single-lane road to the remand centre, I have a chance to gather my thoughts. Whatever happens, I must give Peggy some hope. I mean, I still really like her. What's the big deal about being homosexual? In other countries, gay couples can have civil partnerships. They can live together openly, even adopt children. Peggy's main problem is her drug addiction. Maybe she could persuade the judge to give her another chance?

But as we approach the institution, my heart sinks. There's something so final about being stuck behind hefty stone walls and barbed wire. Coarse female babble floats over from a low-rise building. Big dogs bark. I can't believe that Peg is incarcerated inside.

'I heard that she didn't even bother to put her name on her exam papers,' Wing says, shading her eyes from the sun.

'Passing exams is the least of her worries,' Mimi says.

'She'll get through this,' Steel says, from behind his Ray Ban sunglasses. 'She can re-take. I mean, she's not dumb or anything.'

We all agree.

The walls of the greeting area are covered in graffiti and there's a strong smell of urine. A gruff guard rifles through our bag of goodies for Peggy and confiscates it. 'Where do you think you are, a holiday camp?' he says.

He checks our ID's against typed names on a list. Steel's name isn't on it; he can't go inside.

'Sooooooo strict,' Wing says, running with Mimi to the main building to escape the blinding heat.

'Don't worry. I'll be hanging around,' Steel whispers to me, and vanishes.

A metal gate clangs open and a warder in uniform strides towards us. Her muscular biceps bulge through her shirt sleeves.

'Visitors for inmate number 10893, follow me,' she rasps.

Wing, Mimi and I walk in file down a damp passageway into a bare whitewashed room, squeezing past a middle-aged couple – heads drooped, snuffling into tissues – on their way out. We sit in front of a metal grille and wait for Peg to appear on the other side.

And wait. The steady tick-tock of a square wall clock begins to get on my nerves. Miss Biceps, who's standing behind us, taps her feet and hums. *Has Steel found some shade?* I wonder.

Another warder opens the door and Peggy shuffles through it. She's dressed in a green serge uniform and flip-flops. When I see her downcast face, I'm glad I've come to see her.

She stands by the wall, as if afraid to approach us.

'Peg,' I say. 'Come and sit down.'

Peggy stares vacantly at the opposite wall. Mimi starts snivelling.

Wing is frowning. 'Peggy, we're all really worried about you,' she says.

Peggy's lips twitch.

'How long will you be here for?' I ask.

Peggy shrugs.

'How much were you carrying?'

Peggy points to a video camera suspended from the ceiling and scratches her dragon tattoo. It's not a good idea to talk.

Peggy eventually sits down. She jiggles a knee. Minutes pass. It's hard to find something to talk about. Wing tells a joke but Peg doesn't laugh.

'What's there to do all day, anyway?'

'Watch TV,' Peggy says gruffly.

'What's the food like?'

'Crap.'

'You're not even allowed a mobile?'

'Just letters.'

'We bought you some food but we couldn't bring it in.'

'Instant noodles, Coke, crisps,' says Mimi.

'Thanks.'

'What are we allowed to bring you anyway?' I ask.

Peggy shrugs.

'Maybe we could ask Miss Biceps over there.'

Miss Biceps winks back at us. *Wa!*

'I could murder for some decent toothpaste,' Peggy suddenly says. 'Some Darlie toothpaste, and … '

'Five more minutes,' a voice from a tannoy system blares.

Peggy suddenly whimpers. 'You have to go, so soon?'

'I'll come back on Sunday,' I say.

She slumps forwards.

'I promise,' I say. Wing and Mimi nod.

Peggy's chin jerks upwards and she homes in on me. Her mouth is tense and crooked. 'You're going to turn, aren't you?' she hisses.

Blood rushes to my cheeks.

'What?' Wing says.

Mimi grabs Wing's hand.

'But you are, aren't you?' Peggy says fiercely. Her two

bloodshot eyes stare accusingly into mine.

I panic. I feel cornered, trapped, like a mouse caught between the jaws of a cat. 'Peggy, we can't talk here. Not now,' I say.

'Why not?' She bangs the bars with her fists and wails, and Miss Biceps comes striding over. Wing and Mimi stand up, alarmed.

Then suddenly Steel is standing beside me, his hands gripping the grille. He stares at Peggy and his eyes smoulder with anger. 'Listen,' he says. 'We're here because we want you to get through this, to quit drugs, to get back to school. Anna will definitely … stay around for you. And for her mother. Okay?'

Peggy is crying. With relief, or shock, I'm not sure.

Wing and Mimi look completely stunned.

Miss Biceps is screaming.

A laser-sharp sunbeam of truth zaps me, and I laugh. I'm free and easy. Soaring above the waves. Released from indecision. 'No. No, Peggy. I'm not going to turn,' I say.

And at that moment, the decision feels, finally, final.

Steel has disappeared.

Wing and Mimi are looking at me with saucer eyes.

A superintendent arrives. 'Back to your cell, 10893,' she barks.

There's a flurry of action as two warders seize Peggy by her arms and drag her away.

'I love you, Anna,' Peggy calls.

'I love you too, Peg.'

Wing has Mimi's hand and is pulling her out of the room.

'Darlie toothpaste, and what?' I call.

'Egg waffles?' Peg shouts.

Later that night, when I'm recalling what happened, I think: what love means to Peg, I'm not sure. But I'm not worried about it. I know what I meant when I said I loved her. I'm here for her and it feels good. It's not her fault she's gay.

'Ma!' I cry. She's sitting up in her hospital bed, unaided. Her hair has been combed and her cheeks are flushed with colour.

I rush over to hug her.

'Watch my arm,' she says. It's still in a sling.

My heart is brimming with joy. 'You look … good,' I say.

The man spooning soup to his wife next door rests his wrist on his lap for a second and gives me a doleful smile.

'I feel much better,' Ma says. 'Much, much better. The doctor says I can come home in a couple of days, after she's taken these stitches out.'

Ma lifts a mirror from the bedside table and, looking at herself, cautiously fingers her wounds. 'She says the scars will eventually disappear.'

Her cheeks still look a bit bruised and puffy, to me. Well, if the doctor says the scars will disappear, they will, won't they?

'I'll take care of you,' I say.

Ma sniggers. It turns into a laugh. I laugh too. It's infectious. It's the first time I've heard her laugh for ages. 'We'll manage,' she says.

The idea of coming home seems to animate her. Her eyes are bright and she seems eager to chat. 'Tomorrow I'm booked for an X-ray to see how my leg is mending,' she says, tapping the characters of my name which I'd engraved on her plaster a few days ago.

I shuffle uncomfortably on the stool. It suddenly feels imperative to set a few things straight. *It's easier to talk here than at home,* I think, mentally spurring myself on.

'Ma?'

She puts the mirror down, settles back on a pile of pillows and looks at me.

'What do you actually remember, about the accident, I mean?' I ask.

Ma blinks for a moment. She looks a bit confused. 'You know what? Not much. I was in the barn. There was a mound of lotus roots that Grandma and I had cut and stacked the day before. And I was bending down, filling a pail of water, when I heard some scuffling in the straw. I remember thinking, it must be rats. But then I smelt a peculiar odour. There was a roar and something … someone … from behind … '

'Someone?'

Ma sucks the air. 'Oh dear. I'm not quite sure. I think I must have blacked out. I can't recall anything else. Nothing, until I woke up here at Queen Mary's.'

Phew!

'And Grandma? What's she told you about it?' I ask, still needing to be assured.

'She said that in her village there's a deranged man who sometimes attacks people. He has two vicious dogs; that the attacker was probably him.' Her face suddenly clouds over, as if she's puzzled about something. 'She said you brought two Taoist priests with you. They conducted a ritual and arranged for me to be flown back here.'

'Yeah. In a plane,' I say. And try to gauge her reaction.

Ma's eyes narrow. *Eiya!* She's waiting for an explanation.

'Anna?'

I'm squirming now.

'I've got a boyfriend,' I say. 'He's a Taoist priest.'

'WHAT?'

'You heard.'

'A Taoist priest?'

'Well, an apprentice – of his father, a high priest. It was him and his Dad who came … came to rescue you.'

'Since when have you been mixed up with religion?'

I swallow a gob of spit. 'It just happened. I mean … I mean *(how I hate talking to my Ma about my private stuff)* I was in a bit of trouble, some nasty guys accosted Peggy on the street, and Steel – that's his name, my boyfriend's name – fought them off, with *kung fu.*'

'He's a *kung fu* master?' Ma says, incredulous.

'You could say so.' My mind replays Steel diving through the air to rescue Kung from the fan of flames in Hunan.

Ma is trying to fathom something. 'Wait a minute,' she says. 'Who paid for the airfares?'

Oh no. She's got me. 'No one,' I say. 'I mean, we didn't have to pay.'

'His father charters planes, does he?' Ma says. In jest.

'No,' I say. 'He owns one.'

Ma blinks with astonishment.

'The family owns a house in Kowloon Tong, and another on Lantau Island. They've got a swimming pool, and a stable, with horses, and hundreds of cats.'

'Unbelievable,' she says.

I lean over to hug her.

She repels me. 'But I forbade you to get involved with boys,' she says, trying to sound authoritative.

'Sorry, Ma. I didn't intend to. I mean, I wasn't particularly looking … ' I'm floundering for words. 'And he's … different from the other guys,' I say. 'He's very … very responsible.'

Ma clears her throat. She doesn't seem convinced.

'And very rich,' I add.

Amazingly, she doesn't seem that impressed. 'Does he have a good heart?' she says. Sarcastic-like.

CHAPTER 33
Celebrations

Apparently it was Peach's idea to organise a birthday party, as well as to celebrate that I passed all my exams. (Just!) The big day has arrived and I've been faffing around for ages choosing what to wear.

Ma knocks on my bedroom door. 'Be quick,' she says. 'Steel is waiting downstairs.' It's not easy to find a place to park on the street.

I skim through my dresses one more time and finally put on the pleated white skirt and V-neck top that I've tried for size at least five times earlier. In the mirror, I take one last look at my face and admire my straightened hair. *Thanks for the hair straighteners, Ma!*

I open the door, to find her standing right behind it. She's dressed in her best purple number, with curled hair and a new pair of sandals.

'Where are you going?' I say. Confused-like. I mean, Ma is the woman who doesn't go anywhere.

She fumbles in her handbag and flashes an invitation card.

'You've been invited to my birthday party?'

'Yes, even with a face like this,' she says, rubbing a finger along the scar on her cheek.

'Wear your sunglasses, please Ma.'

'They're in my handbag,' she says.

Her walking stick clacks against the corridor tiles.

Eiya! What if she discovers Steel and his family are vampires? In the lift, I give her a sickly smile.

On the street, Steel is leaning against a dark green convertible: it's a Rolls-Royce! And he's the driver.

A few bystanders have already gathered around to ogle. Steel waves at me enthusiastically, looking drop-dead gorgeous in a black suit and shiny patent leather shoes. Heads turn towards me, including two that are poking out of the back seat window of the car. *Wa!* It's Wing and Mimi.

'What are you doing here?' I cry. They're all dressed up too.

'Happy Birthday,' they say in chorus, and plant a beautifully wrapped gift in my lap.

And then we're hugging and laughing and the Roller is purring down the highway.

'Open it now,' Wing says.

Mimi claps her hands in anticipation.

They've pooled their savings and bought me a beautiful pair of golden lamb earrings, my birth animal.

'They're so cute,' I say, immediately swopping them for the ones I'm wearing.

'Give those to me,' Ma says, storing my old studs in her handbag.

'So Steel managed to keep your guest list a secret?' Mimi says.

I lean forward to gently thump him on his back. He smiles. How sweet of him. *Let's just hope all the vampires behave themselves.*

It's already dusk and the garden is aglow with fairy lights. As Steel turns the car into the driveway, Ma and Mimi gasp with delight at the house. '*Wa!* Amazing!' Wing squeals.

Steel offers his arm to Ma and escorts her down the gravel walkway. Sprays of freshly-picked red and yellow roses adorn the arched bowers above us. They smell divine.

'So many cats!' Ma says, as one brushes up against her leg.

Peach is waiting for us on the terrace. She's wearing a *qipao* dress which reveals her shapely legs. Freddy is running around with his divining stick. I feel myself tense in apprehension as we approach, but there's nothing to worry about: Peach gracefully offers her hand, and after simple introductions, tells us that Kung has a surprise for me in the Chinese garden.

My high heels sink in the soft earth.

The Chinese garden is tucked away behind the house – no wonder I hadn't noticed it before. It is hidden behind a thicket of bamboo and the nooks and crannies of a rock garden full of dinky Buddhist statues. Two stone lions guard an arched Suzhou-style entrance, which leads to a mosaic screen embossed with dragons and phoenixes.

Behind the screen, we meander along a pebbled footpath. Ferns, stones, plants and bushes all have their allotted space. Slippery goldfish slide between waxy lotus leaves in an ornamental pond. A papaya tree groans with fruit. Yellow songbirds coo from wooden cages suspended from mango trees.

We cross an arched bridge towards a red-pillared pavilion.

Underneath its blue glazed roof, Kung is leaning over a canvas on a marble table. 'Anna, I'm writing this for you,' he says, dipping a hairpin in black ink, smoothing away the excess on an inkstone.

His hand moves effortlessly across the white silk, each stroke is lovingly shaped. I stand on tiptoe, feeling a bit nervous 'cos he's using such a flamboyant style I might not recognise all the characters. But I can: *May deep heart wishes come true.*

With a flourish, he dots the final character with a splash of ink and hangs the silk on a rafter to dry. Wing nudges my elbow; I'm in a kind of trance. 'Thank you,' I say.

Kung turns to me and smiles kindly. 'You're very welcome,' he replies. Everyone claps. He reaches for his pocket watch. 'Time to go inside. It's nearly dinner time.'

As if programmed, the doorman bangs a gong.

'Dinner will be served in the dining room,' Steel says. He takes my arm and we lead the way. I glance back at Ma; she has gracefully accepted Kung's assistance.

The table has been set for ten, and ten smart waiters stand to attention as we enter. A starched embroidered tablecloth is groaning with fine porcelain, cutlery, wafer-thin wineglasses and burning candles. Ma looks as if she has seen a ghost. (I suppose there may be a few around.) Smiling, Steel accompanies her to her seat.

Freddy is trying to impress Wing and Mimi with his knowledge of rocks. Steel secretly wraps his leg around mine. His eyes gleam in the candlelight.

I choose from an assortment of starters – smoked salmon,

crabs' claws, caviar, bite-sized pizza. Uniformed servants serve silver salvers of beef rump steak, asparagus, green beans and mashed potato.

One plate of raw meat is quietly passed around the table. Fortunately, the room is dimly lit, Ma is wearing sunglasses, and she doesn't seem to be paying much attention to what everyone else is eating.

Ma's waiter serves her another piece of steak. 'Delicious!' she mouths to me from across the table.

Peach picks at some caviar and smiles at her. 'I was hoping you like Western food,' she says.

'Certainly,' says Ma. The only Western food I've seen her eat before is burgers and chips at McDonald's.

Kung calmly peruses the scene from the head of the table. Just before dessert, he chimes his wine glass with a spoon. 'Anna, we have prepared some birthday gifts for you.'

I feel blood rising to my cheeks. I'm not used to so much attention.

Freddy bounces up to my chair and hands me a large envelope. I open it, and find a handful of hand drawn dinosaurs. 'One for each day of the week,' he says. 'Spinosaurus, stegosaurus, velociraptor … '

'Okay, that's enough,' Peach says, glowing with pride.

'Thanks Doctor D.!' I say.

Steel reaches for something in his pocket. It's small, well-wrapped and heavy. *How exciting!* Everyone is looking at me.

There's no brand name on the top of the box. I carefully tear the wrapping paper, slowly lift the lid and remove the tissue paper inside.

It's a watch, a beautiful Paul Smith watch.

'That's so nice,' I say.

'Try it for size,' Steel says.

It fits perfectly.

'It's stainless steel,' he says.

'Ha ha. That's so funny,' says Freddy.

Everyone laughs.

Peach chimes her wine glass. 'My gift is so big I couldn't wrap it,' she says.

I blink with surprise.

'I'm ashamed to tell you I have lots of new clothes I haven't worn yet this season. Usually I would donate them to charity, but as you and I are about the same size, I would like to give them to you, if you want them, that is,' she says.

Cool.

Peach looks over to Wing and Mimi. 'You may like to go upstairs and have a look too.'

Wing and Mimi clap their hands in appreciation.

'Go now, if you must,' Kung says, 'but don't forget to come down for the birthday cake.'

The three of us run up the marble stairs to Peach's walk-in closet on the second floor. It's heaving with designer-label clothes: dresses, skirts, blouses, coats and furs. There's even a collection of fashion jewellery and handbags. We flick through them, trying the shoes for size, adorning ourselves with necklaces and bracelets.

'Are you coming down, ladies?' Steel calls from the staircase. Giggling, we quickly change back into our party clothes and rush back to our seats in the dining room.

The lights dim and everyone starts singing *Happy Birthday.* The head waiter brings in a cake. It's shaped like a lamb and made of meringues and fresh cream, with chocolate eyes and a red ribbon around its neck.

Everybody applauds. My heart is bursting with happiness.

'Make a wish,' Steel says, passing me the cake knife. He's wearing gold *yin yang* cufflinks. His white teeth glisten in the candlelight.

I close my eyes and take a deep breath. And open them again. 'What if I've got two?'

Ma frowns.

'No problem,' Peach says. She waves to a waiter, who brings in another cake. It's shaped like a puppy and made with chocolate éclairs.

'One cake is not enough for everyone anyway,' Peach says, winking at me.

Ma laughs. I don't know why.

I slice the knife through lashings of cream.

Wish number one: Steel loves me forever.

Wish number two: Ma will be able to walk properly again.

If I had a third, it would be for Peg. I wish she would never take drugs again.

I go to the bathroom (to check my hair) and when I get back, only Peach is left in the dining room. Someone is playing a catchy melody on a synthesizer upstairs. There's a peal of laughter and a door slams.

What's happening?

'How about another glass of champagne?' Peach says.

When I decline, she laughs, and starts humming a snatch of *Happy Birthday.*

Freddy comes dashing down the stairs in a red suit and matching bow tie and asks us to come up to the music studio without delay.

Gaggles of happy Filipinos are sitting on a row of chairs, chatting and laughing with Ma. Rajaram and Ishvar are there too, in their turbans. A greasy-haired technician fiddles with the knobs of a sound system. When I enter, everyone claps.

'We're going to have a birthday jam,' Steel shouts from the stage. Kung, Wing and Mimi are shuffling through sheet music beside him; they have also changed into red costumes. The stage is set up with instruments and bobbing balloons. Peach picks up a golden saxophone and follows Freddy up the steps.

'And now,' Steel says in a sexy voice, 'give a big hand to … The Bloodsuckers.'

Wing and Mimi exchange nervous glances.

Freddy bangs a cymbal.

'And first up is … *Hunt Rock.*'

I wave my arms and cheer.

Steel's feet stomp to Mimi's funky drum beat and he sings in a high breathy voice that makes me shiver with excitement:

> *'Zha' you horses,*
> *Have no fear.*
> *Wotcha cow,*
> *Wotcha deer.*
> *Sleep by day,*
> *Hunt by night,*
> *Join the fray,*
> *It's outta sight.'*

Freddy ups the tempo, and Peach improvises a catchy counter-melody on the sax. By the end of the song, we're all on our feet dancing. Even Ma with her broken leg.

'And now for something completely different,' Steel says. The lights fade to an electric blue. Freddy jumps off the stage and comes to sit next to me.

'I'd like to sing a special song,' Peach says shyly. 'It's one I wrote for my husband on our wedding anniversary.'

'Which one?' I whisper to Freddy.

'Their two hundredth,' he whispers back, giving me a conspiratorial wink.

Kung plays a smoochy sequence of chords on the synthesizer as Peach checks the microphone. Her long hair is adorned with long red ribbons. With her elegant legs and sultry eyes, she could be mistaken for a teenager. Her voice, low and sultry, starts hesitantly.

Kung smiles at her, while accompanying her sweet words with delicate harmonies.

> *'You're the one,*
> *The only one.*
> *We are one –*
> *One body,*
> *One blood,*
> *One track,*
> *One love.'*

Steel is standing behind them. He's looking at me, softly singing the backing vocals.

I love you too, Steel.

From the corner of my eye, I see Ma reach in her handbag for something to mop her tears.

At the end of the song, Kung and Peach embrace.

Freddy covers his eyes and shouts, 'Yuck'.

Steel blows me a kiss. Then he takes up the mike. 'Time for a duet,' he says, looking straight at me.

'What? No way!'

But Wing and Mimi grab me by my arms, and pull me on stage.

No way I'm singing in front of Ma.

Steel takes my hand. 'You can do it,' he says.

'*Bloodswell. Bloodswell. Bloodswell,*' chant Wing and Mimi.

I smile weakly at my stiff-perm, stiff-legged, stiff-brained mother. She's raising clasped hands – like Concubine Lily – imploring me, willing me on.

The lights fade until there's just one spotlight shining above us. Ma has become a ghostly silhouette.

Kung plays the gentle introduction on synthesizer. Steel slides into the texture with a slow-moving chord sequence. Peach floats in on her sexy sax.

Nose-bump close, Steel and I start singing:

> '*Feel the power,*
> *Taste my glory,*
> *Crossed swords,*
> *Blood love,*
> *What's your story?*
> *Drip drop,*
> *Stitch clot,*
> *Silk sheets,*
> *You're neat,*
> *Bloodswell.*
> *All's well.*
> *Ding dong*
> *Bell.*'

We sing in harmony. We breathe as one. Dust motes shiver.

The room shrinks. There's just him and me. Our voices rise and fall: we are waves, lapping against our castle on a distant shore.

And our breath, fading now, floats upwards, to shimmering stars, drifting.

As the final guitar chord dies away, Steel leans towards me, and whispers:

'Forever yours.'

ACKNOWLEDGEMENTS

With thanks to:

Betty Wong

Alan Sargent

Marshall Moore

Mio Debnam

Janet Mann

Lavanya Shanbhogue

Louise Preston

The SCBWI Hong Kong critique group: Irene V Bennett, Elizabeth Grobler, Anne Lim, Jill Mortensen, Darien Muh and Diana Pizzari.

The Park View critique group: Lavinia Chang, Paul Jacobson, Rachana Mirpuri, Ellen McNally and Sandy Sinn-Hussey.

My first readers: Terri Hartshorn (United Kingdom), Malinee Keenan (Hong Kong), Emma Clarke (Canada), Sheree Chua (the Philippines), Arthur Chan (Hong Kong), Anthony Lee (Hong Kong), Michelle Wong (Hong Kong).

Heather Storey

Josephine Wells

Rebecca Dykes

Harriet Dykes